HUMAYUN MIRZA

INDIA • SINGAPORE • MALAYSIA

ISBN 979-8-88815-322-2

About the Author

The author Humayun Mirza, has to his credit above 70 screenplays, including some of the blockbusters such as Zakhmee (Starring: Sunil dutt) , Kasme- Vaade (Starring: Amitabh Bacchan), Love Story (starring Kumar Gaurav), Dhanvan (Starring: Rajesh Khanna), Qila (Starring: Dilip Kumar), Deewangi (Starring: Ajay Devgan), Taqatwar (Starring: Sanjay Dutt and Govinda) Sitamgarh (Starring Dharmendra and Rishi Kapoor) Aap Ke Dewane (Starring: Rishi Kapoor and Rakesh Roshan) and many more.

Recently provided Manuscript of TV series Muskurane ki Wajah Tum ho.

His talent for story - telling successfully continues into a different genre – novel - writing.

Chapter One

"Faithless man, I am not going to shed tears for you all my life, You don't exist for me, right from today right from this moment."

These words; her very own words; the throbbing memory of her past, rose from the depths of her heart and once again gave her a sinking feeling. To get rid of her sore over and done past affair Madhu glanced here and there around her.

Madhu was in a bus full of tourist. The bus was passing through the dense forest of South Africa's Wild Life Kingdom Park. A group of sparkling young boys and girls were in the best of their sprits; laughing and joking, while some honeymoon couples and some youngsters in simple happy live in relationships were taking life the best romantic way not bothering any one or being bothered about any one, were purely lost in each in each other, in each other's arms, some even locking lips passionately. Co-passengers; some mature with age others very young; in category of children, were either enjoying the free show and those not excited and concerned by the blatant couples overtures were focusing their cameras at the beautiful panorama outside the bus.

Suddenly a pride of lions, leisurely crossing the road was seen at some distance. Bus driver gently applied the brakes to stop the bus smoothly. The guide signaled everyone to be silent. The youngsters, honey moon couples, the middle-aged and elderly, all except Madhu were full attention and appreciating the grace, the elegance, the beauty of the king of the jungle and his family.

Sitting on her seat Madhu was once again lost in thoughts of Amar. Her love Amar, Amar who once upon a time belonged to her, Amar who she had lost now, Amar who she had first met in very strange circumstances.

Madhu, a nurse by profession, when off duty was on shopping spree, never alone always with her two friends Salma and Rehman. That particular day 28th of December 2004, the weather was very pleasant in Mumbai (India). Rare and cool was the feel of winter. Even at a crowded place like Crawford Market one felt the chill in the air. Madhu insisted "We must respect this exceptional weather, this cute little chill and have our lunch in the open air."

"Open air, outdoors, but where, on Chowpaty Beach?" Salma questioned.

Madhu replied pulling her cardigan tight on the curves of her shapely figure "No not on the beach, on the hill where the feel of the chill is more."

Rahman, Salma's boy friend inquired joking "Which hill, Khandala hill, Mahableshwar hill or the Himalayas?"

"Malabar hill, just twenty minutes by your new automatic Honda City. But first we will go to Bhindi Bazar, get our Hydrabadi Biryani's packed and then proceed to Malabar Hill." Madhu declared.

At Malabar Hill Hanging Garden, under a more cool shadow of an old and spread out Banyan tree the three friends, Madhu, Salma and Rehman ate greedily their respective, heavy but delicious 'Hyderabadi Biryanie's.

Down below the antique Banyan tree, the cool breeze of rare Mumbai winter was very much relaxing, gossiping leisurely they had dozed off into a carefree youthful sleep.

Some passing steps had awakened Madhu. As she opened her eyes she had first seen two staggering feet, wearing pair of worn out shoes. Raising her head she saw the back of a lean looking boy walking away. The boy was wearing a crumpled but not dirty shirt as if recently washed and worn without the ritual of going under the iron. Black pair of jeans which he wore was loose-fitting and shabby on his underfed belly and lean legs as if reminiscent of those good old days when he was healthy and slightly overweight.

Slow and unsteady he was walking towards a point at Malabar Hill Hanging Garden notoriously known as suicide point.

An alarmed Madhu tried to wake up her friend Salma but she turned away with a do not disturb manner.

The boy had reached suicide point. Yes he was Amar. He had deep dark shadows under his eyes. His lips were dry and parched, cheeks hallow and sunken. It seemed as if he had not eaten since days; his own once fitting clothes hung baggy on his starving body. The drastic weight loss making his looks very weak. Tears in his eyes Amar was looking up at the clean blue sky. Standing at the brink of the gorge a sad smile appeared on Amar's parched lips. Amar raised his right foot to take his life's last step. Suddenly a shriek echoed in his ears "Oh! God!! Oh God!! What are you up to?"

Madhu caught Amar by his collar and pulled him hard with all her strength. Amar landed on top of Madhu. For some moments both kept looking at each other. Then pushing Amar away Madhu questioned "Are you mad, you were going to give your life, commit suicide?"

In reply a sarcastic smile prevailed on Amar's arid lips while his eyes closed in extreme debility.

Hearing Madhu's screams Salma and Rehman came rushing. The sight which greeted them was Madhu lying prostrate on green grass alongside her, hand in hand arms locked, was lying a young man may be in his early twenties, fair and handsome but with sunken sharp features, very pathetic in appearance.

"What is happening?" Salma shot in.

Flat on ground Madhu called back "He attempted suicide!"

"What?" Rehman exclaimed.

Madhu was struggling to get up; inadvertently Amar was not letting go her hand. Rehman pulled Madhu, helping force her hand free and get up. Only Amar remained flat on the ground, the three of them stood towering him.

"Let's hand him over to the police." Rehman suggested. Amar kept lying, not concerned, only a feeble tear rolled out of his wide open eyes. Noticing Madhu commented "Come on Rehman, look at him?"

"Are you sick?" Salma asked.

"He is hungry, starving, can't you see?" Madhu retorted. "You both help him sit; I will get something for him to eat."

Madhu ran to the Banyan tree. They had packed some extra 'Biryanis' to take home for dinner; a water bottle was also there, some water left in it. Madhu rushed back with their picnic basket.

By the time Madhu reached suicide point, Amar was sitting, his both hands stretched and palms fixed on the ground to support his quivering torso. Salma and Rehman were standing watching him in silence. Madhu sat besides Amar, took out the water bottle first, putting it to Amar's mouth, as a trained nurse, said politely "Take a sip of water first."

Amar obeyed, Madhu took out a packet of Biryani.

Salma intervened "Ask him if he is vegetarian or non-vegetarian."

A sarcastic smile came stretching on Amar's dry lips and in a pitiable voice he uttered the first words in front of them "Beggars are no choosers, madam."

The three of them fell silent on his remark and watched him satisfy his hunger with shaking hands, eating every morsel of the 'Biryani' with utmost care, as if knowing the value of every bit.

Half the people who land at the soil of Mumbai from across the entire world are mostly bitten by one bug. The name of that bug is Film Industry.

Amar had also come to Mumbai with dreams of Film making. He wanted to be a director; to be director he had to first find an assistant director's job and this job had evaded him even after his persistent resolute efforts.

It was not that he was not qualified enough or he knew nothing about films. He was a graduate and had done direction course from the famous Film And Television Institute of Poona. All said and done there was only one thing not by his side and that one entity was Lady Luck.

Having lost his battle to fate, starving, shattered and disgusted with his existence he had come to end his life but here too luck had not favored him. Madhu had saved him.

Thus Amar had narrated his sad life story to Madhu, Salma and Rehman.

"Well thank you all so much for your patience to hear me and of course especial thanks to you madam for saving my life." He said looking at Madhu.

Then getting up Amar asked "Do I have the right to know the name of my savior?"

Salma replied "Well the great Lady is my friend Madhu and he is my boy friend Rehman and not the least I am Salma."

Amar as if about to leave said "Thank you all very much once again Miss Salma, Mr. Rehman and Madam Madhu."

"Where are you going?" Madhu asked alarmed.

"Definitely not to commit suicide again, with a full belly I will give it a try once more,"

"Where do you live?" Madhu asked.

"Under the blue sky,"

"I know of a place where you can live on room sharing basis." Madhu had put in.

"I know of many such places but unfortunately none of them are for free." Amar replied sarcastically.

At a guest house Madhu booked a bed for Amar to live in. Amar remarked "In Mumbai if you have a roof over your head half the battle is won. You have won this battle for me the rest I think I can manage; however stupid I may be."

For his daily food requirement, at a nearby restaurant Madhu opened a credit account on her personal guarantee.

The next day having dinner with Madhu in that particular restaurant Amar had made another comment "Such good food that too no limit. Now hundred percent, my struggle will be a cake walk for me."

Madhu joked "Imagine, what you would have missed had you succeeded in your suicide mission."

"More than anything I would have missed you." Amar said simply looking into Madhu eyes.

Madhu said nothing to this approach of Amar. She just kept eating. Amar had stopped eating he was looking earnestly at Madhu "In a way I must thank my struggle; it drove me to suicide and led me into you."

Madhu finished eating; wiping her hands with a paper napkin she gave an intent look to Amar and said with purpose, seriously to make Amar understand "Struggle is essence of life, nothing comes easy and what comes easy goes easy, the bigger the goal the greater the struggle. Your ambition is to be a Director, Director of films worth millions of rupees. Your ambition is too big so struggle has got to be sizeable. It is written in the holly book; after every bad time there is a good time; after grief there is relief; after failure success. Don't give up, keep trying and praying to The Almighty God."

Amar listened to Madhu amazed, impressed and maybe in love.

As days passed a will to live had once again generated in Amar and along with it had bounced immense love for Madhu.

Madhu was also lonesome somewhere. She had lost her father when she was just a child. Her mother had raised her up and when after accomplishing nursing training, Madhu began earning her mother had also left her for her heavenly abode.

Madhu had no one who she could depend upon or who would be dependent on her. Amar filled the bill both ways. Madhu began depending on him because he was very loving, very caring, and of course Amar was totally dependent on Madhu doing nothing other than struggle to find an assistant directors job.

Amar further secured himself completely by conveying his love to Madhu and getting a confirmation of her love in return.

It happened on a very rainy day; 26th of July 2005; later on it was declared a cloud burst. 944mm of rainfall within a span of five hours had flooded entire Mumbai. There were many deaths and hundreds, thousands of people were stranded at Air Ports, Railway Stations, Office Premises, School Buildings, in local and out station trains, single and double décor buses or whatever shelter they could find, if lucky.

Madhu and Amar were more than lucky. Amar had come that morning to visit Madhu at her guest house. It was a week day; most of the paying guests were out on their jobs except Madhu who as a nurse got random holidays. Fortunately 26th of July was her day off.

At 4P.M. It became nearly dark outside. The rain clouds were so thick and overcast that they had eclipsed the sun and it poured real heavy. Within an hour of that severe heavy downpour electricity was switched off all over the city due to the fear of short circuit as very many ground floor flats, shops, warehouses etc. were waterlogged, at some low lying areas even first floors were inundated, so no TV news was available to keep the public informed about the intensity of the heavy rains, mobile networks were also not functioning and landline phones were the first to go dead. Even in the safety of the guest house it was really scary. Madhu was happy to have Amar with her "Thanks God Amar you are here; this guest house is looking like a haunted house, so scary."

Amar made a suggestion "Either we sit here within the four walls of this room; lights off, TV off, phones off, with this creepy chilling feeling or we venture out at least on to the terrace of your guest house and take a firsthand experience, you know this is a life time happening."

To really witness the impact of the torrential rains Madhu and Amar dared on to the terrace of the guest house. They stepped onto the open terrace getting drenched within seconds, looking around they did shudder.

The panoramic view from a top the seven floor guest house was a scene of water-water everywhere. The guest house was located at the center point of Santacruz Market, usually it was a sea of human heads which one witnessed from a top the guest house, it was shocking to find the streets deserted, flooded with rain water, the sea of human heads missing. Madhu came close to Amar and caught hold of his arm tight. Scared she uttered "It seems as if the world is coming to an end."

"In that case I must confess something to you." Amar had very seriously said raising his voice over the batter of the heavy rains.

Surprised Madhu asked aloud shaking the continuous flow of rain from her eyes "Confess what?"

"My love for you…!" Said Amar coming down on his knees at the flooded terrace and raising his hands dramatically in prayers towards Madhu he continued raising his voice over the pounding rains "Oh Madhu my love, my angel, my savior, my knight in shining amour, I love you! I love you! I love you! I shall not mind dying right here in this watery grave, at this moment if you just say yes to me, my love."

For Madhu, suddenly the scary ambience changed into romantic haven. She came rushing into his open arms with such force that with the impact Amar and she ended up flat at the soaking wet terrace.

Nevertheless the strong arms of Amar held her tight; she caved in into them; the torrential rains were adding to their youth, their passion; his lips touched her lips; a sweet wave ran through her veins; she lost and forgot her resolve of chastity; all that mattered for her at that moment was her love for Amar her passion to become one with Amar. Amar was her man; her world. But all of a sudden Amar restricted himself, pulling away from Madhu; breathing heavily he said "No Madhu, no, what you have done for me, I have sworn till the time I be worthy of you, and I put this world at your feet, then and then I will have right on you."

This act of Amar had sealed her love for him.

Madhu brought luck for Amar. He succeeded in getting an assistant directors job with a very celebrated director.

The law or formula of success for one and all is based on three factors; one, one should know well the job one intends to succeed in; two, one should have a need to do that particular work; three and finally lady luck must favor him or her.

In Amar's case he knew the work he wanted to do and succeed in, and of course there was a great need for him to do it, and lady luck had also started favoring him. So he achieved success but till the time he was assigned the job of the Chief Assistant Director. And from there the struggle to become a full fledged independent director began.

In the beginning Amar tracked months that so many struggling months of effort have passed to attain his ambition. Then he forgot counting months began counting years.

Time took flight, seven years soar past. Madhu rationalized to him "God up there brings his people into deep waters not to drown them but to cleanse them. Difficulties you are facing now will be your experience, your power at the time you achieve success. This know-how will help you to defend and shield your position and status at that point of time."

Some times Amar understood, sometimes failed to understand; sometimes a ray of hope other times just darkness.

For Amar the first real silver lining in the dark clouds came in the form of Reena. Reena was the only daughter of a formidable film financier Keshu Bhai. But Reena's interest in films was restricted to film parties only. Amar had met her in one such party and he had even told Madhu about his this meeting with Reena.

Madhu was engrossed in her past life; someone gently kept a hand on her shoulder.

"Madam we have reached Forest Resort "

Little taken a back Madhu looked up. Middle aged, dark and bulky conductor of the bus was smiling at her.

"What is your cottage number madam? I will send your luggage there."

"I have no booking here "

Surprised conductor questioned "Well then where are you going to stay?"

"Some one will be here to pick me up."

"O.K, then that's alright, otherwise there is no other habitation around here."

Conductor went away .Madhu picked up her things.

Forest Resort was a cluster of one and two bedroom hall kitchen self contained cottages. Each cottage had its own small private garden demarcated by well pruned hedge. The cottages were all painted bright white. Combination of green forest and white cottages was very soothing a sight.

Madhu was standing beside her luggage and admiring the peaceful vibes. Rest of the tourists had gone to their cottages. She looked here and there as if expecting some one. She had come from India so far away to South Africa just to forget Amar. She wanted to tear away all his memories set deep inside her heart and cast them out into the wilderness of the jungles of Africa so that they lose their way and never come back to her. This was why she had applied for house keeper job at Forest Conservator Rajeshwar house and on receiving her conformation had come there.

From some distance a jeep was seen approaching leaving behind a cloud of dust. It came and sped past Madhu then screeched to a halt, reversed, closed to her and stopped next to her. The one driving the jeep was a short black man, may be aged between forty and forty five years, his hair were jet black and curly, very broad nose, large eyes and a short neck. On a stunted stout physique he wore black trousers and a blood red T. shirt. In totality his appearance was quite comic.

Sitting in his Jeep he tilted his head to a side and gazed at Madhu with his large red eyes. Madhu also stared back at him confused that how could he be the forest conservator Rajeshwar. He asked Madhu "Miss Madhu?"

Madhu shook her head slightly to nod a yes. All of a sudden he jumped from the jeep, startled Madhu stepped back, he came straight for her luggage picked it up and kept it in his jeep. Totally taken a back Madhu watched all this shocked.

He sat back in his Jeep absolutely oblivious of her reaction and looked back at her innocently. Madhu was standing still appalled. He reacted surprised as if confused as to why she had not sat in his Jeep. Angry Madhu questioned "May I please know who you are?"

Understanding or not understanding the situation, he laughed "I am Johnny – Rajeshwar sahib's driver"

Madhu got annoyed at her for not having guessed so but then the fellow's antics had not given her any time to do any guess work.

Smiling she sat in the jeep. Johnny putting the jeep in gear and taking a U turn drove away in the same direction from where he had come.

The jeep was speeding through the muddy course of the jungle. Some where it passed through the dense growth of trees and at other places it went through the meadows covered with short or tall grass and shrubs. There was a definite typical freshness in the air, a remarkable smell of the green, a very strange youth and strength.

Driving the Jeep, every few moments, Johnny's head tilted and he looked at Madhu; smiled and then seemed to be thinking something. Again and again as he turned and looked and smiled at her, annoyed she queried at his behavior "What are you looking at like this?"

Driving, Johnny asked "You are the new house keeper?"

"Yes"

"How many days are you going to last?"

Madhu was totally taken aback once more and she asked "Beg your pardon."

"I ask how many days are you going to be here?"

"Why do you ask so?"

Johnny laughed and said "No, no, it is like this, before you many others came, I mean house keepers, some stayed for two days, some for four, and maximum was eight days."

Suddenly Johnny applied brakes. Jeep stopped with a jerk. Madhu spotted a group of elephants standing right in the middle of the road.

Their strong creamy white ivory tusks shinning; they were wagging their tails and shaking ears to give themselves some air and ward off the flies as well.

Driving the jeep away from the road to a muddy path, avoiding the elephants, Johnny drove it through the jungle and then came back on the main road, not disturbing the elephants at all.

Madhu, on her part concluded that wild animals must be the reason for the departure of the other house keepers. But the fact was not this; which Madhu was to find out very soon.

The Jeep took a winding turn. Madhu saw a small settlement atop which was a very beautiful bungalow. Jeep reached and stopped in the portico of that bungalow.

Johnny carried her luggage. Following Johnny Madhu entered the bungalow.

Madhu looked around. She was standing in a very spacious hall. At least Madhu had not seen such a spread out living room anywhere else. It was furnished with oriental set of sofas. The wooden center table had a thick glass with some engravings on it. The comfortable seats kept alongside the sofas were so commodious that easily two people could settle on them. But the polish on the furniture was time worn;

no shine left. The drapery hung on the doors and huge windows seemed to be not cleansed since years. Johnny voice echoed "Maji, Maji, Madam is here."

From the two corners of the hall two flights of stairs went up the first floor. One could see a gallery leading to the doors of the first floor rooms. From one open door a wheel chair appeared. Seated on the wheel chair was a lady of fifty or fifty five years of age. Pushing the wheel chair with both of her hands she came near the head of one staircase. Johnny told Madhu "She is Maji, Rajeshwar sahibs Mother"

Madhu joined her hands in a 'Namaste' with a slight smile, Maji replied nodding her head. Even on the wheel chair the personae of Maji was exuding elegance and aristocracy. She was fair, very fair, she had aligned Aryan features. Due to her age her hair was partially white but still thick in growth and long flowing.

As Madhu climbed the oriental stair case to reach her Maji rolled her wheel chair towards an open room door, following her Madhu entered that room. In the center of the room Maji was poised on her wheel chair, she looked at Madhu and said "Madhu is your name right?"

"Yes"

"This is your room, on the right is mine and on the left is Pinky's room."

Nodding her head in a yes Madhu asked "Your grand daughter, Priyanka I mean Pinky where is she?"

"She is out, playing."

As the sight of morning gives inkling of the coming day similarly observing a child acquaints' the family it belongs to; their traditions; their culture; environment they live in, all one can make out simply by watching the child.

At the sight of Priyanka alias Pinky, Madhu understood the people she had come to work for.

The backyard of the bungalow was a huge open space, there were many strong iron cages, big and small, lined up there. In these cages were different wild animals. In one cage was a loin. He was fast asleep and looked weak and sick. Cage adjacent to it was empty. In the next cage were four very cute looking little wolf pups.

Eight years old intrepid Pinky; a school bag strapped to her back was feeding one of them with a milk bottle. She was holding the pup in her hand and was delighted to see it finish the milk bottle. Standing at some distance amazed Madhu watched this and realized that she had come to an animal loving warm hearted caring people world.

Pinky was not as fair as her grandmother nor did she have Aryan features. Except for her eyes, which were deep blue just like Maji she was somewhat different. Madhu contemplated that Pinky might have gone on her mother.

The eyes of the sleeping lion opened. He yawned. A harrowing sound was produced; Madhu shuddered. Then Pinky attention got drawn towards Madhu.

Pinky laughed on seeing Madhu tremble. The wolf pup hanging on her shoulder she came to Madhu "Aunty, don't be scared, Sher uncle is a good friend."

"You are Pinky?"

"Yes and you new house keeper?"

Madhu smiled back in confirmation. The puppy was licking Pinky's cheek, pulling it away Pinky said "Stop it Chintu."

Laughing Madhu gently petted the pup. Pinky passed it over to Madhu and said "See aunty how cute Chintu is."

Fondling the pup Madhu asked "You have named him Chintu?"

By that time the other three pups have jumped out of the open cage and had come to Pinky wagging tails running and rolling over in an excessive show of affections.

"Yes this is Chintu, this Buntu, this Pintu and this Montu and Montu is very strong and naughty."

Madhu picked up Montu "Come I will feed Montu."

"Aunty I have already fed him, if I do not feed him first he will not allow me to feed any."

Madhu gently kept Montu on the ground and picked up the other pup.

"Ok I will feed this fellow, where do I get the milk bottle?"

Happily Pinky took out a bottle full of fresh hot milk from within her school bag strapped on her back and gave it Madhu. Madhu laughed delighted; taking the pup in her lap she gently began feeding him.

"Why these animals are locked here?"

"Some of them are sick. These pups have lost their daddy mummy. Sher uncle is injured and that leopard there is also injured."

"How come they are injured?"

"Fighting, but some are injured by poachers."

"Who brings them here?

Pinky very proudly said "My daddy, who else, Daddy is their doctor, Sher uncle there; Poachers shot him. Daddy did operation, and I saw the bullet, Johnny says daddy got him here in time so he got saved."

Montu who was playing with another pup all of a sudden started fighting with him. Montu was much stronger. The other fellow was wailing. Pinky rushed and separated them then gently smacked Montu "Naughty Montu, biting your sister, now I will lock you in the cage."

Pinky carried him to the cage and locked him up. Meanwhile Madhu had picked up the other one and was looking all over its body to see if he was hurt. Concerned Pinky also joined in. Soon they realized the little one was not hurt. Looking at the loin Madhu asked "Pinky tell me, once Sher uncle is fit will he be left back in the jungle?"

"Daddy says his leg is broken so he will be sending him off to some zoo."

This way in their very first meeting Madhu and Pinky jelled. Pinky introduced Madhu to the rest of the caged animals.

At about four in the evening Johnny brought food for the animals. Madhu and Pinky helped him dole out loins share of meat to Sher Uncle, chunks of meat in leopard cage, green and fresh grass to the sick spotted dear and so on.

Maji, sitting in her wheel chair from her room balcony watched all the doings. She seemed very pleased. God only knew why her heart was hinting repeatedly that Madhu was the silver lining in her family's dark lives. There was a happy glow on her face and hope in her eyes.

Chapter Two

It was midnight when a jeep its strong head lights piercing the darkness of wild night entered and came to a halt in the porch of the forest conservator's bungalow.

Two staggering feet alighted and moved towards the bungalow. He was six feet plus inches tall, broad shouldered, strong physique. But he was drunk; not being able to conduct his hefty burly self. That was the forest conservator Rajeshwar Kumar.

Though Rajeshwar was of wheatish complexion, maybe due to over exposure to sun but his features were just like his mother sharp straight and aristocratic; the Rajputana grace and elegance. He wore a military color safari suit, holding a rifle in one hand, in the other hand carried a lighted torch.

Walking unsteadily he entered the bungalow. The bungalow was dimly lit. Rajeshwar switched off the torch and kept it on a table, laid down the rifle on a sofa, walking up the stairway he moved towards the upper floor.

Madhu was sleeping beside Pinky, in Pinky's room, Pinky head resting on her forearm. Pinky in her deep slumber smiled in her innocent dreams.

Rajeshwar entered the room; shaky he walked to Pinky's bed. Seeing Madhu sleeping with Pinky he reacted slightly confused belching slightly. The old oriental bed had a towering frame; took its support with his hand and leaned over.

Suddenly Madhu eyes opened wide. She could see Rajeshwar face coming on to her as if he wanted to kiss her. Madhu was shocked but to her relief Rajeshwar kissed his little daughter, sleeping beauty Pinky. Then abruptly he turned and walked away.

Flustered Madhu sat up; she could see a staggering Rajeshwar walking out of the room his back towards her. Madhu was breathing heavily she thought 'This must be Pinky's daddy Rajeshwar. Oh! God! He reeked of whisky.'

Suddenly she heard the crashing sound of someone falling heavily. Madhu jumped out of her bed and rushed out of the room towards the source of the crash.

In the dim light she saw Rajeshwar slumped down on the granite floor after bumping into something. Madhu dashed; helped him getup supporting one of his arms.

Rajeshwar looked at Madhu with contempt, then steadying himself, rudely jerked his arm free of her grip and questioned "You?"

"Yes, I am the new house keeper; to take care of Pinky."

In his drunken stupor he snubbed her harshly "Then take care of Pinky not me. You need not bother about me."

Angrily he stamped away to his room and banged the door shut. Tears appeared in Madhu eyes. She stood wondering what her fault was. She had tried to help a fallen man? She mentally made a conjecture of Rajeshwar, a good for nothing alcoholic, ill tempered man. A hurt angry Madhu turned and walked away to her room.

Madhu had decided against working there. Next morning in her room, as she packed her dresses that she had neatly hung the other day in the cupboard allotted to her, back into her suitcase. Maji sat on her wheel chair, tears in her eyes saying "My son Rajeshwar was never like as he is now. He was not ill-tempered or irritable and alcohol he never touched. What a cheerful, happy go lucky, good humored son he was. He loved his wife very much. She betrayed him. She left him. Such despair, such anguish set in him since then."

Having said so tears rolled down Maji eyes and hearing so Madhu felt a pinch in her heart and it ached.

Suddenly she realized that she was also never so touchy. At the hospital being a nurse so many times she came across such ill-tempered, snappy, fractious patients. She always gave them margin. In fact she was too good at handling difficult patients; was confidently allotted the most problematical of them. To co-ordinate and give margin was the basis of her nursing training. There was never ever any question of her relinquishing her job on such issues.

She wondered that how come she got so hurt, touchy and nonprofessional that she was packing her things. Why was she leaving her job? Why was she taking it to her heart? All of a sudden Amar's face revolved in front of her eyes. His betrayal had made her weak. So weak that she had become inefficient even in the job she used to take pride in. So weak that she was failing in her training. So weak that she failed to face a simple problem. Weak people she had seen so many in her life at hospitals that she loathed weakness. Amar had forced this change in her had made her weak.

Hitting her hard that instance, that moment came back to her when faithless Amar had made bare his betrayal.

"It is only Reena who can help me achieve my ambition, that ambition which stands devastated right now. Madhu please try and understand me, my mettle has cracked up, in my own eyes I have become a subject of self ridicule. Reena's father is a very prominent and powerful financier of films he had promised me that for Reena happiness he will set up a very big production house. Then I can make as many films as I want to that too that of my choice."

Rattled Madhu had said "And he will do all this because his only daughter Reena likes you, is in love with you."

An embarrassed and somewhat repentant Amar had tried to rationalize "Madhu I know I don't love Reena; I love you but if I fail to achieve my ambition then what will be there left in my life, it will be meaningless existence, neither of us will be happy, I mean with each other."

Trying to take control of her and contain her tears Madhu had said "No Amar your happiness is in your work, in your ambition. It is dearer to you than your own life that is why you have attempted suicide. I have helped you to an incomplete life. Now Reena will give you complete success. Satisfying life, she will take you to the heights of which you have been dreaming of and living for. Wish you all the best with Reena, Amar."

Guilty but still resolute for his better future Amar had said "May be, maybe, I will never be able to forgive myself."

Knowing Amar well by then, Madhu, a sarcastic smile prevailing on her lips had replied "Amar you will very easily forgive you and forget me. In fact I think you have already forgotten me. And what about me once you are successful you will even forget that Reena."

Suddenly Madhu looked very strange to Amar as she said "Amar you have not known yourself well. Today I am going to tell you what you are."

Saying so, God knows from where a shattered and wrecked Madhu had gathered enough courage and slapped Amar hard "You faithless man I am not going to shed tears for you all my life, you don't exist for me right from today, right from this moment."

In front of Maji, Madhu lost in her past was crying bitterly. A shocked Maji sat perplexed in her wheel chair, totally confused not knowing what went wrong and where.

Madhu sobbing was going out of control. Maji hurriedly picked up a glass of water kept at the side table, maneuvered her wheel chair to Madhu and made an attempt to help her drink the water. Madhu regained her poise and realized that she had utterly confused Maji. She took the glass of water from Maji hand, tried her best to smile, sipped at the water then kept the glass back at the corner table, wiping her tears tried to make up "Maji it is just that I got some what, you see what ever transpired in Rajeshwar Sahib's life, somewhat same happened to a sister of mine."

"Your sister is in India?

Taking a moment Madhu said "No Maji, she is no more in this world."

Trying once more to convince Madhu Maji said "Beti, now other then you, who else can understand Rajeshwar and his suffering better? Forgive him. Please don't go. Do not leave us."

Helpless Maji with tears in her eyes looked at Madhu with hope. Madhu's heartfelt for Maji like no other heart in the world could; sharing the pain; living the anguish; going through the same trauma. Total identification; Madhu kept an appeasing hand on Maji shoulder.

As Maji went on narrating her son's tragic love story to Madhu, the moments of her own betrayal fluttered. Somewhere Madhu saw a great lot of resemblance between her life and that of Rajeshwar.

Just like Amar, Namrata was also the modern picture of the new world. Both wanted to live life their way, their style. Both wanted others to come along; reflecting their colors without any complains.

But in the case of Namrata Maji told Madhu "Rajeshwar had warned Namrata in advance, very specifically that her life with him would be in these jungles, among speechless animals in the dense forests of Wild Life Kingdom Park of which he is the protector."

Madhu thought of Amar; she had also been very honest with Amar; had never kept him under any illusions; always told him that facts of life should be braved boldly. He had also agreed and gone along, thanked her, promised a never ending love to her but abruptly the end came with Reena entry.

Madhu found herself saying "Maji, not only true love but also false love and infatuation is blind. The small difference is; true love is permanently blind false love or infatuation is temporarily blind."

Maji laughed and said "Right you are very right those infatuated regain their senses but the ones who love truly are total loss."

Maji this time along with Madhu again laughed. Pinky was standing there surprised; she had never seen her Grand Ma laugh.

It seemed that Maji was well bent upon revealing all about Namrata betrayal to Madhu. On some pretext or the other she came about it and talked about it.

Pinky had gone to school; Madhu was busy setting her upset room. Maji sat on her wheel chair accounting to Madhu "Namrata sudden marriage to Rajeshwar was not at all a shock to me."

Hanging some frocks into Pinky's cupboard Madhu said "Maji you knew they were in love, so marriage was very much expected."

Annoyed Maji rolling her chair near Madhu said "Expected it was but not the way it happened?"

Closing the cupboard Madhu simply asked "And how did it happen?"

Taking a deep sigh Maji said "First ask me, why it happened not how it happened?"

Madhu smiled, sat on Pinky's bed beside Maji chair, kept her hand affectionately on Maji knee and asked "Well, why it happened?"

Maji taking another deep sigh went on "It had to happen that way, all of a sudden, without any formalities, without any celebrations, with no rituals. I all along expected it. You see the differences between the two families were enormous. My Rajeshwar though a Rajput by birth; from a royal family of Rajasthan in India is just a Forest Conservator earning a fixed salary, fixed benefits for his duties."

Madhu cuts in "And Namrata family?"

"In two words 'Filthy-Rich' mining diamonds out of mother earth is her father's business." Maji replied with contempt.

Ramzan the cook came in asking Madhu what was to be cooked for lunch and dinner.

Maji's knees had given in making her invalid. Madhu sat giving massage with some medicated herbal oil. Maji continued "Rajeshwar had gone on his official work to Johannesburg, the city of dwelling of Namrata's tycoon father Manohar Shivdasani ji and his socialite wife Sheela Shivdasani. There and then it happened, the simmering bubble of Rajeshwar and Namrata romantic relationship exploded right into the face of her parents."

"How?" Interested Madhu asked.

"Don't ask me how, Rajeshwar never told me." Maji continued "All he told me was that Mr. and Mrs. Shivdasani had abjectly disapproved of him and opposed the matrimony tooth and nail."

Madhu thought of better not asking any questions so she simply said "Ok..."

Maji at her age was still sharp and intelligent, she understood in between Madhu ok. She said "More than old age this wheel chair is making me irritable, I am sorry to cut you short."

Pressing her cheek against Maji cheek Madhu confidently and lovingly said "One day you will walk again; I promise. Now tell me then what happened at your son's front?"

"In retaliation to the not just affluent aggression, bold and beautiful Namrata rebelled. In Rajeshwar's jeep they both drove to a Mandir and exchanged 'Var Mallas' and tied the nuptial knot."

Madhu concluded "Thus happed the rushed up Marriage."

"i welcomed my daughter in law with open heart; showered her with gifts I had collected for my 'Bahu' since the time Rajeshwar was born. Namrata was also pleased, very pleased."

"Why not, having lost her parents she must have relished your reassuring love".

"However one and the only gift which her beloved husband Rajeshwar gave her made her more than wince."

Madhu just could not resist, with a naughty touch asked "Maji may I ask what was that?"

Maji went on very nostalgically "Rajeshwar very gently and affectionately placed a ten day old chimpanzee right in her lap."

Maji felt silent for few moments as if the scene was flashing back in her memory. Madhu kept watching her eager to know what happened next. Maji finally put in the picture "Namrata got up with a start shrieking, jerking the poor thing away from her. Rajeshwar jumped and in the nick of the time and caught hold of the little fellow or it would have flown out of the window into the rocky jungle terrain."

Madhu had finished massaging Maji knees; she just looked at Maji, not knowing how to react or what to say. Maji said "It was the very first day of her married life in this house. Both Rajeshwar and she were shaken."

Madhu sat without any reaction thinking something. Noticing Maji asked "Am I boring you."

"Oh no Maji not at all, it is just that I am wondering trying to understand God's point of view what purpose He intends in getting two people totally different in nature, in backgrounds, in out looks, together? The crash sometimes destroys lives."

"How very right you are, did somewhat same happened to your sister also?"

"Very similar Maji; that fellow my sister was in love with was a very ambitious man where as my sister; she happily lived the life as it came."

"What exactly went wrong?" Maji asked.

"Forget it Maji it hurts bad to think about it."

"But I feel light talking about Namrata to you."

"Go right ahead Maji I am all ears."

That day the go ahead came to an abrupt end because Rajeshwar came fetching Pinky from school. Pinky, throwing her school bag at the sofa came straight rushing to Madhu calling "Aunty, Aunty"

Maji remarked as Pinky embraced Madhu "So now you love your Aunty more than me?"

"I love you both." Pinky happily said.

Looking at Rajeshwar who stood silently watching, Maji asked her granddaughter "And your Daddy how much you love him?"

Before Pinky could reply Rajeshwar cut short the topic rudely and pronounced a dictate to Madhu "From tomorrow on wards dropping Pinky to school, taking her lunch there during her recess and then getting her back when school gets over is your responsibility."

Madhu shook her head in agreement but Maji intervened "You mean Johnny will drive them to school?"

"Yes, till I find some other driver for them."

As Rajeshwar turned to go Madhu said "I can drive but my Indian driving license needs to be endorsed or whatever the legal procedure."

Giving it a thought for a moment he said "We will see" and went away to his room.

Pinky once again held on to Madhu and said "It will be fun driving to school with you Aunty. I will show you all the ways around here, I know all the roads."

"But first your Daddy had to get her license done." Maji said thinking something.

Next day after dropping Pinky to school with Johnny Madhu came to Maji's room. Maji still in her bed was having her bed tea served on a specially designed tray which was safely kept on her bed. She brightened up seeing her and asked "So how was your trip? Must be very refreshing?"

Sitting beside Maji on her bed Madhu replied "I missed you Maji; I promised myself that one day you will be there with me, together we will go to drop Pinky to school."

Tears appeared in Maji eyes; she was touched, greatly touched by the concern and again comparative Namrata image came to her mind and she said "You know once a week, at least, Rajeshwar used to take Namrata out to town. Mornings they used to leave and come back late at night. During the two years of their marriage Rajeshwar spend major part of his savings taking her to places of her choice on his annual holidays. You know London, Paris, New York, Switzerland.

And on her return home whenever I asked her how her trip was? Her reply was always one and same 'out of hell; back to hell.'

Maji fell silent lost in the tragic past of her son. Madhu felt like changing the topic but then she also by then was very much interested in knowing more and more about Namrata. It gave her a vicarious satisfying feeling; helped her understand that other faithless people like Amar very much existed in the world. She was not the only one to have encountered one, there were other victims also. Madhu initiated "Maji, how gradual Namrata love fever recede?"

"Very fast, she was regularly in touch with her friends on internet. Day and night she just sat on her lap top. The truth is memories of her glittering high society never left her. The affluence and grandeur brought by her father's enormous money power; the limousines; the capacious gorgeous bungalows; the lavish parties thrown in them."

Maji again got lost in her past. Madhu, overflowing from her own experience with Amar, shook Maji by what she uttered lost in her own past "The moving around honorable esteemed people; their hoity toady lofty ways; the games of the affluent; the show of money power; the wish to reach the more prosperous and the desire to subdue the vulnerable."

Surprised Maji kept looking amazed at Madhu who continued thinking of Amar designed as Namrata "All that was not possible in this natural world where the extensive spread out greenery is for every one;

the smell of the flowers; the freshness of the air has no price; and there is a limit to being big; hold to being small."

Excited Maji couldn't contain herself she sliced in "Well, very well you speak from your heart."

Johnny came in the room to remind Madhu "Madam we leave for Pinky baby's school at 12.30 noon, her recess at 1.15 we reach there in time."

"I will be sitting in your jeep at 12.30 sharp you better be there in time, morning you were late and you drove very rashly."

"You drive rash that is why Sahib never lets you touch the family car and why were you late?" Maji inquired.

"Sorry Maji, to drop Sahib at office and come back in time for school is difficult Maji." Johnny excused grimacing.

"Johnny how to get my Indian driving license endorsed here?"

"Sahib can get it done, very easy, RTO people very happy with Sahib, all his friends."

Maji making a mental note said "I will remind Rajeshwar." Then she told Johnny "Johnny sit here."

Johnny sat easy on the carpeted floor, Maji told Madhu "Madhu when you were not here I used to talk to Johnny, I mean about Namrata. He also has very fond memories of her."

"Please give an example Johnny?" Madhu put a straight question to him.

"She never tipped me, always was angry with me." Johnny said thinking of the past, Maji and Madhu laughed, then thinking something Madhu said reminding Maji "Maji you know my sister's that faithless man, he and Namrata were one of the same characters only their gender different."

"But I bet the female was more deadly." Maji very confidently voiced. Johnny was all confused. With a dash of humor Madhu said "Please do put on view one instance in support."

"No problem at all, there is many in account, for example a hard fact of this Forest Conservator job is to save wild animals; Rajeshwar often ran into armed poachers."

Johnny nodded in agreement as Maji continued "One day in such an encounter with poachers one of Rajeshwar forest guards was shot and killed. Namrata raised all hell. First time she openly confronted Rajeshwar and exhibited her utter contempt for his work.

"What a primitive & ignorant life you are living. In my father's mansion stuffed animal heads, skin and fur are of use as decorative pieces. Hunting is a sport but in your eyes those very hunters are poachers, criminals. To protect these worthless wild animals you risk your life. If you want to safe guard & defend something go to the borders & defend your country. There if you are shot and killed at least you will be awarded a medal posthumously, here if you die protecting these wild animals & wild trees only thing you will get is a decent cremation in lots of freshly cut jungle wood; and will finally disappear in smoke and ashes."

Repeating her daughter in law tears sprang up in Maji eyes. Johnny remarked "Bad, very bad days they were."

"These words of my own daughter in law for my only son are so deep embedded in me, I don't think even my funeral pyre will help burn them out of me."

Madhu anger rose within her, she did realize that Namrata had gone even beyond Amar. She felt angry also on Rajeshwar, why was he taking all that shit from Namrata after all he had admonished what her life would be with him. Madhu questioned Maji "Why did Rajeshwar sahib never remind his wife that he had warned her life with him would be in these jungles?"

Defending her son Maji said "I know my son well he simply wanted Namrata to realize on her own without any persuasions or compulsions and adjust with the facts of life with him."

Next morning at dining table Maji sat alone in her elevated wheel chair having breakfast. Madhu brought her fresh hot toasts, as she put them in front of Maji and was about to go Maji caught hold of her hand "If I do not tell you right now what I want to tell you I will get digestive disorder."

Madhu immediately settled next to Maji on a chair, very much eager "Go right ahead Maji, I am once again all ears."

Remember the little baby chimpanzee; Rajeshwar wedding gift to Namrata I told you about?"

"Yes the one she almost threw out of the window."

Maji with pleasure applied butter on her fresh toast as she said "That fellow was a constant irritant to Namrata. Rajeshwar had named him 'Bholu'. It was not that Namrata had not tried making friends with Bholu. One day when he sat cool in Rajeshwar's lap Namrata brought a full bunch of bananas. You know she kept peeling bananas and fed him and he kept eating till his tummy was full then to make Namrata stop you know what Bholu did?"

Inquisitively raising her eye brows Madhu inquired as to what he did.

"Bholu rudely showed her teeth and snarl at her sending shivers through her body while Rajeshwar laughed."

Madhu also laughed to her heart's content. Maji watched her delighted, love in her eyes.

"Where is Bholu now Maji?"

"He will come any day. Be prepared for him, he is Pinky's best friend."

"I will also like to make friends with him."

"You will, I am sure you will." Maji said confidently and came back on Namrata topic "You know right where you are sitting Namrata sat that day; I very distinctly remember Namrata was four months pregnant, we three, I, Rajeshwar and Namrata were having our breakfast. Bholu came after a gap of many days and joined us as if he was also a family member."

"Right here on this table?" Excited Madhu asked.

"Yes, yes he sat on this table opposite you there next to Rajeshwar; cried asking food then all of a sudden before anyone could offer any food he snatched Namrata's breakfast from right in front of her and started eating; once again showing his growing fangs only to Namrata. Angry Namrata walked out."

Amazed Madhu sat there trying to contain her laughter. Johnny had come by then, adding to Bholu and Namrata breakfast encounter he said "Madam Madhu, all of us workers loved Bholu, for this brave fellow was never scarred of Namrata ji."

Madhu and Maji were amused at Johnny's expression. Maji remarked "You see a chimpanzee also had to be brave to counter Namrata."

Another merry laugh then Maji further elaborated "Rajeshwar tried to explain to Namrata that the animal had not forgotten its first encounter with her. She had sarcastically questioned."

"Well in that case, one day, he will have me for breakfast."

Rajeshwar reassured "This fellow will never harm you, as he grows up he will understand that you are my wife the madam of this house. If he wants to be welcomed in this house he better respect you."

Shocked Namrata asked "You mean he will keep coming here even when he grows up?"

"Bholu kept coming as and when he pleased." Maji further told Madhu.

"Namrata gave birth to Pinky, among those who celebrated Pinky's arrival the first and foremost was the chimpanzee. As soon as Bholu saw infant Pinky he jumped around, tossed things, made sounds which made Namrata shudder."

Johnny added "Pinky baby was one year and not even little scared of Bholu sometimes even sat in his lap."

"She very much played with Bholu and Namrata very much petrified fought with Rajeshwar." Maji recalled.

Rajeshwar had misplaced his jeep's key the previous night when he had come home late drunk as usual. Next morning he searched for the key all over.

"I am getting late for work, Johnny has to drop me at office then come back and take Pinky school. She will also be late at school."

His temperature rose every moment. Maji came rolling her wheel chair "Take out some time from your busy schedule, go to the RTO with Madhu, get her license done, then she can drive Pinky to school every day in our car."

"Ok, ok, Maji but first we have to find the dam key." An irritable Rajeshwar countered "Johnny, don't stand like a stupid dumbstruck idiot search the key."

Madhu appeared with the key dangling in her hand and handed it over to him. Annoyed he questioned "Where was it?"

"Sir it was at Pinky's bed."

Rajeshwar reacted confused, not remembering how and when he dropped it there. Madhu clarified "Last night it might have slipped out of your shirt pocket Sir while kissing Pinky good night."

Maji remarked "Yes you never forget to kiss Pinky good night however drunk you may be."

Not caring for the sarcasm in Maji remark Rajeshwar questioned Madhu rudely "Then why didn't you come and give it to me earlier?"

Madhu looked at Rajeshwar; a smile opened out on her pretty face as she replied "Well Sir earlier I didn't find it. Right now while making Pinky's bed it just dropped right in front of my eyes."

Giving one additional smile to Rajeshwar she made her exit. Perplexed Rajeshwar kept looking after her. Maji looked pleased.

That day after Rajeshwar drove away with Johnny to office Madhu convinced Maji to take a trip to school.

"Change is must in life; sitting day night in this house on this wheel chair is not done. Maji I am a nurse and I am here to take care of you, I know for you to get well physically you must get prepared mentally first and to get mentally prepared you must move and move you will with us to your dear Pinky's school." Madhu said decisively.

Pinky was jubilant her 'Dadi' (Grand Ma) was coming to drop her to school, first time in life. Madhu, Johnny and the cook Ramzan had helped Maji get on the jeep, lifting her from the confines of the wheel chair.

As the jeep sped on the road to school fresh lease of life emerged conspicuous on Maji face. She was seated on the front seat in between Madhu and Johnny. Pinky was at the back, she never sat all the while stood; her hands around her dear grand ma neck talking-talking and talking "Dadi you see this is a new short cut to school ok, the old road went through the Forest Resort, long road took one hour to reach, this is by pass ok, Johnny how much time it takes us now to reach school?" She shook Johnny's shoulder asking shouting into his ear.

Johnny laughed shouting back at Pinky "Baby not more than 35 minutes."

Pinky moved away from Johnny complaining "Johnny your mouth smells of whisky, you drink too much."

Johnny felt embarrassed then all of a sudden applied brake, at a turn of the road, a herd of elephants was crossing over, and jeep came to a halt to let the magnificent animals pass by. Madhu remarked as the elephants triumphantly crossed the road and Johnny put the jeep back in gear and drove on "A million dollar sight."

"To you but to some it was horror glorified."

Madhu understood that Maji was back to Namrata but before she could react or say anything Pinky cut in "Dadi where is Monu?"

Madhu asked "Monu or Bholu?"

Pinky explained "Monu not Bholu, Monu is the elephant and Bholu the chimpanzee."

Shocked Madhu looked at Maji who further clarified "Monu was also just one month old when

Rajeshwar brought him home. His parents and family were shot and killed by poachers."

Pinky went on "He is also my best friend like Bholu ok. Monu has grown too big, lives in jungle, has a family of his own but he comes to meet me whenever he is free, you will like him aunty, ok."

Madhu trying to comprehend shook her head in a yes uttering "Ok."

They had reached school, Pinky jumped out of the jeep then before proceeding to her school called out to her grand ma "Dadi will you come at recess with aunty to feed me and stay back to take me home?"

Maji laughed saying "Oh no baby, one trip is enough for me to begin with."

Madhu reassured "Your Dadi one day God willing be fit and fine, you just pray for her and keep her happy."

Happiness is contentment, if one is content with what one is and what one has then one is happy. Rajeshwar was content with what he was, a Forest Conservator but was not content with what he had. He had lost his First Love Namrata, so not having his love, his wife, he was not happy and was suffering and was also powerless to do anything about it.

There was only one thing with in his power to end this suffering and that was to forgive. Yes if he could bring himself to forgive Namrata then he could have very efficiently got rid of the suffering; that is why to forgive is divine and divine everyone is not because to forgive others is a very difficult task. However to forgive one own self is a much easier task but to forgive oneself one should first acknowledge the mistake one has committed. For example in Rajeshwar case the obvious mistake was that of Namrata but Rajeshwar was also somewhere wrong. His mistake was in his desire. He desired Namrata who was different by birth, by upbringing, by different mindset. At the time of marriage he was confident that Namrata would change and he would help her to change. However that never happened. He held Namrata at fault for not changing and never forgave her and was helpless to do anything either; like taking revenge, so he suffered. Had he held himself responsible for not succeeding in reconditioning her then he would have come to terms with the tragedy easier and faster because certainly he would have forgiven himself over a period of time and taking revenge from his own self would never have occurred to him. Mere realization that his desire was wrong he was not fit for Namrata would have helped him to forget and forgive and in turn spared him a lot of pain.

Simple fact; to forgive and forget others fault is difficult; to forgive and forget one's own faults is easier. But to do so one has to acknowledge the fault not in others but in self.

And also, one should not try find faults in others, because correction of others faults is not always with in ones power; yes to correct oneself is always with in one's hands.

Same was true with Madhu. Madhu should have realized that Amar was of a different kind, she and Amar were two different people; their union meant inviting trouble. Realizing her mistake Madhu should have had convinced herself that the world is vast there existed different people of different cast, creed, cultures and thinking. Some of her kind was very much there in this world. Lamenting for Amar was no good; looking for some one of her own kind was a much better option. And Rajeshwar was one such better option.

However many a times, time is the biggest teacher and always the best healer.

Chapter Three

Rajeshwar contentment with his job of Forest Conservator was the only silver lining in his otherwise dark life. Poachers were a head ache for him and he took them in line of his duty.

Poachers used to hunt not for pleasure or sport but for business. They very well planned and contemplated their every move. One such group of poachers was headed by Michkle. Rajeshwar and Michkle have had come across each other many a times. A forest guard was also killed in one such confrontation. Then Rajeshwar had pledged to get Michkle at any cost, dead or alive.

One day Rajeshwar was returning home when a villager informed him about Michkle and gangs entry in to the jungle. He also reported that Michkle inquired about elephants.

Rajeshwar very well understood that the hunt was for ivory. He immediately ordered Johnny to speed up the Jeep towards the part of the jungle where Michkle was seen and then on wireless ordered his forest guards to reach that spot.

Michkle and his group spotted a family of elephants. Among the family there were six elephants with full grown tusks. For Michkle and his men the worth of elephant ivory was much more than their lives.

The elephants were hit with a hail of bullets. All the six elephants with tusks collapsed then and there. The rest of the family ran for their lives.

Michkle and men got set on their job. They were cutting the tusks of the dead elephants with battery operated saws. One of their comrade was a top a huge tree keeping vigil looking around through binoculars. Suddenly he saw Rajeshwar Jeep at great speed approaching. He yelled the warning to Michkle. Michkle shouted back at him to shoot at Rajeshwar. The man fired, the bullet shattered the windscreen of Rajeshwar's Jeep.

Rajeshwar countered by firing back. Johnny was scared but Rajeshwar ordered him to keep driving ahead.

Michkle and his man were recklessly trying to cut the ivory free. Some more gun shots were heard. The man atop the tree saw some more Jeeps full of forest guards approaching. He barked a final warning to Michkle. Michkle instructed his men to pack whatever ivory they had succeeded in detaching from the dead elephants into their Jeep and leave. Taking their contraband they left along with the man atop the tree. When Rajeshwar reached there he saw the devastated dead bodies of six elephants in their prime.

Michkle and his men in their Jeeps had left a cloud of dust in route they have escaped. Rajeshwar told Johnny to wait for the forest guards and himself drove after Michkle.

Rajeshwar was speeding through the dusty road with little visibility, and then came into his view the dim image of Michkle's Jeep speeding away.

Rajeshwar driving with one hand aimed his rifle with the other hand and fired. One of the tires of the poachers Jeep had burst open. Michkle lost control of the vehicle. It dashed into a tree. Michkle and his men fell out of the hood less jeep. Some of them were hurt.

Rajeshwar's Jeep approached fast. They opened fire at him. Trying to escape their bullets Rajeshwar also lost control of his jeep. The jeep got stuck in a ditch. With the impact his head had hit the broken wind screen. His forehead bled but he jumped out with his rifle and counter fired at Michkle and his men. Johnny also reached there with the rest of the forest guards.

In the encounter two of Michke's men were arrested but Michkle jumping into a river escaped along with the other two and the ivory,

Wounded Rajeshwar was on his way back with the arrested men and forest guards. The one month old baby elephant was standing wailing among the dead bodies of his parents and other family members.

That was how Monu, the baby elephant had met his savior Rajeshwar.

At night Pinky had gone to sleep Madhu was on her routine massaging Maji knees and legs "What happened when Rajeshwar Sahib brought Monu home. I mean how Namrata reacted?"

"It was just too much for Namrata she pronounced her final decision."

"Rajeshwar you will have to relinquish your job and this jungle."

"Then what will I do?"

Proud Namrata had replied "You have so much to do that others don't get to do even after taking many births. I am the only daughter of my billionaire father. I will get you the charge of his as many companies as you may desire. Just let us get out of this isolated hell."

Rajeshwar had smiled sadly. Looked at Namrata with pain in his eyes and said "Namrata at least let my wounds get dressed then you can fight as much as you want."

Furious Namrata retorted "Rajeshwar the quota of fights between us is over. Enough is enough. Now this is my final decision. I am going away from here. If you want to come with me you are welcome otherwise."

A cool Rajeshwar questioned "Otherwise what?"

Proceeding to pack her things Namrata looked back and had said "Otherwise you will get the notice of my lawyer."

A distressed Maji had intervened "Beta! Beta! Please stop her."

"But Rajeshwar had not stopped Namrata. Yes he had not allowed her to take away Pinky. Namrata had also not been very assertive about the custody of her child."

Madhu asked "Very strange?"

Maji explained "She was constantly in touch with her parents and kept them regularly informed about her dwindling relationship with Rajeshwar. Once during those days they came here on a visit. I heard with my own ears, they telling her.

"Namrata you want a new life, good family, good house, good husband, no one will marry mother of a child."

Maji lamented "Namrata, anyhow wanted to forget her past and go back to her society as the only daughter of a diamond merchant, she knew her society well, she knew they will simply overlook her past and welcome her with eager open arms."

Madhu prepared Maji's bed and helped her lay down. Maji summed up Rajeshwar's tragic love story "After a few days divorce papers arrived. Rajeshwar signed them."

Madhu thought 'So had come to pass another sad love story.'

The tragic love story of Rajeshwar very sincerely told by Maji touched the very core of Madhu heart. She and Rajeshwar were sailing in the same boat; glimpse of her life was very much there in Rajeshwar heartbreak. So when Rajeshwar was irritable or angry she sensed the pain in it.

The very next day Rajeshwar was again very much off mood. Reason; rot in system. Some unscrupulous men of position have maneuvered clearance of a hundred acres of forest land adjacent to a Town Ship, basis; need of agricultural land; motive to build another Town Ship.

Rajeshwar came home angry and thirsty craving for liquor.

Back home, it had happened so; Madhu was putting the mess of Rajeshwar room in order. She noticed a case of whisky kept on the bed side table. She decided to keep it at its proper place, the small but well done up bar at the rear end of the copious bedroom. She never told the maid, helping her, to carry the fragile item to the bar. She herself was safely transporting it when all of a sudden Pinky came dashing and clung to her legs in motion; lovingly calling "Aunty! Aunty!"

Madhu lost her balance, tripped, the case of whisky jumped out of her hands, crashed on the hard floor.

Right then she was standing in attendance to Rajeshwar "Who gave you permission to enter my room?"

"No one did Sir."

"Then why did you?"

"Sir...It was messy...It is my job to tidy it up."

"Take it straight from me, now on you will not interfere with me. This is the second and the last warning to you. Do you understand or not."

Madhu was quiet. This annoyed Rajeshwar more "In case you have some other designs then forget them, I knows females like you very well. You better clear your accounts and leave."

In spite of her resolve Madhu was hurt. Rajeshwar had raised doubt on her character. Tears sprang up in her eyes; just then Maji came wheeling her chair hastily. Madhu went out of the room. Maji exploded on Rajeshwar "You are sickening! How can you talk to a lady in such a manner? Frustrated I know you are but your frustration can put such thoughts in your mind this I never knew."

It was Pinky who had rushed to Maji and informed about the debacle, she entered tears running all over her face "Daddy it is my mistake, I accidentally pushed Aunty."

Rajeshwar, who by then felt somewhat guilty hearing that it was his daughter's fault was uncomfortable "Well then why didn't Madhu tell me so?"

Maji said in Madhu defense "She is not one of those who dodge responsibility and put blame on others. She is good my son, very good but I am afraid her days here are over."

Pinky was still crying. Rajeshwar sat beside her, wiped her tears with his hand and said "Go and tell your Aunty I am very sorry."

Maji reproved "No you personally go and say sorry to her."

Madhu was pressing Pinky's school uniform. Rajeshwar knocked at the door saying "I am sorry."

Madhu turned and looked, there were no tears in her eyes she had already forgiven him. His bad experience with his lady love had left him bitter to women kind however her own experience with Amar kind had not made her bitter to all male kind, she felt one up on Rajeshwar; so she smiled at him just then little Pinky came rushing to her saying "Aunty! Aunty! Daddy said sorry."

Madhu held Pinky in her arms and once again smiled at Rajeshwar and said "On the contrary we should apologize to your daddy for forcing a dry night on him."

Not understanding dry night Pinky reacted confused. Rajeshwar was also mystified at Madhu demonstrating good humor, after his hard talk he had expected an angry Madhu packing to leave but there she was doing her job, efficiently pressing Pinky's clothes, smiling and friendly.

Maji was very happy to see Madhu ignore her son snubs and treat with contempt and Rajeshwar was very much amazed to see Madhu so well jelled with Maji, Pinky and the rest of the house hold in such a short time, it seemed as if she was one of the family.

Rajeshwar was on his routine jungle patrol. He spotted a very severely injured leopard. It seemed some enormous lion or a pack of rivals had done the damage. Rajeshwar and Johnny carried the half dead leopard to their jeep and rushed him to their make shift hospital.

On reaching home as they were transporting the unconscious leopard from the jeep to the hospital, Madhu from her first floor room witnessed the display of human benevolence.

A wooden table in the hospital room served as operation table. Rajeshwar and Johnny had prostrated the leopard on it. Rajeshwar told Johnny "Quick strap him well and make sure his jaw is securely tied up."

Scared Johnny nodding a yes said "Yes sir, I know, I know, while cleaning his wounds if his eyes open we will be lying here."

He quickly started strapping the leopard with the straps attached to the table. Rajeshwar was checking the wounds. Suddenly they saw Madhu standing there. In her hand was a surgical tray containing surgical appliances, medicines and gauge and cotton. She kept the tray on a table. Picked up some cotton, soaked it with some antiseptics then professionally began clean-up the leopard's wounds.

Rajeshwar silently observed her, Johnny was thoroughly surprised. Accepting what he saw Rajeshwar prepared an injection. The leopard body showed some movement as if he was gaining consciousness.

Maybe to assess more Rajeshwar very causally passed over the injection to Madhu. Madhu without any conscious effort expertly administered it. Johnny reacted once again shocked. Leopard's body relaxed. It went into an unconscious sleep.

Being a trained nurse Madhu assisted Rajeshwar expertly. She helped him first in cleaning the wounds then in stitching them and finally in dressing them.

Finishing the job at the operation table Madhu, Johnny and Rajeshwar together picked up the leopard and gently placed him on a mat in an enclosure.

Madhu and Rajeshwar were washing their hands at the wash basins Rajeshwar asked "You are not scared of these wild animals?"

Smiling Madhu replied "Humans are scarier."

She gave a meaning full look to Rajeshwar and left. Rajeshwar kept looking at her.

At Pinky's age her hair was ideal showcase for any hair care product; her inheritance from her grand Ma.

Pinky stood in front of her cute dressing table dressed in her neatly pressed school uniform. Madhu was combing her long flowing hair. As usual Pinky was in her chit-chat mood "Aunty when I grow up will I be as pretty as you?"

"You will be very pretty, more than anyone else. Look at your hair they can put any lady to shame, including me."

"Never mind my hair they are a big bother too, I just want to be as pretty as you." Pinky insisted.

"Why?" Madhu asked laughing.

"Because I like you, I like your eyes they are large and very attractive, your lips also I like and your nose is very cute and your figure..."

Madhu cuts in saying "Enough and thank you." Maji rolled in on her wheel chair "Good news, Madhu today Rajeshwar will take you to RTO, you take your passport and driving license with you, after dropping Pinky to school you straight go to the RTO with Johnny, Rajeshwar will meet you there."

Jubilant Pinky screamed "Hey."

"That's good, come Pinky we must leave early." Madhu said.

Maji intervened "Not like this."

Surprised Madhu asked "Maji what do you mean not like this?"

"I mean not dressed like this."

"Maji we are going to RTO office not to any party?"

"But you are going with Rajeshwar." It slipped out of Maji. She immediately tried to cover up "I mean at the local RTO everybody knows us so not this jean and top, something Indian; may be a sari will be better."

Somewhat wary Madhu said "Maji other than the casuals all I have are some shalwar suits, I have no sari here."

A trunk full of saris flashed through Maji mind. Whenever Maji went to India she had brought saris for her would be daughter in law, but her 'Bahu' Namrata, when came home thought sari to be too demanding a dress. When Maji got the blouses stitched Namrata had only once worn one sari and discarded the lot of them commenting that they were difficult to wear and walk in the jungle though she never ever went into the jungle.

Wheeling her chair out Maji said "Wait I have a sari along with its blouse which I am sure will fit you."

Maji went out of the room without waiting for Madhu reply or consent. Absolutely apprehensive Madhu inadvertently looked at Pinky who spoke innocently "I am dying to see you in a sari, I am sure you will look your best."

"But why must I look my best?" Madhu as if asked herself, pat came reply from Pinky "Because Dadi and I want you to look your best."

Anxious Madhu questioned Pinky "Why?"

"Because you are the best."Once again, instant, simple, honest and innocent reply from Pinky came.

Madhu had to give in to the pure love of Pinky and Maji; starved she was of such love; she wore the sari which Maji had once brought for her would be daughter in law.

Rajeshwar was at the school. Pinky jumped from the jeep and rushed to her father who stood next to his personal Honda CRV, waiting for them.

"My very good Daddy I am so happy you are taking aunty to the RTO to get her license done. Now I and Dadi will take a spin whenever we feel like. I will show aunty all the ways around here."

"Not without my permission." Rajeshwar issued a command.

"When Dadi is there, why must I take your permission? Dadi is your mother?"

Madhu, yet sitting in the jeep smiled at the prompt reply of Pinky. Rajeshwar held Pinky by both her arms and made her stand in front of him and said firmly "Your Dadi has the right to tell me this, not you, understand."

Scarred Pinky shook her head obeying. Rajeshwar released her arms telling her "Now run to your class."

Pinky ran to her school, Madhu not liking his rude attitude got off the jeep. The jeep was in between Madhu and Rajeshwar so as Johnny drove away the jeep she and he stood facing each other.

Rajeshwar was stunned to see Madhu; the hidden beauty in the casual dresses which she wore sari exposed; the curves; the cuts; the absolute measuring comparative figure oozing sensuality as well as grace, poise and beauty and her Bengali oval attractive facial features on a fair skin tone; Rajeshwar was just dazed for a moment and Madhu observed so without making her notice obvious.

Rajeshwar, coming out of his shocker, moved towards the driving seat of his car gesturing Madhu also to sit in. Madhu for a second thought whether to sit at the rear seat or in front along with Rajeshwar then opened the front door and sat in.

On the way to the RTO Madhu sat quiet. Rajeshwar concentrated on his driving to come out of the sudden invasion of sensuality. After Namrata exit his masculinity had become immune to feminine charm, however a while ago the female in Madhu revived it. He was finding it hard to keep his eyes and mind off her, Madhu though not looking at Rajeshwar but was conscious of him glancing her way while driving, suddenly he asked "In India how long have you been driving?"

"Five years."Madhu replied in two words and was hit by her past once again.

Rainy season it was; Amar came home soaked to the skin in rains. He had a bike; Madhu gave him a key "Congratulations…"

"What for? And what key is it?"

"Car key, your car key."

"My car, come on Madhu I am wet and tired."

"Stupid I bought you a car today, a Maruti 800, and happy birthday."

Amar had hugged Madhu passionately, both had learned driving together, date of issue on both their driving license was the same, both used to drive around in the car together, but the car belonged to Amar, in his name, a gift to him by his lady love, so Madhu had left it behind with Amar.

"What car did you drive?" Rajeshwar was asking, the words rang in Madhu ears, she came back to present "A Maruti 800"

"Well here you will have to drive this car."

"This is an automatic car, easy to drive." Madhu said confidently "A friend of mine had one, I have driven it." Madhu said thinking of Rehman.

Rajeshwar drove the car to the side of the busy road and parked it. He could not restrain himself from looking at Madhu once more, but with a smile, for a change "Come, drive..."

He got out of the car; she also alighted from the passenger seat but kept standing. Walking around the car when he came to her she asked "What about the license?"

He took a good look at her and said "It is a simple formality, just a letter to the consulate asking a permit to drive in South Africa attached with your passport copy and your driving license copy. In a week's time you will get your permit. Meanwhile you can drive on your Indian license."

"That's it?"

"Yes that's it, I have the letter with me, you sign it, and my man will do the rest, now come on let's see how good you drive."

Madhu drove well, she was confident so always was good and comfortable at driving. Amar was nervous and shaky at driving; Madhu all the time drove when they were together. Madhu felt strange instead of Amar Rajeshwar sat beside her while she drove. Thoughts of Amar again invaded Madhu. Amar would be driving Reena's limousines; he liked big cars, he should be confident; Reena sitting alongside him in a limousine; reason enough to be confident or was he yet nervous; letting Reena drive while he sat mentally working out a story for his some ambitious film project.

The signal turned red, Rajeshwar voice jerked Madhu senses back "Stop red signal."

Madhu applied brakes in time. The car screeched to a red halt just before the white line. Rajeshwar simply watched her; embarrassed she said "I am sorry."

"You drive well even in your thoughts but as drinking and driving doesn't mix well so do thinking and driving."

"I will take care next time."

Rajeshwar gave no reply, simply kept starring at her. She was very much conscious of his attention. A thought came to her that may be he is trying to make up his mind whether to allow her a next time or not. She asked "If you do not want to give me a second chance that is ok." Madhu said her eyes downcast.

The signal turned green. She drove the car ahead to a parking lot and parked. Right across was an open air restaurant. Getting out of the car Rajeshwar said "Let's have some coffee."

At the coffee table there was an awkward silence, and then coffee got served. Taking a sip of his coffee Rajeshwar said "Second chance, will you give yourself a second chance?"

Madhu a little taken a back said "Sir, I don't understand?"

"Well, I asked you will you give yourself a second chance."

"I don't know sir."

"I know, you must give yourself a second chance, haven't you heard 'man is to err' we commit so many mistakes in life; if we don't give ourselves second chance then how are we to survive?"

Madhu smiled, once again thinking of Amar, he too had given himself a second chance. Reena was his second chance; she asked "Is giving second chance always right?"

"If one commits murder then giving second chance is not right." Rajeshwar said with a hint of humor.

Madhu smiled at the thought as it relayed in her mind; Amar had committed murder of love. She said "Right I have not committed any murder so I should get a second chance, sir"

"I don't like you calling me sir. Respect should be in heart, deeds, the way of performing duty, I have seen that respect in all what you do."

Madhu looked puzzled, Rajeshwar further imposed "I would like to deal with you on equal terms in first person. It will make things frank, easy and better, and remember I make the rules here."

"But sir?"

"No more sir." Rajeshwar admonished raising a finger then continued "Coffee is over, shall we make a move, I want to show you a shopping mall close to our place, and you can visit with Maji and Pinky."

Rajeshwar beckoned for the bill. Madhu gathered her purse and got up. Rajeshwar moved on, paid the bill at the counter and went to the car, opened the passenger side front door and sat in. Madhu came; sat at the driver's seat. Took out the keys from her hand bag, started the car, reversed with ease and drove on in the direction pointed by Rajeshwar. Anyone could have taken them as to date couple.

Since the time Madhu had come to Rajeshwar house as house keeper on routine she was the first one to get up early every morning. Then she woke Johnny, the cook Ramzan, the maid Leela and last of all Pinky who she got ready for school. By the time Pinky was dressed for school her breakfast and morning tea was prepared in the kitchen. Maji would be up by then, tea and Pinky's breakfast was as a rule served in Maji room where Madhu and Pinky would join in.

It was Johnny's duty to take Rajeshwar bed tea to his room. Who just took a few sips. Since he had started drinking heavily at night he had lost his taste of morning tea. He would rush to the bathroom;

a quick cold water shower was his permanent immediate requirement courtesy the hangover.

By the time Madhu and Maji finished their morning tea and Pinky her breakfast Rajeshwar would be ready and off to office without any breakfast because his hangover killed his appetite, a glass of any fresh fruit juice was all he had for breakfast.

While Johnny drove Rajeshwar to office in the jeep Madhu sat with Pinky at home revising her home work, this morning fresh mind revision helped Pinky a lot in her studies. As the revision got over Johnny would be back dropping Rajeshwar at office to transport Pinky and Madhu to school.

This routine was little altered when it was Pinky's holiday. Madhu allowed Pinky to sleep as long as she wanted to.

That day also it was Sunday, Pinky's holiday. So she was sleeping to her heart's content. Madhu covered Pinky with a blanket and came out of the room. As Madhu passed through the corridor she happened to glance down at the hall. She was shocked out of her wits; a huge elephant was loitering around in the hall. In size he seemed to be full grown but his tusks were still short and young. At leisure he was moving around the hall. Scared Madhu rushed to Maji room. On Sundays Maji also slept late. Madhu woke her up saying "Maji, Maji, there is an elephant down in the hall."

Getting up a sleepy Maji said "Yes beti it must be Monu."

Baffled Madhu inquired "Monu? Who Monu?"

"Same Monu I told you about whose father and mother were killed by the poachers when he was one month old and Rajeshwar had brought him home."

"Oh yes, but he is down in the hall room?"

"Don't worry beti he has grown up with Pinky he really loves Pinky."

"Loves Pinky?"

"Yes and Pinky is also mad after him, you go and wake up Pinky and see the fun."

Very much taken a back Madhu asked "Do you mean Pinky is going to go near him?"

"Please go and wakeup Pinky and then see for yourself."

Talking to Maji Madhu realized that at least there was no danger. Her inquisitiveness increased. She wanted to see what the phenomenon was. She proceeded to wake up Pinky.

"Pinky getup, getup…"

Sleepy Pinky complained "Aunty let me sleep, it's my holiday today."

"Yes it is your holiday today but down there some body has come to meet you."

Still sleepy Pinky asks "Who?"

"Your Monu."

Hearing Monu's name Pinky jumped up in her bed "Monu my Monu."

She leapt out of her bed and ran. Running through the corridor and down the stairs she kept calling "Monu, Monu, Monu!!!"

When Monu saw Pinky he raised his trunk and thundered happily, whole house echoed. Rushing to Monu Pinky clung to his huge leg. Very gently and lovingly, Monu with his trunk caressed Pinky. Pinky caught Monu's trunk then looking at him angrily said "Why have you come after so many days where were you? Have you found some other friend? Go I will not talk to you."

Pinky Stamped away went and sat on a sofa. Monu came and heavily settled alongside her with a thumping sound, with his small eyes looked at Pinky, kept moving his large ears and wagging its tail. Warning Monu with her little finger Pinky said "Promise you will not do this again, every Sunday you will always be here."

Monu shook his head as if saying yes. Madhu, Rajeshwar, Maji, Johnny and other servants were all watching this scene.

Amazed Madhu was witnessing such a show for the first time in her life. Her eyes were wide open. But there certainly was no trace of any fear on her face. She seemed happily surprised.

Rajeshwar looked at Madhu and he did appreciate what he saw. Suddenly why, God only knew why, that scene flashed in front of Rajeshwar eyes when he had brought one month old Monu home Namrata was screaming.

"Throw him out of the house. This elephant of a thing is not going to stay in my house,"

Just antithetical Madhu was standing there admiring the scene of grown up Monu. Pinky was telling Monu "Come Monu I will make you meet my very nice aunty,"

Pinky called Madhu who was still standing at the staircase.

"Come Aunty, please come down, meet my Monu, he won't do anything."

Madhu came down the staircase; a little hesitant, a little scared she approached Monu, who was sitting next to Pinky, Pinky issued an order to him "Monu shake hands with aunty."

Monu looked at Madhu then he held out his trunk to her. Madhu though a little afraid but totally amazed took Monu trunk in her hands. Pinky exclaimed "Aunty, will you come for a ride on Monu!?!"

Madhu shook her head in a no. Pinky reassured "See I will show you how I go ridding."

Pinky promptly mounted Monu's neck. Monu steadily got up, moved to the entrance of the hall with Pinky on top. While passing through the huge oriental hall door Madhu was thoroughly surprised to see Monu bend his neck a little, so as to easily pass through it, as Pinky clung to him. Rajeshwar very proudly watched his daughter ride the elephant, Madhu asked him "Where is Monu taking Pinky?"

"Forest camp resort."

"Why there?"

Rajeshwar smiled and said "Come with me, I will show you why?"

Ridding Monu Pinky went out of bungalow. Rajeshwar and Madhu were following at some distance.

As they passed through a jungle path four-five other elephants emerged and joined Monu, Madhu was once again shocked.

Now this band of elephant along with Pinky avoiding the main concrete road strode through the jungle ways to the forest resort.

Very much at ease they were treading through the resort. Tourists rushed out of their cottages; cameras focused on elephants and Pinky. Some tourists even fed elephants fruits, cakes, bread, and biscuits. The bolder fed with hands while others kept the offerings in the center of the road. Elephants helped themselves picking with their trunks. Rajeshwar was telling Madhu "Pinky, Monu and these elephants have become so famous that tourists from all over the world come to see them. Pinky had been interviewed many times she is much more famous than me."

Appreciating all this Madhu said "The proverb elephant's memory is so true. Monu has not forgotten his adolescence and Pinky's friendship."

Rajeshwar reaffirmed "And will never forget."

Some tourist came to Rajeshwar and Madhu they asked Rajeshwar about the jungle. Some praised him and showed him articles and news items published in different magazines and news papers about him and Pinky; about the precision with which he performed his job; about Pinky the wonder child; her dauntless caring and loving enormous wild elephants. The mammoths obeying her innocent at will commands. They told him that they have come there after reading those articles. How eager they were to meet Rajeshwar and Pinky along with her brigade.

Madhu came to know more about Rajeshwar. How much he was respected how much he was loved. One elderly couple asked Rajeshwar and Madhu to have a cup of tea with them.

They sat having tea at the elderly couples cottage. Husband presented Rajeshwar a magazine in which there was specific mention of his forest conservation. Pinky was among the rest of the tourists endlessly giving free show with her Monu. The elderly woman asked "Your child, this wonder girl Pinky, was she born here?"

She put the question to Madhu taking for granted that she and Rajeshwar were husband and wife and Pinky their daughter. Rajeshwar not noticing her objective replied "Yes she was born here and this elephant is her childhood friend and also a full grown chimpanzee; the fellow is absent today."

Madhu was helpless; she got no chance to clarify the old woman's misunderstanding. The lady continued "Oh really, I would love to take some photographs of your daughter with that chimpanzee."

She again put the request to Madhu taking her to be Pinky's mother. Busy reading the article in the magazine Rajeshwar said once again before Madhu could clarify "Give your mobile number to Madhu she will call you if the fellow appears while you are here."

Madhu was caught in an awkward situation. The old lady remarked "Madhu is such a sweet name. What does it mean?"

Rajeshwar kept the magazine away, looking at the lady replied "Madhu means exactly as you said 'sweet'."

Madhu smiled helplessly. The old lady put one more question this time to both Rajeshwar and Madhu "You both are so young and look totally made for each other, both of you must plan another child may be a boy this time?"

Rajeshwar was shocked, Madhu never knew where to look, and she felt extreme difficulty controlling her laughter. The elderly couple was confused. Rajeshwar finally realized the ambiguity and laughed and laughed. Yes after many years; laughing he felt what he had missed.

Around mid-night at Rajeshwar forest bungalow everyone was fast asleep. Madhu was wide awake fighting the memories of Amar trying to extricate them tear them apart from herself and throw them out of her existence, but as ever the invasion of the memories overwhelmed her, penetrated her left and right. The bed felt too claustrophobic, too small an arena to deal with the memoirs of that Amar. She left her bed. She came to the terrace of the bungalow for a better breathing space, for a wider outlook, to get lost in something else, the only way she knew, the only power she had over the sore memories.

It was a wide spread out terrace. The moon was in full bloom. Somewhere from far away distant jackals howled, a moment later a lion roared, an elephant triumph was heard simultaneously; even after so many wild varied hollers there was tranquility, serenity, there was peace.

The open and the fresh air helped. Worries, tensions and anxieties were reduced. Over the clear blue sky the glittering stars bathed in full moon light, and down below them were lush green meadows and tall green trees swinging in the breeze singing the song of nature. Perhaps Amar should have been there, again the same memories. Once again all got revived.

The strong arms of Amar; her caving in into them; his lips touching her lips; a sweet wave running through her veins; she losing her resolve but Amar restricting himself, breathing heavily saying "No Madhu, what you have done for me, I have sworn till the time I be worthy of you, till the time I put this world at your feet. Then and only then I will have right on you."

"Washed your hands off me and on all the rights on me; what a way to pay off my love…" Lost in her thoughts Madhu spoke out to herself. In the still calm night Rajeshwar voice rang "Alone you talk to yourself?"

Startled Madhu turned and saw him standing at some distance. Possibility was he might not have heard Madhu exactly but at least he did assume or made out that she had uttered something, all alone, to herself. An embarrassed and a little nervous Madhu said "No, no, sir, it is just like that…"

Rajeshwar thought it better not to press the 'sir' bid right then, he just repeated his query "Well, I heard you talking to yourself, what is bothering you?"

Madhu brood over for a moment then said "There is a lot of difference between this world and the world I have come from. So some memories were just bothering me."

"The memories that bother are not good. Maji was telling me you had a sister?"

"Oh, yes some body's betrayal chocked her to death."

It was then Madhu saw a whisky glass in his hand. Taking a sip he said "Is that why you never mind my attitude, I mean my bad behavior. Some where you do see that I have been knocked down the same way as your sister had been and if put rightly and truthfully you have been?"

Surprised Madhu looked at Rajeshwar thinking how he had discovered the fact. As if reading her face he explained "Madhu the pain which one can see in your eyes is very personal."

Madhu just failed to give any adequate reply. She merely stood still and quiet. Observing this Rajeshwar continued "Now that we know we are sailing in same boat please put some light on one thing."

Taking one more sip of his drink he questioned "Why is it so difficult to forget a Perfidious, Treacherous, and Faithless First Love…?"

"Because attached with every unfaithful lover's bad memories are some good memories also and the more good memories; more difficult to forget."

Spontaneously Rajeshwar realized the truth, shaking his head in a yes with an appreciation in eyes for Madhu he said "These good memories, which keep bothering again and again; keep coming back repeatedly; as much as you try to forget them. Let us medicate them, treat them, heal them and get rid of them in a novel way."

Taking interest Madhu asked "How?"

"To forget these memories is proving not possible so let us harp on to them, talk of them and grow on them. May be trying hard to call back them they may leave us. Let our heart be free again."

Madhu laughed. Rajeshwar said "In this exercise we will have to help each other out."

"How?"

"I will keep telling you about Namrata and you tell me about whatever his name be. By the way what is his name?"

Smiling sad Madhu said "Amar,"

"Ok, so tell me about the great Mr. Amar. About the good time you have had with him."

Thinking about Rajeshwar contemplation and somewhat approving it also Madhu said "Your theory is very appealing sir. However since the concept is yours so it will be better if you initiate. It will be of help for me to follow suit. I do sincerely hope that by sharing heart aches may be our torments might lose weight."

Rajeshwar reassured "Correct, hundred percent correct. God willing they will evaporate in thin air. Let's begin the experiment and be friends, be honest, truthful, and frank and forget the 'sir' bid."

Both laughed; laughed with their hearts to their laughter and their hearty laughter echoed in the silence of the woodland night.

Rajeshwar initiated "One feat of Namrata I will never ever forget. She is the only daughter of a prodigious father. Still when her parents kept condition that she marries me, she gets disinherited, will not be entitled to a single penny of their enormous wealth. You know what she did?"

Madhu was very much intrigued, looked keenly at Rajeshwar anticipating some dashing exploit by Namrata and of course was not let down as Rajeshwar let know " She rang me up, told me to immediately buy for her a pair of jeans, a T-Shirt, a set of undergarments and a pair of shoes and come at once to her house."

Madhu curiosity increased. Rajeshwar went on "I asked her why, what the matter was? She curtly told me "Don't ask questions, right away get going, I am waiting."

"She switched off her phone, carrying all the stuff she had ordered in a hand bag I reached her home. Her parents were sitting in the hall all tensed up, I asked where was Namrata, from the side room she emerged, walking briskly she took the hand bag from my hand and went back in to the room banging the door shut after her. I stood baffled. Her parents starring at me; hate and scorn striking through their looks, just within two minutes the door of that room opened and Namrata came out wearing the outfit I had brought her."

Surprised and impressed Madhu laughed saying "Really!"

Rajeshwar went on "She told her parents "Daddy Mummy I have stripped out of the clothes brought by your money and this is your chain and locket."

"Saying so she took off the chain and locket, kept them on a table and said a final goodbye, took hold of my hand and moved to the exit, then thinking something she stopped, turned, looked at her parents with tears in her eyes, the lipstick on her lips, she rubbed it off with her hand then brushed her hand with a curtain hanging there and told her mother."

"Mamma you had once given it to me, I am leaving it here."

"Holding my hand she walked out on her parents."

Madhu was more than amazed. Namrata certainly had her own way of doing things, her own style one may say. Madhu said "I do truly admit she had her own attitude and stance."

Rajeshwar added as of his own experience "Very high stance and attitude, also very adamant she was. For one full year her parents kept on trying to make up with her, asking her to forgive and forget however she did nothing of the sort, never met them. It was only when Pinky was born. Her parents all of a sudden came to our house. After a lot of my insisting she met them. And then gradually things became normal. Now you tell me something about your Mr. Amar."

Looking at her watch Madhu said "It is quite late; tomorrow early morning Pinky's school is there."

Rajeshwar agreed saying "Ok then tomorrow be it, I will come along to see how you drive Pinky School, and you can tell me about Mr. Amar, on the way."

Madhu smiled and turned to go. Rajeshwar passed an observation "Listen by telling you about Namrata I am feeling a little light and at ease."

Laughing, Madhu went back to her room very much feeling at ease.

Chapter Four

Pinky and Madhu, ready for school, came out of the house. Instead of Johnny Rajeshwar was waiting at the jeep. Pinky was all excited to see her father coming to drop her school.

"Daddy, Daddy you are going to drop me school?"

Relishing his daughter's excitement he said "Well, after long Daddy is back on Pinky Beti's duty."

Happily Pinky called out to her grand mama who as usual was in the balcony of her room on her wheel chair to see her dear Pinky off to school.

"Dadi! Dadi! See who is going to drop me to school?"

Tears of bliss appeared in Maji eyes .She blessed raising her hand. Rajeshwar could see the happiness around; Maji, Madhu and Pinky were beaming. He said to Madhu "I want to see how good you are at driving my jeep, so please go ahead." He pointed out the steering. Nodding a confident yes Madhu positioned herself at the driving seat. Pinky all the more excited called at Grand Ma again "Dadi see Aunty will drive."

Somehow Maji was also confident of Madhu, she blessed once more. Pinky sat in between Rajeshwar and Madhu.

As the jeep disappeared from the range of Maji chasing eyes a thought generated in her mind. Her face brightened up. Folding her hands she spoke to her God "Oh God, I know you have finally heard my prayers. This girl Madhu, yes she is the answer to my plight. Please God let me witness this bliss in my life time."

With eyes closed in devotion Maji prayed.

All the way to school Pinky talked and talked and talked. Amused Rajeshwar and Madhu loved it. Dropping her at school on their way back Madhu said "Pinky was really very happy today. Laughed and talked all the way."

"Thanks God she has no memories of her mother."

"Yes, I do not see any pictures of Namrata ji anywhere in the house?" Madhu commented.

"She took them all along with her, you know her attitude, never wanted any reminders behind." Rajeshwar laughed then came to the point.

"You also lose little weight. Tell me something about Mr. Amar."

Depression came over Madhu she uttered "What to tell. Let it be"

Rajeshwar insisted "This is going against the agreement. You will have to tell."

Madhu very flatly said "I saved Amar's life. You know how we first met?"

Madhu narrated the complete incident of her first meeting with Amar; how she helped Amar to begin life the second time; how Amar had then succeeded in getting assistant director job and how then he had met Reena and betrayed her. Rajeshwar quietly listened to all this then commented "Well I wanted to know something good about Mr. Amar, some good memories that bother you."

Once again very simply and honestly Madhu said "I was madly in love with Amar. I belonged to him heart, body and soul, and Amar knew this, still he never took advantage of me."

Madhu eyes filled up with tears. Rajeshwar noticed this and remarked "Honorable man that Mr. Amar."

Sarcasm in her tone Madhu pronounced "Honorable but too ambitious."

"Yes this ambition often proves destructive. One runs after some thing, many a times his eyes closed to other important obligation and responsibilities. In case ambition is achieved, usually all gets well. In case of failure obligations grow to be debts and do haunt bad."

Suddenly a villager appeared in front of the jeep. Rajeshwar slammed the brake foot. The jeep screeched to a stop. The excited African, very excited, said something to Rajeshwar in his verbal communication. Rajeshwar reacted alarmed. Madhu inquired

"What is it?"

"Bad news, some poachers have injured a lion."

"Then what is to be done?"

"We have to search for the lion. I will drop you home."

"Leaving me you will lose a lot of time. I will also come along. I promise I will not panic."

Rajeshwar smiled and started the jeep. By that time the African had already jumped in to the back seat.

Jeep entered the dense forest, reached the spot where the lion was shot. Rajeshwar stopped the jeep there. At some distance from there forest guards have surrounded a dense spreading shrubbery. Some guards came running to him and informed him that the lion was in the dense thicket ahead.

Madhu was sitting in the closed jeep. The jeep was at some distance from that thicket. Rajeshwar with his men moved towards that thicket.

A forest guard pointed out the paw prints of the lion. He also told Rajeshwar that early morning the lion was heard roaring from the thicket.

As Rajeshwar moved ahead he saw some fallen blood on the leaves. The blood was hard and dried up. Rajeshwar checked it rubbing it in between his fingers; the blood seemed very dry and stale.

"The blood is at least two days old this means lion was wounded two days back. He must be very hungry."

Johnny had reached there with some more forest guard. Scared he remarked "Meaning the danger is much more."

One more Jeep of Forest guards came in carrying a huge strong net. Rajeshwar ordered the net to be spread at one particular end of the thicket. By that time some villagers also reached there; they helped.

The trap was expertly hooked with iron clamps. The clamps in turn were slightly entrenched in ground so that when the loin ran on the net the beast would get tangled in the net and the iron clamps get pulled out of the ground and help in trapping the pugnacious loin.

Trap set, the Hounding of the lion from the other end began. Shouting, beating drums and tins the villagers and the forest guards penetrated in the thicket to force the lion out in to the waiting trap. The guards were armed with rifles as well as tranquilizer guns. Rajeshwar carried a Thirty Springfield Rifle in his hand.

Madhu came out of the jeep and stood next to it; her eyes fixed at that thicket where the hounding was on full blast.

Sleeping lion awoke. Opened his eyes, he was not in that thicket which was hounded and across which the net fixed to capture him. He was in a small shrub very near the jeep and Madhu.

Disturbed by the clamor the lion got up. He felt an excruciating pain in his leg where the bullet had pierced him. A roar came out of his jaws but was lost on Rajeshwar and his men in the rumpus. The roar definitely did reach Madhu.

Shocked Madhu turned and looked; the lion was emerging from of the bush. He saw Madhu and stopped in his track. His eyes were fierce and stomach famished. Madhu was resting bodily at the jeep. She turned icy and froze. Her hands, feet and total self were as if paralyzed, immobilized, eyes wide open, mouth ajar; however no sound or shriek came out.

Lion's stomach was skeletal and emaciated. He was very hungry, limping with his hind leg he moved towards Madhu.

Seeing the lion come towards her a shiver ran thorough Madhu but she was too stunned to move or pitch out a scream.

Jeep was parked under a huge tree, on top of which a band of monkeys watched the scene. They too were terrified and panicky; squealing loudly and jumping from branch to branch.

The lion was about fifteen to twenty feet away from Madhu. Angrily he looked at the noisy interrupting monkeys and roared. Stunned a monkey lost balance and fell from the branch it was perched on. It landed at the bonnet of the jeep. The crashing sound brought some of Madhu sense back. Quickly she entered the jeep and closed the door behind her.

On the other hand the booming lion roar amidst the clamor faintly reached Rajeshwar. He reacted alarmed.

The lion charged, with one powerful stroke of his enormous claw he shattered the window pane of the jeep closed door standing its full height at it, horrified Madhu shrieked. She pressed to the other side of the jeep interior. The sharp claw of the lion was trying to reach her. Trembling, with horrified eyes, she looked in to the snarling and reeking face of the lion.

Rajeshwar rushed out of the thicket, desperately looked here and there for the roaring lion.

The lion was then a top the bonnet of the jeep. With a single strike he smashed to smithereens the wind screen; forced his head through the broken screen. Madhu felt the hot and stinking breath of the lion brushing past her.

Rajeshwar was in the open by then. He spotted the lion. In one second he and his rifle were aiming at the lion atop the bonnet of the jeep. But in face of the danger his hands were not steady. He fired, missed; the bullet hit the bonnet of the jeep. The echo of the bullet rang in the lion's ears. The fear and the pain of the poacher bullet revived; the lion backed withdrawing from Madhu proximity and pulled its half self out of the jeep's wind screen metal frame. Rajeshwar fired again but in that fraction of the second the lion had jumped off the jeep. Lion escaped.

Rajeshwar ran towards the jeep with all his strength and speed. Madhu had lost her consciousness.

On the way back home Johnny drove the Jeep. Rajeshwar sat at the rear seat holding Madhu in his arms. He sprinkled water on her face to get her back to consciousness and then shook her gently calling her name.

"Madhu, Madhu its ok now, please open your eyes."

When she opened her eyes tears emerged and ran down her face, she kept looking at Rajeshwar, yet dazed. Her Lips began to quiver and she caught hold of his arms tight, he helped her close to him, she held fast to him. Buried her face in his strong arms and kept sobbing. Rajeshwar made an effort to calm her "Madhu it's over now, the lion is gone, we will be home soon, I am sorry, I am so sorry."

Weeping Madhu looked at Rajeshwar her tear full eyes telling him that there was no need to be sorry. The lion closing in on her, once again flashed through her vision. She holding Rajeshwar tight took refuge in his arms.

They reached home. Rajeshwar helped her out of the jeep. Leave aside walking Madhu was not able to stand on her own. Rajeshwar picked her up in his arms and carried her in.

In her room as Rajeshwar put a trembling Madhu to bed a distraught Maji entered on her wheel chair asking "What happened?"

"Poor fellow had had a second life."

Maji managed the wheel chair close to Madhu. Madhu held Maji hand and began crying. Maji understood that something terrible had happened. Demonstrating great coherence she thought it better not to put forward any more questions. She pacified Madhu keeping her other hand on her shoulder.

Though Rajeshwar had saved Madhu, but held himself responsible for the predicament. He went out to his room and got some medicines for Madhu.

"Madhu please, this is sedative, it will help you relax. "

Understanding Madhu nodded a yes and took the tablet. Maji offered her a glass of water kept on the side table of the bed. Madhu gulped the tablet down.

She was exhausted. The medicine worked quickly on her. She fell fast asleep. Rajeshwar covered her with a blanket. Both mother and son left the room silently.

Sitting outside her room Rajeshwar and Maji were thinking the same thing.

'Will Madhu go away?'

The horrendous occurrence Rajeshwar told Maji. She kept quiet for a while; thinking all sort of negative things forced by the complexes of her past 'Madhu is very different from Namrata but what has happened is too precarious a happening, born and brought up at a metropolis like Mumbai she will think twice to live life here at the risk of her being. Namrata left us, broke all relations with us, divorced my son who she loved once; Madhu is in no relationship with us, there exists no bondage to hold her to us. If she goes…' Maji broke her silence "Beta you should not have taken Madhu along."

"Maji I told Madhu that I will drop her home first but she insisted to come along, any way you are right, I should not have listened to her."

"What a nice girl she is, how well she had put our house in order. Pinky is crazy after her."

Taking a deep sigh Maji continued "If she goes we will not get any one like her again."

"Mama you don't worry, I will speak to her, try to make her understand."

Wiping her tear Maji said "I will also talk to her; I will not let her go."

The sleep helped Madhu a lot. When she woke up she was almost fit and fine. The shock seemed to have receded. Madhu straight away got herself busy in her routine house hold cores. When Maji came to know of it she was happily surprised. She came rushing to Madhu and asked "Beti what are you doing? You should be in bed, taking rest."

Ironing Pinky school dress Madhu said "Maji to forget Sher uncle one should get busy at work."

A sea of love and appreciation appeared in Maji eyes. Breathing relaxed she told her "I did chide Rajeshwar for taking you along."

Madhu was visibly disturbed and disappointed "Why did you do so Maji, I insisted on going, Rajeshwar sahib saved my life. Had he not reached there in time by now I would have been completely digested in Sher uncles system."

Tears of love and affection sipped in into Maji eyes "You must not talk so."

Recognizing the concern and emotion in tearful eyes of the old lady, Madhu was very much touched, she gently wiped Maji tears "Maji how much you have started loving me in such a short time, oh God these tears for me."

Crying Maji said "Beti I was scared that you might go away, even Rajeshwar had this fear."

Now tears appeared in Madhu eyes also "Maji I have no one to go to, I will never ever leave you people on my own however if you people cast me out…"

Very much emotionally charged, Maji sitting on her wheel chair spread her arms opening both her hands towards Madhu. Madhu moved to her. Both vehemently embraced each other. With Madhu close to her heart Maji said "Your coming made all the difference to us, we were so incomplete."

"And I so alone..."

Suddenly Madhu seemed to remember something. She looked at her watch saying "It's time for Pinky School coming who has gone to get her?"

Just then sound of the approaching jeep was heard, Madhu looked down the window. Rajeshwar and Johnny were home with Pinky.

Jumping off the jeep Pinky rushed in the house. Rajeshwar and Johnny followed her.

Running Pinky stopped in her tracks seeing a hail and hearty Madhu standing alongside Maji "Ok! Aunty is fine, thanks God."

She came running to Madhu. Madhu took her in her arms.

"Aunty nothing happened to you."

"Happening, happening I got saved. Your Daddy rescued me."

Laughing she looked at Rajeshwar who had just entered with Johnny. Seeing Madhu hale and hearty Rajeshwar commented "How come you are not in bed?"

"In bed Sher uncle visited me so much in my dreams my sleep ran away."

"Thanks God only your sleep ran away. "

Madhu read in between the lines and said "I am not the one who runs away. Now it is Sher uncles turn to be scared. Get hold of him fast. Lock him in the cage. Then you and I will very lovingly take care of him."

Saying so carrying Pinky's school bag Madhu went up stairs along with Pinky; making light of the serious event. All kept watching her, amazed.

It was also a very strange affair that Monu used to visit Pinky only on Sundays. God knows how he knew that Sunday was Pinky's holiday so he could play with her, take her for a ride. That day also it was a Sunday and Mr. Monu sat all his heavy self in the hall.

It was sugarcane season; Rajeshwar had brought and dumped a full cart load of sugarcane in the compound. All meant for Mr. Monu. When Mr. Monu came he had picked up a full load of sugarcane in his trunk and walked straight to hall entrance, had given a slight push to the close door with his huge heavy leg. The door had given in and flown open.

Many latches of that door had been replaced by Rajeshwar on account of Mr. Monu.

So that day also Mr. Monu was standing conveniently in the hall and enjoying sugarcane; it being scattered all around. As per schedule Madhu got up first and beheld the scene. She straight away went and woke up Pinky. Pinky rushed down to the hall, Monu was busy with his sugarcane; just acknowledged Pinky's coming by a slight wave of his tail and ears but no triumphing around. Pinky came and stood by Monu for a moment, touched him with love and made a suggestion so as not to disturb his feast "You have your sugarcane, I will just go have my bath, breakfast and come down ok, and then we will go out ok."

Monu shook his head as if he had understood.

Persistent Pinky convinced Madhu for a ride on Monu .Teasing, Rajeshwar remarked "Oh, yes, you have faced Sher uncle Monu is just a kid of the house no point getting scared of him."

Madhu laughed but insisted "I will sit on Monu outside the house, not here; my head will bang against the top of the door."

Rajeshwar happily agreed "Ok, ok this is perfectly alright."

Pinky held Monu ear and pulling it up said "Up Monu, up."

Obeying Monu got up. Holding his trunk Pinky leads him outside the house. Then gesturing to him said "Monu sit, Monu sit."

Monu sat. First Pinky mounted him. Then with Rajeshwar and Johnny's help Madhu conquered Monu; astride his neck, behind Pinky, legs resting both sides. She also held Pinky tightly with both hands. When Monu got up Madhu went a little off balanced. Rajeshwar called to her "Madhu press your legs against Monu neck."

Madhu did so and regained her balance. Perched on the balcony Maji called out to them "Beta Rajeshwar you also go with them don't send them alone."

Now Madhu was enjoying the ride, waving to Maji she called back "Maji everything will be all right. Don't worry we are with great Monu he will scare Sher uncle away."

Pinky also joined Madhu "Yes Dadi, yes."

Ridding Monu they went ahead towards the Resort, Rajeshwar turned back into the bungalow to have his bath and then the glass of juice.

Once again some more elephants joined Monu on the jungle path. Once again they were roaming in the Forest Resort but the difference was along with Pinky Madhu also sat perched ridding Monu.

Tourists were feeding Monu and the other elephants, photographing them. Somebody emerged from a cottage a Video Camera stuck in his eyes recording the phenomenon. As Madhu appeared in that somebody's camera he reacted shocked. The camera slipped and almost fell from his hand. He was Amar.

When Madhu saw Amar she almost slipped from a top Monu. Pinky helped her to regain her posture. Beads of perspiration appeared on Madhu forehead. She asked Pinky "Pinky please tell Monu to take us back home."

Surprised Pinky questioned "Why aunty?"

"I am not well. Please tell Monu to take us home."

Pinky taped Monu jaws with her little hand "Monu… Monu … Home… Home."

Shocked, camera in hand Amar was watching the scene. Monu was taking them back home.

As the shock of seeing Amar in South Africa settled down, Madhu brain began to function rapidly. 'May be Amar is here with Reena on his honey moon. But no, a girl like Reena will never come to South Africa for her honey moon and that too in this forest resort. She would rather go to Switzerland, London, Paris, New York. Then may be Amar had come here to make some film. Yes this can be. But if it is so, any film unit of Hindi films was to come here, at least Rajeshwar must have been in know of it and he certainly would have talked about it.'

Then a thought came to Madhu which convinced her to some extent 'may be Amar had realized his mistake and somehow found out, may be through Rehman and Salma, that she is in South Africa and had come searching for her'

The feel of this thought certainly increased her heart beats. However she felt not happy about it. Was there no emotion for Amar left in her heart? If it was so why did she react so vehemently on the sight of Amar? Why her hands and feet had turned numb? Whatever it was, the first question was why Amar was there?

Amar was there to make a documentary. He was on the assignment given to him by Mother Nature Channel.

Along with his camera man Amar was there at Rajeshwar office. He gave a letter of recommendation from his channel to Rajeshwar, requesting assistance. Rajeshwar assured Amar that he will help him in all possible ways.

Amar had introduced himself as Amar. However since Madhu had told Rajeshwar that Amar was to marry a financier's daughter; was to manage his own film production house so right then it did not occur to Rajeshwar that he was the same perfidious Amar who had entered Madhu life and gone. Simply a case of two different identities having a common name was all that came to Rajeshwar mind.

Whereas Amar on seeing Madhu at the forest resort had inquired about her and had found out that she was the new house keeper at Rajeshwar house. Amar made an attempt to augment friendship with Rajeshwar "Today early morning I saw your daughter astride an elephant, you know there were five six of them but the one she was ridding seemed so amenable. Very cute child she is. When striking at his jaw your daughter said home the elephant simply turned towards your home. Really it was an out of the world scene for me."

It struck Rajeshwar and he deliberately to confirm his doubts about Amar identity said "Yes she and Madhu went ridding today, it was first time for Madhu."

Amar did not react at all on Madhu mention. Rajeshwar suspicion was put to rest. Amar went on to say "I must say your daughter is a wonder, what is her name?"

"Pinky." Rajeshwar replied relaxed.

"Sir may I know how come a little girl like Pinky became friends with an elephant?"

"Monu's family was killed by the poachers."

Amar cuts in "Monu, you mean that elephant?"

"Yes that elephant fellow he was one month old, I brought him home, he grew up with Pinky."

"Great wonders, Sir I have a request, please let me interview your daughter, I want the word to know through her innocence how an animal and human can be friends."

"Well, you see her exams are…"

Amar beseeched Rajeshwar to permit him the interview "Sir my entire carrier depends on this documentary. If I make this documentary well there will be a bloom in my life otherwise it will remain bankrupt as it is."

Rajeshwar laughed. Amar seemed to be an interesting person to him. "Ok, ok you both come over for dinner tonight we will see what can be done."

Amar was happy to be invited for dinner; a chance to meet Madhu.

After Amar was gone Rajeshwar rang up Madhu "For dinner two guests are coming please get some food made for them."

"Will they prefer veg. or non veg?"

"Well I didn't ask them, you get both veg. and non veg. made."

Talking to Madhu on phone all of a sudden the doubt repeated itself in Rajeshwar mind.

"And here, listen Amar is the name of one of them. He has come here to make a documentary. By any chance can he be your Mr. Amar the great?"

Coolly Madhu replied from the other end of the phone "Rajeshwar sahib he is the same Amar. I saw him today at the Forest Resort."

Rajeshwar was alarmed, all the more because Amar to him seemed not a straight person. He had not reacted at all on the mention of Madhu; the man was playing games, shrewd games. Angry Rajeshwar said on phone to Madhu.

"Don't go through the trouble of preparing anything for the bastard, I will cancel the dinner."

But Madhu from the other end insisted "Please do not cancel any thing, please let him come, I want to know his well being. Just want to ask what happened to his film making factory? How come he had come down to documentary making. Please Rajeshwar let him come."

Madhu had called him Rajeshwar; by name, for the first time. Rajeshwar saw some good tidings. May be Madhu needs to drive some sadistic pleasure out of it he thought and said "Ok..." putting down the phone

Madhu cut the phone at the other end. Suddenly Rajeshwar felt very much perturbed for another reason.

A very heavy sort of jealousy had crept into Rajeshwar. Apprehensive he thought what was the reason for him to feel so, to think so? Friends with Madhu he was, a feel of some satisfaction in being with her also existed when in her company. All this had transpired so gradually with time and events that he had never even given it a thought. But the extent of jealousy he felt then, the deep fry burning of his heart and the beads of perspiration he felt on his forehead. Was it happening again? He asked himself. The reply came immediately to him.

Split with Namrata had created a cool vacuum in his heart. That vacuum was no more there with Madhu coming. And he was very wrong in his accepted wisdom that after Namrata no other woman would get place in his heart and that his heart will not go again for someone else. As of now he realized that love was an emotion; the need of a good man life; this sentiment cannot die with some ones deceit; yes it could lose its awareness, and if somebody right can kindle the awareness once again, then time healed very fast and the love starved tormented life yield to the assistance of that right enlightened person. Madhu was that one such person for Rajeshwar. That was why he felt so apprehensive and dead jealous of Amar.

Amar reached Rajeshwar house alone. He rang the bell Madhu opened the door for him. For some moments both kept looking at each other. Amar with down cast eyes and Madhu her eyes fixed at his face, very much bold and intrepid. Madhu standing right there at the door bounced her first question.

"How come you have scaled down to documentary making? What happened to your own film company?"

Amar slightly laughed and replied "Well… I discovered that disloyal and faithless people like me are not at all in good books of lady luck; the one for whom I left you; she left me."

Surprised Madhu asked "Why so?"

Endeavoring light humor Amar said "You may call it a rich father's only daughter's luxury or attitude. Got fed up of me, as soon as I said yes for the marriage Hundreds of my defects became glaringly visible to her."

Madhu was very much tickled. She laughed willfully to her heart's content. Rajeshwar entered. Seeing Madhu laughing so blatantly he asked "Madhu what is it? I have never seen you laugh so before."

Trying to soothe her laughter Madhu said "What to do, I just heard a very funny joke."

She pointed Amar, while laughing a tear had come out of her eye. She took it on her finger and jerked it aside. Rajeshwar remarked "Mr. Amar you make people cry while laughing, you are a very dangerous person."

"You have very well recognized me Mr. Rajeshwar. That is why I am here in your jungle to play along with it dangers."

Rajeshwar pointed to a sofa for Amar to sit "Jungle dangers are very straight forward, one knows this is a lion it is dangerous this is a dear; harmless."

Rajeshwar sat while Amar settled facing him. Madhu came and sat next to Rajeshwar. A pinch Amar suffered at his heart; Madhu sitting with someone else not him weighed on his heart and mind; an ironical look came over on his face. Complimenting Rajeshwar Madhu said "What Rajeshwar sahib means is this that in jungle everything is an open book there are no illusions or deceits, the one who is friend is a friend, the one who is an enemy is an enemy. Not like your metropolises where neither the friend ship is genuine nor enmity permanent."

Amar laughed as if on him and said "Miss Madhu you have just given a very good subject for my documentary. I will prove this one point; rules of the jungle are straight forward; what is that is. No wolf hiding in sheep coat."

Rajeshwar made a comment "It will be a very good lesson for some "

Nodding a yes Amar said "Yes sir those who commit mistakes must be taught lesson so that they do not repeat the same mistakes again."

Just then camera man entered with his camera. Introducing him to Madhu Amar said "He is Mr. Dilawar Khan my camera man. I have had a talk with Mr. Rajeshwar about little Pinky's interview, I took a chance I mean if we can do the interview now?"

Madhu replied in a flat, cool tone "Pinky is sleeping. Tomorrow early morning is her school; her exams are due so no time for your interview."

Rajeshwar intervened "You are very much out of luck Mr. Amar, Madhu had outright rejected your plea and her word is final so I am sorry."

Amar was not the one to give in so easily, calm and composed he said "I am here for a long time, I can wait, later I will try my luck with Miss Madhu's permission but today we can at least have dinner?"

Going towards the kitchen Madhu said "I will get dinner served."

Madhu went out of the living room out of the sight of Amar; he felt a pain as if someone had squeezed his heart. Cursing himself he sat there quiet. Rajeshwar and Dilawar talked about the wild life, about the documentary to be made. Amar was lost in his thoughts. Rajeshwar though talking to Dilawar was very much attentive to Amar, and his thoughts which were in a mental process of making good the bad he had done. 'I have committed a grave mistake, a blunder, left my true love for that pin-up of lust and sex. I have to win over Madhu again. She will forgive me, after all I am her first love and no one forgets ones first love. I will keep on begging forgiveness till she pardons me. I will tell her that I am not going to run any more after big name or fame or money, whatever is, we will live happily in it. All this I will explain to Madhu. I will not leave this jungle without her. She must understand. After all I love her and I am sure she still loves me. I am her first love.' With such thoughts of confidence and resolve Amar was in full mood to win over Madhu once again.

Rajeshwar interrupted his reverie with a pinch of humor and sarcasm mix "Mr. Amar you are somewhere else please do come back, dinner is waiting."

Dinner was waiting but not Madhu. She had gone up stairs to Maji room. She never came back even to say goodbye to Amar as he left.

"This is Wild Life Kingdom Park"

Amar announced on his mike. He was standing in an open jeep driven by Rajeshwar. His camera man Dilawar was shooting the scene and the scenery as described by Amar.

"Here is a treat for your eyes, a herd of antelopes, specifically known as spotted deer, you see they are grazing care free, may be they know there is no danger around, no carnivore sitting ducked to launch its lethal attack. And just a little ahead to the right, if I ask my camera man Dilawar to pan; you will see giraffes, with their long necks nibbling at the tall green tree leaves."

Dilawar's camera captured at places herds of antelopes grazing at the green grass. Then the giraffes with long necks nibbling tall tree leaves.

Jeep approached a huge lake. Hundreds and thousands of water fowls were floating across the lake, geese, ducks, and flamingoes.

Amar was so amazed by the sight he requested Rajeshwar to stop the jeep there for a while. Rajeshwar did oblige. Dilawar got busy shooting the captivating visual as Amar went on with his commentary "This is what makes it true that the world is made of land and water, there are some lives who live and feed on land and some lives who float and swim to live their lives and feed themselves."

Amar stopped in his course as he saw a lone flamingo wading here and there on its long legs as if searching for someone calling for some one. Amar questioned Rajeshwar "Why is that fellow so restless?"

"It is a flamingo; you must have heard flamingoes are great lovers, parting with their partner means death to them. He is a male his female seems to be lost, may be shot by some poacher or killed and devoured by some carnivore. This fellow is going to keep searching and calling for his mate for the rest of his life."

Amar was literally taken a back. He sat quiet, thinking of Madhu but Dilawar asked "Rajeshwar sahib will he not get some other female?"

"He might get but both will except each other or not cannot be said. Only time will tell."

Rajeshwar drove his jeep ahead. In his language Amar smelled Madhu. It seemed to Amar that Madhu had revealed at least something to Rajeshwar. But within such a short time had Madhu come so close to Rajeshwar so as to tell him about her private life. Last night also their conversation seemed to be very much in tune and sink 'No that cannot be so' Amar thought 'I am just being skeptical, I have definitely betrayed Madhu. But Madhu is a girl of integrity; such a girl in whom faith is deep rooted. She cannot forget me so fast. Somebody else can't attract her so soon. I am just being cynic.'

Some forest guards stood surrounding a place. Jeep stopped near them. As Rajeshwar got down from the jeep to find out what the matter was, one guard informed "Sir it is a trap."

Rajeshwar looked at Amar, found him yet lost in thoughts. Smiling he called out to Amar "Mr. Amar your attention please this is some material for you."

Rajeshwar motioned a guard to move aside dry leaves which were spread in rather a uniformed manner. Dilawar focused his camera at that spot. Guards brushed the leaves away carefully with long leafy branches. A net made out of thin bamboo sticks appeared from underneath the spread out leaves.

There was a huge pit on which the net was laid out. As Dilawar shot the net was pulled away and removed from atop the pit, Rajeshwar explained “This is a trap for some big animal. Had we not discovered it some big game like a rhinoceros, lion or even elephant could have got trapped.”

Amar remarked “These poachers must be a big headache for you.”

“Yes they are a big nuisance for us and we are a big bother for them. Very often we confront each other.”

“Meaning?”

“Meaning bullets are fired some time lives are lost.”

Excited Amar saw a scene for himself. He made an earnest request “Rajeshwar sahib please let us be a part of such an encounter if it happens again, you people shoot with your guns we will shoot with our camera.”

A serious Rajeshwar made a sarcastic comment “Amar sahib this is no film shooting. No dummy bullets are fired.”

Amar replied in tune with Rajeshwar sarcasm plus loads of humor “I am also not making a fictitious film. I am making a real authentic documentary. On clean truth full straight life of this jungle which is being poisoned by these poachers. Rajeshwar sahib you will be my hero and those poachers my villains. One day I will get award for this documentary, you will also be famous all over the world.”

Looking deep at Amar Rajeshwar remarked “Mr. Amar my life is in these jungles. What will I do with a big name and fame here?”

"Why, you can do a lot here with that name and fame, for starters more tourists, more government grants."

"And what will I do with more tourists and more government grants?"

"Have a much better life, may be move out to a bigger Park with better prospects."

"With better prospects will I have a better life?"

"May I ask Why not?" Amar was the one to question.

"For starters Mr. Amar I have struggled to set life here, I will have to struggle again to reset it at the bigger park."

"Sir there is no harm to struggle for better prospects in life."

"Prospects in life, not life in prospects; Mr. Amar my life here, with the decent prospects I have, is very much content, and to me, there is no bigger success in life then to achieve contentment. To keep trying for more and more with no end to it, is not my idea of life."

Rajeshwar got busy instructing his men. Amar was yet more disappointed with Rajeshwar; he analyzed self thinking 'This is the difference between me and a common man. I even after being beaten and battered can't stop thinking big. Even here in this Jungle I am positive; maybe it is God's will; may be my life is to flourish from these green pastures.'

Amar got busy in the describing the poacher trap on the visuals being recorded by camera man Dilawar.

That leopard which Rajeshwar had brought home in very precarious condition and Madhu had helped him in treating had recovered a lot. Fully conscious it was quietly sitting in its cage. Preparing an injection Madhu came. Rajeshwar was inspecting the already set medical tray. It was time to change his dressings. Rajeshwar said "Madhu he is sitting just right juxtapose to the cage. Have to inject his hind leg. Should I or will you?"

Madhu smiled as if recollecting something. Then looked at Rajeshwar, her cute smile casting a penetrating and lasting amorous effect on the poor fellow, said "Back in India, at the hospital patients use to say that I have a very light hand, while injecting no one felt anything. Human beings never felt let us see if this animal feels or not?"

Rajeshwar thought 'Well your hands may be light but your smile is certainly not light, it is sharp and piercing and does inject sweet pain.' However on the obvious facade he raised his hands as if permitting Madhu to go ahead and administer the injection.

Madhu dealt the injection. The leopard did not react at all. Slowly his eyes went drowsy and he lost consciousness.

Rajeshwar opened the cage then with Madhu help carried the animal out. They lay him down at the table. They strapped him carefully. Rajeshwar set a net on his jaws and fastened it. Now both began the job of changing its dressing. First they removed the old dressing then cleaned the wounds which seemed to have healed considerably and then applied fresh medicines. While at the job Rajeshwar said casually "He is very much guilty."

Caught unawares Madhu was confused; she failed to place he who, she asked "He who?"

Smiling satisfied with Madhu not placing Amar right on and looking in to her eyes Rajeshwar replied amused "One and the only…"

Madhu then understood. Composing herself and helping in the dressings of the leopard she said in a no bother flat tone "Guilt ridden he is because in deceiving me he got deceived himself. A cheat when cheated; only then realizes the worth and the pain of deceit."

Rajeshwar to explore her heart more planted one more question "Suppose if he sincerely apologizes will you forgive him?"

A rage came over Madhu; as if the question of forgiving Amar she was waiting to be asked for so long, as if she had prepared the answer many times in her mind, revised it over and over again; the opportunity had come at last, Rajeshwar had asked the damned question. Very vivid Madhu replied by heart "Forgiven are those who not deliberately commit mistake, in the heat of a moment, but a wrong which is done intentionally; after a lot of thinking and calculating; keeping some personal benefit in mind to forgive such a man is utter stupidity."

Rajeshwar noticed the feel and the deep anguish in Madhu; prove enough that she loved Amar too much and too much is a thing which always had bothered

Rajeshwar. Too much is bad even of good, even of love. Too much means much more then one's own capacity. Too much reflects, too much rebounds; too much is counterproductive, Like Namrata too much wealth was. Rajeshwar was worrisome again. To delve more he asked "He must have heard about this hospital. Is asking very much to see it you know for his documentary purpose. I think he is just looking for excuses to meet you."

Madhu had gained her composure; calm as ever she said "For me he is just a stranger. If he meets me it is ok. If he doesn't, then too it is ok."

But Rajeshwar in his heart of hearts decided that he will not encourage any such meeting. Tryst with a repentant lover can prove dangerous. It can give went to dying love flame.

Chapter Five

Somewhere very far, deep inside the jungle, that wounded lion, starved sitting in some bushes, licked his leg injury. It had almost healed but had made the leg very weak.

Some spotted deer were grazing nearby. Feeding on the grass they were coming near the lion. Their herd leader picked up his graceful head, turning his beautiful neck a little glanced at the resting lion. Snorted through its thick nose and then carelessly began to graze yet again. May be he knew the lion was wounded but the wounded beast was also very hungry this he was ignorant of. Lame lion had no other alternative, was under the compulsion to cool the hunger fire burning in his stomach to help heal his wound absolutely; to regain his lost might. His sixth sense cautioned him; without his wound healing totally his death was certain; either due to debility or vulnerability. As it was some hyenas were on rounds around him.

Grazing the deer closed in to the lion. The lion changed posture. Sitting on his paws gathered his hind legs together in readiness to strike. Alarmed the leader of the deer, the dominant mail raised his head and looked at the lion once more alert and vigilant. Sensing definite danger he rattled his ears and threw out an admonishing snort through his puffed up nostrils. Others in the herd took heed. Lame Lion instincts told him that he should not stall any more.

He pounced. The deer ran for their lives the lame lion after them. Marking one deer he was trying to reach it with his full speed and force but the pain in his leg kept increasing and speed decreasing. In a matter of moments the deer vanished from his sight. Lame lion stopped exhausted, kept looking blankly at the fading sight of his meal. Then he sat panting. He was very much underfed, lean and famished. His eyes were blazing in anger.

It was the marriage of the neighboring village chief's daughter. Rajeshwar and family were especially invited. Chief Jumbo uncle was six and a half feet tall, heavily built man. At sixty years of age he kept a very athletic body. Though his complexion was very dark there was a very attractive glow on his dark face which gave away a very nice and accommodative heart. His hair was curly, in his eyes there could be seen a depth of understanding. His lips were not as thick as his race people. In totality he looked a huge man with whom one would like to be friends and meet again and again.

Jumbo uncle was a very influential person. Many tourist buses of the area belonged to him. Adjacent to the jungle was hundreds of acres of his farmland. In the village he had a palatial house. Above all he was one of the major share holders of the Wild Animal Kingdom Park.

Rajeshwar was like a son to Jumbo uncle. His experience was that since Rajeshwar had taken the charge of Wild Life Kingdom Park as of then the number of tourist had increased many folds and poaching of poachers had diminished considerably. That was why using his influence he had stalled Rajeshwar transfer elsewhere.

Pinky was very dear to him. Often in her holidays Pinky came over to live in his house. She was very friendly with Jumbo uncle's grand children.

When Namrata had left Rajeshwar and gone, Jumbo uncle and wife had shifted and lived with Rajeshwar for many days. Trying to comfort Rajeshwar and Maji and look after little Pinky.

The marriage ceremonies at Jumbo uncle's place were to continue for many days. It was just the commencement then. And right from the inception Rajeshwar had to shoulder certain responsibilities. Rajeshwar also was looking forward to introduce Madhu to jumbo uncle and his wife and family. Some where Rajeshwar felt that Jumbo uncle and his family could help him to make the ends meet with Madhu.

For his this personal favor, on a prior occasion, he had praised Madhu a lot, in presence of Jumbo Uncle and given the necessary hint to Jumbo uncle's eldest daughter in law Niku. Niku was very much eager to meet Madhu and lend a helping hand playing cupid.

When Madhu met Jumbo uncle and family, on the first look and meet she realized that whatever Rajeshwar had talk good about them was right and true.

Madhu had driven the Honda CRV with Maji and Pinky in it to go to Jumbo uncle mansion.

The all decked up ladies were in no mood for the rough Jeep ride. The jeep was a must for Rajeshwar because from Jumbo uncle's place he had to proceed on some official work deep in the forest. So Rajeshwar led the way driving jeep with Madhu following in the CRV.

The CRV in toe Rajeshwar jeep came and stopped in Jumbo uncle palatial Mansion, Jumbo uncle was there with his entire family to welcome Maji. All crowded the side of the CRV where Maji was sitting; everyone was in a hurry to help Maji alight, welcoming hands propped Maji up and out.

It was then Jumbo uncle realized the need of the wheel chair. The thought that the wheel chair had to be positioned first had skipped all minds. Maji was dangling in the strong hands of Jumbo uncle he called out "Someone get the wheel chair fast."

In seconds Madhu appeared, expertly maneuvering the wheel chair in between the extensive family and positioned it neat right in front of suspended Maji. Very much obliged Jumbo uncle gently made Maji comfortable in it. Then he looked at Madhu; appreciation in his eyes. Rajeshwar voice rang over introducing Madhu "She is Madhu, the one I told you about."

Happily Jumbo uncle jumped slightly and shook hands with Madhu saying "Rajeshwar you were wrong, she is not good, she is too good, she is superb."

Everyone laughed Maji was heard saying "To me she is a God send angel."

During this marriage; with every ones joint efforts to make Madhu say yes for Rajeshwar was not a big bargain. Niku had briefed her younger sister in law, Jeena and even the bride to be. They all were excited; within the marriage celebrations had appeared the opportunity of one more very lovely entertaining activity.

Rajeshwar was no less than a real brother for all of them. His divorce had hurt them all bad. When they met Madhu an instant approval by one and all was made very much obvious. Madhu was confused as to why they all were reacting so happy seeing her, talking to her. Some of them were always around trying their level best to be extra friendly.

Madhu was very good at applying 'Mehndi'. A ritual very popular among ladies in India; the hands of young and old ladies are adorned with beautiful designs; the paste made by the green leaves of 'Mehndi' plant is packed in a pointed cone; it is very artfully applied on hands, even feet, then is allowed to dry out. When finally it is washed; the green captivating designs are transformed into red beautiful, exotic, sensual illustration on pretty delicate feminine hands, also giving a cool, smooth and clean sensation to the skin.

The "Mehndi" plant Madhu found grown as a hedge around Rajeshwar flower garden. Madhu had quietly picked up a bag full leaves; grind them in the kitchen grinder; applied the paste on Maji, Pinky and her own hands a night prior coming to Jumbo uncle's mansion. Morning, when Pinky washed her hands, she had yelled happily; ran up and down the house showing her hands to everyone, amazed, excited and loving them.

At Jumbo uncle's mansion, Madhu was on instant demand. From bride to bride's kin to maid servants all wanted a piece of Indian art.

BrideS Niku and Jeena were the first applicants. They sat in a room around Madhu watching her first apply 'Mehndi' on bride's hand; happy for 'Mehndi' as well as for getting Madhu all to themselves. The idea of initiating Rajeshwar seemed easy.

But complication and impediment cropped up in the form of Amar who was there on Jumbo uncle's request to video record his daughter's marriage. Other then Rajeshwar nobody had any inclination about Amar and Madhu past. Ignorant Jumbo uncle had thought Amar to be of advantage not knowing he was otherwise.

Madhu was busy with her "Mehndi" job at one of the bride's hand, Niku winked at her sister in law Jeena. Jeena was the youngest daughter of Jumbo uncle. She was just fourteen but very smart and cute as well. Niku said "Madhu you must teach this 'Mehndi' art to me or else who will apply 'Mehndi' at your hand on your wedding."

Taking the hint Jeena asked Madhu "Is there any chance you getting married here in South Africa?"

"No chance getting married anywhere. "Madhu replied laughing.

The bride questioned "Why?"

As if in reply to the why, Amar appeared camera stuck in his eye. Madhu hand shook losing concentration at the unexpected sight; the application went wrong at the bride's hand. Madhu expertly made the correction.

Amar camera, not off his eye, was at his job, very systematically recording every delicacy of Madhu and her art. His camera registered the touch of his presence in Madhu erring, he zoomed into the big close of Madhu face; the twitching of her cheek, the sudden blinking of her eyes, the color fading out and in on her fair complexion, all was captured in camera. Amar saw his chances in brighter light.

Love lost gained new hope, new energy, desire of Madhu multiplied. The focus of the camera automatically became the pretty charming beautiful face of Madhu; her smile; her expressions of satisfaction as she reviewed her work; then close shots of her hands, doing the work; Amar felt a pang in his heart. Inadvertently a sigh came tearing out of his heart and reached Madhu touching her heart. Madhu was distraught and off mood she had finished doing both the bride's hands. She got up making an excuse "I have to give Maji her medicine can we do your hands later."

"Any time but before the marriage gets over" Niku joked.

Crossing Amar Madhu was gone.

All through the marriage ceremonies the meetings between Amar and Madhu became a constant affair. Madhu had said that Amar was a stranger for her but Amar was not letting it be like that.

During the seven days of marriage ceremonies luckily three days was Pinky's holiday, so it was agreed that the three days maximum by 11oclock Madhu will drive Maji and Pinky to Jumbo uncle's place. At night Rajeshwar will reach there from work and will drive them back leaving the jeep to Johnny.

Next morning Amar was standing by the CRV. His camera man Dilawar was absent again. For the seven days of marriage at Jumbo uncle's mansion no work was to be done on their documentary so he had taken a leave and gone to meet some relatives living in Johannesburg.

When Madhu came out with Maji and Pinky and saw Amar she faced away from Maji trying not to show her but natural disappointment. Amar on his part stepped forward and joining his hands in namaste said "Namaste Maji, I am Amar the video man."

Maji responded blessing him by the gesture of her hands "Oh, yes, yes, I saw you yesterday at Jumbo house."

"I am on my way there only, Jumbo uncle rang me up and told me to take a lift if of course no body minds."

Madhu gave no reply, however Maji welcomed him "Why should we mind, any Indian company in this part of the world is welcome, where from India you are?"

By the time cook Ramzan had come to help Maji into the car, Madhu and Ramzan put their hands around attempting to help her in the car; Amar volunteered and picked Maji off their hands in his arms all by himself. As he gently placed Maji at the back seat Maji thanked him, and then repeated her question to Amar "So young man which part of India you belong to?"

"Maji the whole of India is mine, no north Indian, south Indian, Marathi, Gujarati problem."

Maji laughed loud but Pinky felt strange, confused she asked "Dadi what is the joke why are you laughing?"

"Beta in India some people take this joke very seriously, they fight over it."

Innocent Pinky said "I don't understand."

"I also don't understand." Amar said plainly.

Madhu with Ramzan help was busy loading the wheel chair at the rear of the CRV, as she moved towards the driver's seat Pinky moved to sit with Maji, Madhu called out to her sitting in and adjusting her seat belt.

"Pinky you come and sit with me here in front."

Pinky rushed to the front seat happily "Oh I thought uncle was going to sit in front, I love to sit with you.

On the way to Jumbo uncle's mansion Amar made friends with Pinky; broached the topic of the interview.

"Pinky I want to take your interview; want to ask you how you met Monu and Bholu and made friends with them."

Pinky was all excited "Go right ahead, take it right now ok, I am ready, I can tell from the beginning."

"Not here in the car, I want the interview in a green valley when Monu and Bholu are around."

Pinky complained "Bholu had not come since so many days."

Deliberately changing the interview topic Amar inquired "Had he forgotten you?"

"Never, Bholu is a good friend he will never forget me ok."

"Correct." Amar agreed "Good friends must never forget each other." Madhu was concentrating on her driving; not concerned.

Maji intervened "Right, I have so many friends back in India none of them have forgotten me though we have not met since so many years but still we keep in touch."

"Absence makes heart grow fonder, makes one realize the worth of good friends." Amar said meaningfully for the benefit of Madhu. Madhu took no notice, kept driving.

"Even bad ones we don't forget." Maji puts in with light humor; may be thinking of Namrata again.

Amar added "In my opinion bad one's are most difficult to forget, Maji you know why?"

Interested Maji asks "Why?"

"Well God is very kind He wants to give the bad one's time enough and a chance to expiate their sins."

Madhu reaction spoke of no interest.

"What does expiate mean?" Pinky asked.

"Making amends for the wrong done to someone." Amar said looking at Madhu from the rear seat, sitting alongside Maji.

A sore expression came over Madhu face, distorting her pretty features a little.

Maji was definitely thinking of Namrata, she countered "But some wrongs done cannot be undone."

"Right Maji but at least one can try and then nothing is impossible if one earnestly tries, God may take pity and help, show the way." Amar was pathetic. Madhu was somewhat attentive. Maji also noticed pitiable tenor and made a comment "You talk as if you wish to expiate some sin?"

"How very right you are Maji, there is a list of my sins I want to expiate. Maji bless me to live long enough to do my penance." Amar said joining his hands in devotion and prayers, Madhu eyes were showing signs of heaviness.

Maji appreciated "There is no one in this world who has not sinned, but very few who want to make amends; it is good to know a young man like you."

Massaging Maji legs Amar said "It is a blessing to know you Maji, my mother died at my birth; father had died earlier fighting a war for the country. There was no one to guide me to tell me the difference between right and wrong. I am one of those who learn from their own mistakes. I sincerely beg of those who I have wronged to have pity on me and forgive me."

Amar was very solemn once again, Madhu could see very well in the rear view glass he looking down as he attempted to jerk of a tear. Not willing to give in but still Madhu had no control on her heart, it was touched by that unseen tear of Amar and the touched heart designed tears in her eyes which she somehow managed to contain not letting them float up on her face. Pinky was there next to her and she was conscious of the little child. Maji affectionately throwing an arm around Amar took him close and said to Madhu "Madhu the young man is very God fearing and lonely let us invite him to live with us till he is here."

Before Madhu could object, Amar cut in "No…no Maji, my channel had provided me accommodation at the Resort, just allow me to visit you all off and on."

"You are most welcome do come whenever you feel like my son." Maji assured.

Madhu may have looked at Amar or not but she was always aware of his beseeching eyes pleading, entreating forgiveness. Madhu did try to stay clear of him but Amar kept his heart at her feet.

Madhu, after a very long session of marriage preparation chores was relaxing with Niku. They sat in a corner of the huge hall cups of coffee in their hands.

Daughter in law of Jumbo uncle, Niku, was a well educated girl in her late twenties. Even after giving birth to two sons she kept her figure very much in shape; attractive features; whitish complexion; her long flowing hair thick and black; cheerful and outgoing in nature; to her Rajeshwar was brother. Niku was all set to finally broach Rajeshwar to Madhu.

Amar was also around. He was advising an electrician on setting up the lights for his camera job but was all ears to Madhu and Niku. A premonition that this marriage may vicariously contribute to another relationship was haunting him.

Niku plunged into a direct talk of Rajeshwar "My brother Rajeshwar, I am worried about his drinking compulsively."

Agreeing Madhu said "His job demands an alert mind; you know dealing with poachers and wild animals."

Niku added "He is lonely."

Madhu may be on purpose or innocently suggested "You are his sister. Do something about it."

Niku smiled, looking intently at Madhu and punched in "I am at it."

Madhu very well understood Niku's 'I am at it'. Her reaction could have been positive but for Amar presence.

Amar was within hearing distance. He heard 'I am at it'. His heart skipped a beat. He said nothing nor came in their way, just a heart rendering sigh exhaled out of him once more. The coffee cup in Madhu hand shook as she took it to her lips, upset, but smiling she got up saying "I think we have relaxed enough. Let's get on to work, so much is to be done. Just four days left for the reception."

Rajeshwar's subject was broached to her by the cupid playing trio not only on every opportunity but also abruptly, at random. Jeena was the youngest, only fourteen. Rajeshwar took care of her as his real sister and Jeena adored Rajeshwar; she was in great rush to see him settled again. From the first day itself when she was introduced to Madhu she saw no occasion, waited for no opening or chance, precisely went on praising Rajeshwar to Madhu right from day one.

Jeena was introduced to Madhu by Rajeshwar "Madhu this is Jeena my very dear kid sister."

Jeena broke the ice "And he is my best brother, you know why?" she asked Madhu.

Liking her attitude, Madhu asked "And why?"

"Because he is the best, all my pretty looking friends say so, once I introduced him to a lady professor of mine, she passed me when I had failed my test."

An uncomfortable Rajeshwar admonished her showing wide eyes, amused Madhu laughed,

The other day Madhu was in the crowded kitchen, preparing a special sweet dish for a ceremony. Jeena came from behind and held Madhu tight and said without any inhibition "I want a sister in law like you and I can't find anyone else other than you, tell me what should I do?"

Madhu wriggled out of her grip and ran after her the large cooking spoon in hand. Every one present in the kitchen laughed amazed.

Amar had been haunting Madhu, the endeavor to get rid of the past was being made more and more difficult. Madhu found some moments to herself. She sat all alone at a far end corner of the mansion's spread out garden sipping a cup of coffee. Jeena came and sat beside her. Madhu looked at her suspecting she was up to something. Jeena smiled and caught her both ear lobes by her hands, as if promising to behave, and sat quiet for a moment then all of a sudden asked "Are you in love?"

Madhu suffered palpitation thinking if she had found out about Amar "Why do you ask so?"

"Because if you are not in love, you better be, I mean your age factor, you might miss the bus, Rajeshwar bhaiya..."

Madhu cut her short annoyed "You are going overboard Jeena. Stop it."

Madhu got up and left. Jeena was taken aback a little but was confused more.

None understood her non receptive mood except Rajeshwar. Rajeshwar had disapproved Amar presence from the very first day. All through he kept an eye on him. To Rajeshwar all the exploits of Amar were deplorable drama. He decided to explain all this to Madhu on way back home.

That night a native folk dance group was to perform after dinner. Very famous dancers, men and women were summoned by Jumbo uncle to give a special performance. For that performance there actually was a general invitation. People had thronged from all directions. Stage stood constructed in the open. Performances were on in full swing; the crowd all around.

Rocking to the tune of African folk music were dark, very well shaped sexy figures, Slim waists, expansive brimming thoraxes, shapely legs, glittering in white revealing dresses; conveyed and demonstrated that beauty lies not only in white. Dark color has a class of its own, an attraction of its own.

The scent of so many human bodies had allured the wounded and starved lame lion. Both hunger and hate had compelled him to come close and close.

Taking shelter of tall grass and dense shrubs he was very much there. But the bright lights were daunting him. Cars buses and trucks were parked all around. The lion was so famished that his sixth sense was continuously warning him that if he doesn't hunt fast and fill his belly the hunting potency will give way completely. Gathering courage the lion moved between the parked vehicles.

An ill-fated man felt the urge to urinate. He never knew that the excuse of the urge was actually his death warrant. Taking the cover of a bus he began to relieve himself.

Suddenly the lion appeared in front of him. Terrified the man froze; the process of relieving himself got abruptly cut. With wide open eyes he starred into the face of the lion.

Before he could turn and bolt for his life the lion struck. Power full claw slashed through the abdomen. Legs gave way. A horrifying shriek and the man collapsed. Lion seized him by neck and dragged him along.

Approaching tempo head lights lighted up that dreadful scene. People coming in the tempo saw a man being dragged by the beast. Shouting they jumped out.

Sticks and spears in hand they rushed to save the man. But the distance gave the lion an edge and enough time to drag his prey into thick bushes.

There rose a blaring outcry that a lion had dragged a man away. The function came to an abrupt stop. Madhu was unable to comprehend because all the shouting and screaming was being done in African dialect. She enquired of someone "What happened?"

"Lion! Lion! Man…Gone."

Rajeshwar, Jumbo uncle and some men with their guns ran towards the jungle. Amar snatched the camera from a dead scared Dilawar hand who had come back that particular night after visiting his relatives, and followed them.

At one place aflame torches were distributed among men. Men carrying these burning torches entered the jungle.

After many hours of search a half eaten body of the ill fated man was discovered.

The Lame lion had transformed in to a Man Eating Lion.

Rajeshwar made an announcement to that effect to one and all declaring the lion a 'Man Eater'.

That night Madhu, Maji and Pinky stayed back at Jumbo uncle house. Rajeshwar along with his forest guards and Amar in toe, searched for the lion all through the night. They also set different types of traps in their exercise to catch the lion alive. Tranquilizer guns were also kept handy in case of need.

Dilawar Khan had flatly refused saying that shooting a Man eater lion was not there in his contract. Not bothered Amar was there with the camera accompanying Rajeshwar at every step, very much to his annoyance .Rajeshwar had warned him bluntly "This is a very dangerous affair. I do not take any responsibility of your safety."

An all excited Amar replied "Rajeshwar sahib that God up there is responsible for our lives, we live as long as he wishes neither more nor less."

At his excitement Rajeshwar remarked "But while living one must accomplish something great, make a big name. Am I right Mr. Amar?"

Amar confirmed "You are sent percent right sir. Dying without making a good name is an insult to living."

Rajeshwar complimented "Ok, Then come along, a golden opportunity is here for you waiting in the wings of life and death."

That night and the next full day they searched the Man eater lame lion.

Its hunger satiated the lion was fast asleep in a thicket. Resting he recuperated and gathered his lost strength back. The taste of human blood he had liked very much. The other good thing was that the two legged animal was a very easy prey. Its number had also increased very much in his jungle. Now whenever he felt like he could satisfy his hunger making a kill of the slow weak thing. Otherwise also since the time that two legged animal had injured his leg he had developed hostility to its kind. Now he will hunt it whenever he liked and take revenge from the two legged animal.

Rajeshwar very much aware of these deliberations of the lion had explained them to Amar, so that Amar through his documentary reached this fact to the world. How much human beings are responsible for transforming carnivores in to Man Eaters.

Dropping Amar at the forest resort Rajeshwar reached home. It was evening time. He saw Madhu standing at the terrace as if waiting for him. All of a sudden Namrata flashed through his mind. She had never waited like this for him but then another thought pinched him. May be Madhu was waiting not for him but for Amar. But then he realized that Madhu knows that Amar lives in forest resort. Why will she stand and wait for Amar. But once again a lover's thinking whispered to him 'May be she wants to enquire the well being of Amar from me' he got annoyed at himself and uttered "Dam it, you very well know she has said that Amar is a stranger to her now "

Driving Jeep, Johnny got startled he asked "Sahib did you say something?"

An embarrassed Rajeshwar replied "No, no, nothing."

Johnny was so exhausted and sleepy; he simply shook his head disappointed at himself.

By the time Rajeshwar entered the house Madhu had come down she told him "Hot water is ready in the bath, you freshen up I will get dinner served."

His tired eyes were great full to Madhu. He smiled and said "Thank you."

"What about Sher uncle?"

"Till now there is no trace of Sher uncle must have gone far deep in to jungle."

Worry and sorrow came over Madhu as she informed Rajeshwar "Jumbo uncle had appealed to the government for the wife and the kids of the man who is killed and on his own he has filled their house with food grain. He told me to tell you this."

Going towards his room Rajeshwar said "See I told you Jumbo uncle is a very fine man."

Smiling Madhu walked towards the kitchen. She was thinking 'Amar was also with Rajeshwar God knows how he is?'

Then as if annoyed with herself she uttered "Come what may, why should I care."

Johnny had just come in he asked "Madam did you say something?"

Nervous Madhu said "No, no, nothing."

She quickly went in to the kitchen. A confused Johnny stood scratching his head as if asking himself 'Am I hearing things.'

At the dinner table, having dinner sat Rajeshwar, Maji and Madhu. Pinky was sleeping tired and exhausted. Rajeshwar told Madhu "Now when Pinky's school reopens extra care had to be taken. An armed guard will always be there with you when you drive her to school."

Maji asked "What about the resort, the tourists there are also in danger?"

"Armed guards will patrol the resort day and night and I have issued orders restricting tourists not to go in the forest interiors." Rajeshwar glanced at Madhu he wanted to note any relaxed feeling on her face on coming to know that, that Amar was safe; he wanted to know her concern about Amar. He saw none. She ate her food without looking up. Rajeshwar felt relaxed. He was wrong; nibbling her dinner Madhu was thinking about Amar; whether to ask Rajeshwar about him or not she was in a double mind.

Double mind was another human weakness which Madhu detested. She was a confident character, in one second she had decided against faithless Amar, why then same Amar was becoming the reason of her demerit, was her first love making her a mentally weak; unable to decide good and bad for her. No she thought; she would rather die than to live like a confused feeble mental jerk. Whether to say yes to Rajeshwar or not and go into a new relationship or not was another matter. But to revert back to Amar was against her female vanity. She made her decision then and there.

Rajeshwar was exhausted; her silence was annoying him. He ate his food occasionally glancing at Madhu. He also hated confusion, he and Madhu were very much same characters, may be that was why their pattern of lives was similar. Right then he wanted to know the meaning of her deep silence. He was satisfied that she had not asked about Amar but he himself wanted to talk to her about that Amar. Tell her that all the emotional antics of Amar were mere drama. Then another apprehension crossed his mind, should he utter any such thing or not. By even talking ill about Amar should he keep Amar alive in Madhu heart or not; again confusion; a lover's confusion.

Next morning coming back from the village market Jumbo uncle paid them a visit. Madhu told him that Rajeshwar was sleeping tired and exhausted. A distraught Jumbo uncle informed Madhu that that particular night's marriage program had been cancelled. Next night after full security arrangements the schedule will continue. Just then on top of the main gate a chimpanzee appeared perched. It jumped inside. Shocked Madhu shrieked. But Pinky who had just got up happily ran towards the chimpanzee calling "Bholu, Bholu."

Laughing Jumbo uncle told a bewildered Madhu "He is the same baby chimpanzee who Rajeshwar had brought home. Maji raised him fed bottled milk, like Monu Bholu is also Pinky's child hood friend."

At a distance, Madhu saw Pinky very amicably telling Bholu something, maybe complaining about coming after so many days. Just then Monu entered pushing the gate open Madhu remarked "Great, both friends have come together."

"Yes, yes, and I very well understand why they are together here."

An amazed Madhu questioned "And why so?"

"You may believe me or not, but I am sure these two friends have come here to protect their little friend Pinky."

"Meaning what?"

"Animals are no nonsense; they have great sense. They have come to know somehow that one lion had become Man Eater. Both of them are here to safe guard Pinky from him."

Skeptical Madhu asked "Jumbo uncle can it be so?"

Convinced and confident Jumbo uncle replied "It is happening so my dear."

Then Pinky came running to Madhu. Bholu followed her. Monu proceeded to the heap of sugarcane. Pinky introduced Bholu to Madhu

"Aunty meet my friend Bholu."

Jumbo uncle produced a huge bunch of bananas from his jeep. Keeping the bananas near Madhu he said "Madhu feed Bholu if you want him to be your best friend."

Apprehensive Madhu plucked a banana and offered it to Bholu. But Bholu was eyeing the full thing. Madhu understood and pushed the full bunch to Bholu. Bholu greedily kept the whole bunch in his lap and guzzled the bananas one by one. Amazed Madhu sat there with Pinky. Departing Jumbo uncle said "O.k. Madhu beti I am leaving. Tomorrow you must come and yes get that documentary fellow with you, I heard his camera man left scared, but this fellow, Amar, had all along being with Rajeshwar."

Jumbo uncle went. Madhu was somewhat happy hearing some good about Amar. Inadvertently a slight smile came to her face but then angry at herself she discards it annoyed.

In the church Jumbo uncle's daughter marriage was solemnized. After the ceremony the bride and bride groom stepped out of the church. The bride held a bouquet of flowers in her hand. As per the ritual she faced away from the crowd assembled there and flung the bouquet to them. It landed in between Rajeshwar and Madhu. Instantly both Rajeshwar and Madhu caught hold of it. The bouquet was in their hands. Jubilantly the entire crowd including Jumbo uncle and family, Maji, Pinky, all clapped.

Amar was at his job recording all that; the camera trembled in his hands.

Dinner was served in the lawns of Jumbo uncle's mansion. Celebrating the marriage many guests were drunk including Rajeshwar. Seeing Madhu approach Rajeshwar hid his liquor glass behind him. She came and simply took away the glass hidden behind his back from his hand saying "You have to drive and Sher uncle is still not found dead or alive."

Tipsy Rajeshwar proclaimed "We have full security all around. My men and Jumbo uncles' men will not leave him if he dares to appear."

Madhu smiled nodding but said "Yes, I know, I know but then too if you eat food it will be very nice."

Going along with Madhu Rajeshwar was saying "Yes ...Yes ... Madam ... Your wish is final nothing matters more ... I will eat ...Will eat ......"

Saying so Rajeshwar walked a little ahead of Madhu. She was following him when Amar all of a sudden appeared in front of her "Madhu, I thought you hated drunkards?"

Madhu retorted "Yes then I used to hate drunkards now I hate someone else."

Madhu moved ahead but thinking something stopped, turned and gave a deep penetrating look to Amar and said very decisively "Amar don't waste your time on me, I am not the one to be knocked down by the same stone twice."

Giving a very stern look to Amar she moved towards the dining table. A heart shattered Amar watched Madhu go away. Then there right in front of his eyes Madhu served food to Rajeshwar.

Rajeshwar on his part, even in his drunken stupor, had noticed the brief encounter between Madhu and Amar.

As Madhu gave the food plate to Rajeshwar he gave a loathing look to Amar and said "That bastard there... All his sigh business is fake, those cold exhalations, sad tears in his eyes all is again a conspiracy...a drama..."

Madhu looked at Rajeshwar surprised; the man had been observing, the thought brought a smile to her lips; she made a morsel of food from the plate he was holding and fed him "I know him better than anyone else in this world."

"But you see, I don't trust him, beware of him, he is shrewd, cunning, scheming..."

"He is worst." Madhu said laughing.

Amar watched her talking and laughing and feeding a drunken Rajeshwar. Tears dropped from Amar eyes.

Chapter Six

Early in the morning Amar set out for a morning walk, but not forgetting his camera, it was very much in the tight grip of his hand. Walking through the natural beauty and fresh air Amar thoroughly enjoyed himself. Only one thought disturbing his rejuvenating walk; Madhu was not there with him and the chances of his lost love coming back were very much on decreasing power.

On his way came the valley of flowers; hundreds and thousands of color full flowers and above them millions of butterflies swaying as if to the tune of the winding breeze in rhythm with the swinging rocking trees.

Delighted Amar stood still watching for a moment. Then automatically his camera came to his eye. Through his camera eye on its lens appeared Pinky the angel, playing between the flowers and butterflies. Then Madhu appeared watching her play, and along with Madhu Bholu and Monu entered the frame.

The view of Madhu with a chimpanzee and an elephant did not shock Amar, he knew about Monu and Bholu but watching Madhu so familiar with them was a very disturbing sight.

Madhu saw Amar. He had stopped recording the rare visual; he gestured to Madhu asking what was happening? Was Madhu alright? Madhu gestured back to him conveying that she was absolutely fine and reassuring patted Bholu's head with her hand. Amar again gesticulated trying to say that he does not understand. Bholu saw him. To Bholu Amar was behaving strangely. Bholu reacted alert. He wanted to know who the funny man was. In an aggressive mood he moved towards Amar. Amar folding his hands begged Madhu to save him. Madhu also realized the predicament; coming after Bholu she called "Bholu ... Bholu... It is alright ... Friend ... Friend ..."

Pinky had told Madhu that by uttering 'friend' Bholu understands that the person concerned was o.k. Bholu came near Amar and took a stand confronting him. Madhu rushed there in time and gently stroked Bholu repeatedly saying "Friend ... Bholu ... Friend..."

But Bholu was not in a good mood. Madhu turned and looked at Pinky playing at a distance. Pinky was busy with her butterflies. Madhu was apprehensive calling out to Pinky. Doing so might excite Bholu more. Suddenly Amar caught on to some idea. He quickly put his hand into his jacket pocket. When his hand came out, it was full of dry fruits, which he always carried as emergency rations. He extended hand full dry fruit to Bholu. Looking at the dry fruit Bholu hostility reduced. One lick of his tongue and all the almonds and cashew nuts disappeared into his mouth. Amar again put his hand in to his pocket but this time only a few pieces of dry fruits came out. This was not appreciated by Bholu. He put his own hand into Amar pocket and over turned it. Whatever emergency ration was there spilled out on the green grass. Bholu got busy picking and eating it. Amar and Madhu took a sigh of relief. Amar smiled at Madhu and said "Thanks a lot for saving my life once again."

Without responding to him in anyway Madhu called out to Pinky "Pinky it is enough, now let's go home."

"Aunty please; some more time."

Seeing Pinky playing among the flower and butterflies Amar appreciated "I have never seen such a beautiful sight in my life, with your permission may I"

He focused the camera once more on the visual. Madhu gave a cool look to Amar and said "Your camera man ran away is it right?"

"Yes, he loved his life very much."

Madhu taunted "And you love your work more than anything."

Taking the camera off his eye Amar took a deep sigh and said "For someone I can sacrifice both work and life."

Madhu retorted "Humans sacrifice, not working machines which are available to anyone who can pay well."

A repentant Amar looked at Madhu with tears in his eyes and said "You may say so Madhu you have all the right to say so, I never knew myself that I am such a bad man."

Just then Rajeshwar jeep was seen coming speeding toward them leaving a cloud of dust behind. It pulled up with a jerk next to them. Rajeshwar was definitely feeling bad seeing Amar and Madhu together. That was very well written on his face "Amar sahib poachers have entered the jungle I am going to take care of them, you want to come along with your camera or are you busy?"

"Mr. Rajeshwar I was coming to you only, walking all the way but this eighth wonder of the world held me back."

Saying so he pointed to Pinky, butterflies and flowers, Johnny with two rifles was sitting besides Rajeshwar. He jumped to the rear seat. Amar sat besides Rajeshwar who drove away.

On the way two more forest guard jeeps joined them. Amar put a question to Rajeshwar "Rajeshwar sahib what is more urgent, going after the poachers or the Man eater?"

"Mr. Amar these poachers create Man eaters. More over no carnivore kills unless hungry. Right now that lions belly is full. But these poachers kill to fill their pockets; for business. The bones of animals; their skin; their teeth, even their horns; claws are marketed. If they are not stopped they will annihilate these jungles."

Suddenly at a distance a Rhino darted out of a thicket, running for its life. He was hit by bullets. Blood oozed out of its wounds but it was running with all the force of life left in him.

Chasing and shooting at the Rhino then appeared two jeeps full of poachers. Rajeshwar and his men in their jeeps spread out confronting and blocking the escape of the poachers, the poachers panicked. Reversing their jeep they tried to flee the way they had come from but by that time one forest guard jeep appeared blocking that exit also. Rajeshwar picked up a mike and announced warning them to surrender. But in reply they shot back. Rajeshwar and his men counter fired.

The poachers realized that they were outnumbered by the law men and their attempts to escape were blocked. The vehicles of law cornered their jeep from all directions as they made their escape bid. Constrained, at a point in dense forest, they jumped off their jeeps and ran in to the jungle. Rajeshwar and his man also abandoned their jeeps and chased them on foot.

Bullets were continuously being fired from both sides. For Amar it was a God sent opportunity to show his talent to the world, to the people who never acknowledged his worth, never gave him a chance to prove himself. Amar got so engrossed capturing the encounter in his camera that he came in between the cross fire.

Rajeshwar tried his best shouting to caution him but Amar was so lost in his job that he paid no heed. For him the bullets riddled encounter was a gift of God; priceless shots. To the best of his abilities he was recording the scène of both sides firing at each other.

For Rajeshwar it seemed a single choice; to save Amar life let the poachers go off his hands. He could have very conveniently got Amar killed in the cross fire and washed his hands off the trouble shooter but Rajeshwar was not cut out a man that type.

Impelled Rajeshwar ordered his men to cease fire. Getting their clearance the poachers escaped.

Rajeshwar was furious. Amar very well understood, the poachers' escape was due to him. Standing at a distance Rajeshwar was fuming at Amar. Amar walked to him and said "Rajeshwar sahib your anger is very well justified. Definitely because of me these poachers have escaped but the faces of those very criminals are very well captured in this camera. Also their efforts to stall the government officials to perform their duty; firing at them; charging at them to kill. All this is also so well captured in this camera of mine; the dangers of the encounter from the law point of view will seem to be that between the heroes and the villains. And before this entire happening are those moments when prior to commencing firing you had warned them to surrender but they initiated firing at you first. Then you and your men returned their fire; at the stake of your lives; you and your men discharged your duties. You may also appreciate that I too played on my life to perform my duty; acquired the proof for you to get the enemies of your Wild Life Kingdom behind bars and in the process I too have captured some award winning shots for myself."

Rajeshwar burst into an appreciating laughter on his logic, reason and effort.

That late night, having dinner alone with Madhu, Rajeshwar narrated the entire incident to her. She was not amused at all. To her Amar had not changed .She told Rajeshwar "Rajeshwar sahib we people work to live but Amar lives to work, just to earn name, fame and money at any cost; it can be someone else's life or happiness or even his own existence. His purpose and idea of life is just to work and work. Name, fame and money, is the essence of life to him."

Rajeshwar agreed saying "Yes, workaholics in my personal opinion are very self centered people. They rationalize that they work for their near and dear ones but the fact is the passion of work is all that matters for them."

Madhu gave her assent as if from her personal experience "And such workaholics have no family life, always constrained and tensed relationships, with just name and money no one can buy contentment and happiness."

"The pact of happiness is the deal of heart but sometimes one loses even then." He said indulging in his past.

Understanding what Rajeshwar meant Madhu added "The deal of hearts should be from both sides. I and you dealt one sided deal. On the other side was the same glitter of money, fame and acclaim."

Rajeshwar pointed out "There is a little difference between my happening and your happening. Namrata never looked back at me but Mr. Amar had very well realized his mistake and is repentant."

"Repentant he is because leaving me he never got what he wanted. Had he got what he wanted he would have simply vanished."

Rajeshwar smiled and nodded a yes.

Next day at Rajeshwar house the newlywed along with Jumbo uncle and his entire family were invited. Amar was also there very much at it, doing his job, his camera on and his mind set on Madhu. After the last encounter he had argued with himself that Madhu had very rightly rebuffed him and he should very rightly keep begging her forgiveness. What he had done to Madhu was not easy at her so how could it be easy for him to undo the wrong done by him.

Maji had asked Amar to cover the party, Rajeshwar had not objected on purpose. He, by then was confident of Madhu but wanted to see if there were any more lengths left for Amar to go on.

As soon as the family arrived, Jeena came straight to Madhu, who was in Maji room collecting brides present kept there. Jeena said teasing "I saw you feed Rajeshwar Bhaiya last night at our house. Say yes and end the matter, what is the problem?"

"You, you are the problem; you are making me think twice." Madhu said lightly.

"Why me?" Jeena asked innocently.

"Sister in law like you will be a head ache."

Madhu said smiling while carrying a tray well decorated inside which was an expensive dress for the bride. Jeena blocked Madhu way standing right in front, hands stretched "Sister in law like me will be of great help to you in all matters A to Z just try and see."

Niku came to the rescue of Madhu "Is she giving you problem again?"

Madhu, gently brushing aside Jeena moved ahead towards the hall where everyone was, replying Niku "Sorry I can't tell you the problem; it's a very private business between us."

It just shot out of Jeena mouth, loud and clear "Oh I know now, you are just playing hard to get."

Madhu stopped in her tracks; Niku showed eyes to Jeena.

Madhu walked back to Jeena who felt and reacted scarred and sorry, once more catching her ears "It just slipped out of my tongue, I am sorry."

Niku came in reprimanding "You better be, I will tell your brother."

There were tears in Madhu eyes, with a gesture of her hand asking Niku to be calm she said to her "Don't be angry at her, she is still a child." Then to Jeena she said "Jeena you have made me feel important by saying that I am playing hard to get and the truth is I would love to have a sister in law like you but I need some time, please give it to me."

Tears sprang up in Jeena eyes, she hugs Madhu, Niku also came close, and Madhu put the tray aside on a show case and took Niku also in her fold.

Nevertheless the buzz around the party was of one more marriage on the cards. The names of Rajeshwar and Madhu were in the air. Amar got not any chance to come near Madhu and his heart continuously went through a sinking feeling.

To give him some fresh air Amar came out of the house into the Garden. Pinky was playing with Jumbo uncles grand children. A thought entered his mind. 'What type of mother Namrata is? How could she leave such a cute child and go?'

He saw Johnny loitering around, sitting on a lawn bench he called out to Johnny "Johnny just a minute, please."

Johnny came, with a gesture of his hand Amar requested him to sit beside him on the bench. Johnny happily sat saying "Sahib, get ready for one more wedding. After all my Sahib will get married again."

Preferring not to indulge in the topic, Amar asked Johnny the question bothering him "Johnny please enlighten me; what type of woman your Namrata memsahib was?"

"She was tall. She was fair. Her hair was always cut short."

"I mean how she could leave such a beautiful cute looking child and go."

Johnny replied not defending his onetime Madam "For her money, little proud no, no very proud of her money."

"Then why did she marry your Sahib?"

"Confusion…Sahib…confusion…full confusion… she the only daughter of very rich father… Her father mother more bad then her, Too bad … They hate my sahib much … Not happy with the marriage."

During the conversation Johnny informed Amar that some time back he had gone to Jonesburg. He had met Namrata "Very strange…Till then … Not got married again …"

"May be not forgotten your Sahib." Amar said a hope building in him.

"That I not know...But When I talk of Pinky Baby ... Her eyes become watery."

Hearing this God knows why Amar saw a silver lining in his dark romantic clouds. He inquired further "Do you know her address?"

"Manohar Shivdasani's daughter my Memsahib... in total Jonesburg anyone tell ...What bungalow ... What cars ... some say they have one plane also?"

Amar mind was racing. His hopes were increasing. As it was Amar had to go to Jonesburg on official business. He had to submit his tapes to the channel office. He was confident of his good work and sure of getting extension of his contract and good money as well. There in addition he would meet Namrata also.

Amar's mother had once said

"A Girl is born to be a Mother"

Now he had to find out how true the saying was, how much power motherly love had over the female called Namrata. But for that he had to first meet Namrata.

Reaching Jonesburg, Amar manipulated to get Namrata invited to a lavish party thrown by his channel. Namrata never showed up.

A film unit was there in South Africa from India for Film shooting. Namrata was much found of Hindi Films. And all the stars did oblige Namrata. They attended her dinners; her invitations of opening ceremonies of her organizations.

Through Namrata they availed many facilities in South Africa. Limousines to go around, discounts in hotels. Her father was also into construction business, so huge bungalows were available on discounts for shootings.

Amar reached one such party thrown by Namrata for the Indian Film Unit via a good old friend of his.

When he saw Namrata he was stunned. In looks she was no less than any heroine. And what high and mighty she was; at her finger tips all was available. The hero and the heroine never left her side for a moment. The producer and the director were at her service constantly, the poor producer obliged her serving her drinks personally.

Amar failed to reach anywhere near her. The friend who had invited him prohibited him; less the friend may lose his job.

Namrata had a P.A. Personal Assistant, a forty-forty-five year's old Indian woman. Very balanced figure she had for her age, whitish complexion, very attractive Bengali features, very grace full and of course well educated. To Amar she seemed to be a very understanding woman and was also accessible to him.

Amar introduced himself to her. He told her that he was making a documentary for Mother Nature Channel. He had just returned from Wild Life Kingdom Park. From there he had brought a gift for Madam Namrata. He took out an envelope from his jacket pocket and gave to the P.A.

"I will be very great full to you if you can just pass it over to Madam Namrata."

P.A. opened the envelope. It contained some very cute photographs of Pinky .P.A. watched them carefully, trying to make out something of it because as soon as Amar had mentioned Wild Life Kingdom Park she did feel something fishy. Amar then told her "This is Pinky, Namrata ji's eight year old daughter,"

P.A. kept back the photographs in the envelope and coolly said "Namrata ji has no lineage with them anymore."

Amar also coolly replied "Lineage is not manmade. It is God made. We humans are just a via media. That is why blood relations do not end even after death. Get connected with the next generation next genealogy. Madam I do not intend anything wrong. I want to meet Namrata ji for the well being of her daughter."

"And why are you interested in the well being of Namrata Ji daughter?"

Very simply and plainly Amar replied "In the well being of this little innocent child is my well being."

"May I ask what the connection is?" questioned the P.A. giving Amar an intent look.

"That I must say is of great personal concern for me, as well as I am sure, for madam Namrata. She might also appreciate me telling her in person only."

Amar had being so truthful and straight forward that the well experienced P.A. kept watching him for a moment. Then she placed the envelope in her handbag.

"I will give this envelope to Madam after the party gets over, what is you contact number?"

Amar gave his mobile number to her and left the party.

Party got over by four in the morning. Namrata had had a few drinks more. Back in her luxuriant bedroom she was feeling exhausted and sleepy. Her maid helped her disrobe her tight fitting dress. P.A. Chatterji entered. Selected a beautiful night tie for Namrata then as Namrata stepped out of her dress P.A. held the nigh tie open for her to move in. A drained Namrata said "I am very tired, sleepy, just wants to hit the bed."

Showing her the envelope Chatterji said "Ok, I will give this to you tomorrow morning."

"What is it?"

Giving the envelope to Namrata "Please see for you self."

Opening the envelope Namrata took out the first photograph. Looked at it and kept looking. All of a sudden all the sleep as if had dissolve away from her eyes. Intoxication clouding her brain evaporated.

Slowly she pulled out the rest of the photographs and gently laid them down on her bed. She continuously looked at them. She failed to understand why those souls less photographs were reaching her heart. Watching and understanding her Chatterji said "The one who had given these to me said they are your Pinky's photographs. May be he is wrong?"

Without looking away from the photographs Namrata uttered "He is not wrong. This is Pinky."

She picked up some photographs. A shiver in her hand was visible. Looking at them closely she said "Pinky was two years today after six years also she looks just like me."

A thought of Rajeshwar blocked the tears in her eyes. The same old herself, the same flare flashed again. She looked at Chatterji and questioned "Who gave these to you?"

Chatterji told about Amar. She told that Amar was saying that for Pinky's well being he wanted to meet Namrata.

"And?"

Chatterji continued "And he also said that in Pinky's well being is his well being, on the first look the man doesn't seem to be a wrong person, in my opinion Madam you may meet him."

Thinking something Namrata replied "Ok, I will call you."

Namrata had planned that she will go to sleep and when she wakes up she would ring up Chatterji and tell her the time to meet Amar. But the sleep which vanished on beholding Pinky photographs evaded her all through.

After maid servant and Chatterji had gone, the images of her little daughter kept her engaged; her own flesh and blood in form of the beautiful photographs went on refreshing her memories of the two year old she had deserted years back.

Then she got up; pulled down all the photo frames displayed in her room. She replaced the pictures, paintings in them with her Pinky's photographs. At her bed side she put up that snap shot of Pinky in which among flowers and butterflies she was laughing brightly. And another photo in which Pinky was in an English bride dress that also she placed at the side of her bed.

Lying on her bed she kept watching; the past flashing when she left Rajeshwar, the memories of Pinky. One year old Pinky laughing, crying, two year old Pinky learning to walk, giggling at her, Namrata dressing baby Pinky up, giving her bath, feeding her milk, changing her diapers. So on the memories of her daughter kept haunting her.

Often on Pinky's issue she fought her parents; why they did not let her bring Pinky with her, why they brain washed her that no decent boy from any good family will marry a mother of a daughter. Today there were so many suitors for her from rich and famous families. Still she was not married. The reason was only one; she herself had not approved of any one. In one and all she found something or the other missing or wrong. Her parents and friends assumed and felt that she had lost faith in men, all because of Rajeshwar, his betrayal. But Namrata knew that it was not right, she simply did not feel for any one as she had felt for Rajeshwar.

The fact what she failed to realize was, that in every man she somewhere looked for Rajeshwar. That was the reason why she could not approve of any one.

Again on the thought of Rajeshwar she got annoyed but in that was hidden her love for Rajeshwar. The lone fact was she was not in know of and no one else ever explained that to her. All her near and dear ones hated Rajeshwar, were repulsive to his name. He was always discussed in bad light.

That day in her life a new person Amar had entered with some news of her daughter. May be it was Rajeshwar who had send that fellow. Suddenly she was eager to meet Amar.

Amar had gone to sleep at about two in the morning. At eight Am. he was in deep slumber when consistent ringing of his mobile woke him up. It was a call from P.A. Chatterji. Namarta had summoned Amar at 9 A.M. at her bungalow. Getting ready fast Amar was thinking 'Party must have got over by morning, Then how long did this Namarta sleep? She had called him at 9 in the morning. Must be, must be, Pinky's thoughts; they have hijacked her sleep.' Reasoning so Amar smiled at the first good sign. It was his first step towards success. More over it was a very clean and fine job. Uniting segregated mother and daughter. Settle an unsettled family. Madhu was a very fine girl. She was bound to understand the human side of it. Along with being benevolent he would get back his Madhu, he just had to make understand this Madam Namrata.

Namrata parents were out of the country. They were in London on a holiday.

Namrata was sitting alone in the lavish living room of her grand and spacious Bungalow waiting for Amar. The Butler entered with Amar and very respectfully announced "Madam, Mr. Amar."

Taking two steps backwards he walked away from there. Amar bowed his head a little to wish Namrata. She did not respond at all neither gave any hint for Amar to sit. In a very reserved manner put forward a question.

"Why did you want to meet me?"

Though Amar had not succeeded in becoming a director but he had all the qualities of a good director. He immediately understood that Namrata was a hard nut to crack. Would like straight talk; to the point.

"Rajeshwar sahib is getting married again. This means a step mother for Pinky."

Namrata reacted with a twitch of disappointment but she did not make that obvious, instead questioned "So what is your problem? Why have you come to tell me this?"

Amar again answered straight to the point "The girl Mr. Rajeshwar is going to get married to, is the girl I love. I can't live without her."

Amar looked at Namrata with sad and honest eyes. Namrata smiled. May be at the game of destiny then she pointed towards a sofa for Amar to sit down.

Amar understood that the stone had lost some weight. In an attempt to shift the conversation to humanitarian grounds, Amar said "My Madhu is a very nice girl but this relation of step mother and step daughter is very dicey. Often good also turn bad."

Amar sat on the sofa, Namrata questioned again "You want your love back, how can I help you?"

Gaining confidence Amar said "There are two ways, one is legal, you can file a lawsuit, claim custody of your child on the ground of your ex-husband getting step mother on your daughter. But this way Pinky will be dragged into court proceedings. This may leave a bad impression on the innocent child, so I think other modus operandi is better."

"And what will that be?"

"Rajeshwar sahib is to be made to understand that he is committing a mistake getting a step mother for Pinky. Maybe during this course he might even realize the mistake he committed in leaving you."

Hearing this shiver ran through Namarta entire body. A new hope sparked her up. One such happiness which she had not experienced for long her heart felt. And she failed to conceal this excitement.

Amar not the least made obvious that he had read the vibrations in her; very wisely not offending her. He on the contrary appealed to her; fed her ego "Namrata ji, I am a very ordinary man, an orphan since childhood. This Madhu is the sole excitement in my life. If you help me I will get her back in bargain. I am not worth anything to be of any use to you but that God up there He sees everything. For this benevolence of yours he will definitely reward you."

Just then the butler came and respectfully informed Namarta "Madam your breakfast is ready. "

Namarta ordered "Mr. Amar will also have breakfast with me" Then she led Amar to a huge dining room. An extensive dining table was well set with glittering crockery. The cutlery was not golden but was of gold. Breakfast both veg. and non. Veg. was laid on the extensive table. During the course Namrata inquired about Madhu "How is that you love Madhu so much and Madhu leaving you is getting married to somebody else?"

From the beginning Amar had anticipated that this question was inevitable. He had decided to tell Namrata everything very truthfully, very honestly.

Amar told her about his and Madhu's first meeting when Madhu had saved his life. Stopped him for committing suicide and then for seven years how their love had blossomed. Then he narrated how he had betrayed Madhu for Reena to achieve the goal of his life, and then how Reena deserted him. This slap of destiny had brought his senses back. He came to make a documentary in South Africa. Here the Almighty made him meet Madhu again however now his Madhu was going to belong to someone else.

Amar's tale made Namrata feel somewhat familiar. It seemed that both were made of the same mould. Time and circumstances had brought them together. As of then both had the need of each other. The advantage lied in helping and assisting each other, but to Amar Namrata said no such thing. Of course her name was Namrata which meant politeness, being nice, but she knew no such thing. Since her childhood she had known no such values. She told Amar "Ok I will help you but to do so will I have to go back to that jungle?"

Amar requested "Madam it is just a matter of few days. More over during past five-six years that jungle had urbanized a lot. There are five star resorts and hotels to live in. Tourists from all over the world come there."

Namrata retorted "They then also came, tell me when we have to leave."

"We will have to leave as soon as possible Madam. If they get married and then we reach there then no point madam."

Chapter Seven

Every day early morning Rajeshwar left in search of the Man eater and came back home late at night, tired and exhausted. To find one particular lion in that vast spread out jungle was indeed a very tricky and hard job. Jumbo uncle was of the opinion that the lion was dead for sure, for the reason that the lion had not killed again. Injured, he might have fallen prey to some carnivore or rival. But as per Rajeshwar instructions his forest guards were always on the alert as it was also possible that the lion had fed on some other carnivore's hunted prey.

In fact the fact was also that. The belly of the lion was full. He had fed on his brother's kill. The brother was of his own age and was as ferocious as him. Both were born together, brought up in the pride together and when together they reached adult hood their own father disinherited them. Drove them out of the pride so that they do not start family of their own; claim lionesses and produce their own off springs.

There after both the brothers roamed the jungle together. They hunted together. Both grew very powerful and impregnable concurrently. The day was not far when they would have laid claim to some pride. Would have killed its leader or driven it away and themselves become the protector of the pride as dominant males. But before this could happen the dammed poachers' spotted them and one was shot and injured. The other brother had escaped.

Time passed, when the injured and hungry brother's roar reached other brother, searching him, he came, both met. Now he killed and fed his lame brother.

After tasting human blood the injured lion did eat the kill, a deer, killed by his brother but it did not taste as good as the flesh of the two legged animal.

Man is one beast which eats the best of the food which produces the best of the blood and flesh. His mind has thinking power this makes the marrow of his bones much tastier.

Brother lion sensed some change in his lame wounded brother but this change was due to the taste of human blood this he was not able to make out. Lame lion was waiting to recover completely then he would make his brother understand and may be transform him also in to a Man eater.

That evening when Rajeshwar reached home after his search tired and exhausted, he saw Madhu once again at the terrace. He deliberated if it was her habit to take a walk on the terrace daily evening or she waited for him.

Enough of that confusion, he decided that he should find out the fact. He parked the Jeep. Straight away using the lift reached the terrace.

Yes Rajeshwar had got the lift installed especially for Maji. So that Maji could freely use the terrace or come down to the lawn garden as and when she desired.

Rajeshwar stepped out of the lift; he was shocked to see his mother's wheel chair vacant.

At one corner of the terrace Pinky was standing on the other side was Madhu and along with her was standing Maji supporting a stick. Rajeshwar was bemused. Pinky called out to Rajeshwar "Daddy hold on ok. See Maji is going to walk to me, Ok Dadi,(Grand Ma) start walking now."

Slowly taking the support of the stick Maji moved forward, beholding his mother walk after year's together tears swelled up in Rajeshwar eyes. Walking with caution Maji proceeded to him instead of Pinky. As she reached him an emotional Rajeshwar moved and embraced his mother asking "Maji How this miracle had happened Maji, how?"

Tear rolling down her eyes, Maji with a shaking hand gently held her hand towards Madhu. A delighted Rajeshwar uttered "Madhu, Madhu did it?"

By this time, both Madhu and Pinky had come near them. Lovingly Maji touched Madhu saying "Since the time she had come here every evening she had been working on me. First she gave me my happiness back, then my courage, then made me walk supporting me, persevering with me and now finally this stick. if she stays on you will see even this stick will go."

Rajeshwar made up his mind to propose to Madhu then and there only. Madhu was saying "Rajeshwar sahib, please excuse me for keeping this a secret. In fact Pinky insisted on giving you a surprise."

Wiping his tears with his sleeve Rajeshwar proposed to Madhu right in front of Maji and Pinky "Madhu please give us one more surprise. Just say yes to me, to us."

A surprised Madhu looked at Rajeshwar not understanding exactly, but Maji understood. Holding Pinky's hand she whispered "Come my dear, you come with me."

Holding Pinky's hand and with the support of the walking stick Maji moved to leave. Madhu intended to stop them but refrained as Rajeshwar said "They will be down there at the hall waiting for you to say just that one yes."

Madhu understood. She looked at Rajeshwar a little diffident. May be her past was yet coming in between. Rajeshwar very well knew Madhu by then, said "Madhu our past had made us come together. It is the will of God. We must bind to it. I will not hear anything other than 'yes' from you."

Confidently he held his hand out asking for her hand. Madhu looked up to his hand then at him. She saw a total picture of sincerity in Rajeshwar as he said "Madhu have faith in me I am not a faithless man."

A flash of decision flickered in Madhu eyes; reason her inner voice calling out to her, asking her how long she was going to dwell on the sore memories of that faithless man and why. Next moment she offered her hand to Rajeshwar.

Holding Madhu hand Rajeshwar was standing, happiness sparkling in his eyes through his tears.

Madhu was looking at Rajeshwar smiling, once again feeling not all alone.

Maji and Pinky were in the hall, Maji very eager and restless, Pinky confused and angry at Maji "Dadi why did you make me come down? I wanted to be with Daddy and Aunty."

Pinky had not understood that her father had proposed to Madhu. Maji was in double mind whether to explain to little Pinky or not. In case Madhu said yes it was ok but if she refused then?

At the steps leading to the hall appeared Rajeshwar and Madhu hand in hand coming down towards the hall to Maji and Pinky. Happiness sought palpitation into Maji; she was standing taking support of her walking stick. She sank down into the sofa near her. Madhu hurried to her asking Rajeshwar "Get a glass of water quick."

As Madhu rushed to Maji; Maji looked fixed at Madhu. Madhu shook her calling "Maji…Maji…" Rajeshwar brought glass of water, Madhu took it from his hand and made Maji drink it slowly. Taking a few sips she relaxed. Holding Madhu tight close to her heart she cried shed tears of bliss. Pinky was all the more confused as to what was happening. Rajeshwar realized how much his mother loved him, how much she sought his happiness. He sat besides his mother reassuring "Ma, she is your Madhu now she has said yes to us."

Pinky intervened "She had yes to what?"

"To be your mother." explained Maji. Pinky understood and jumped in to Madhu open arms calling "Mummy my mummy."

She held Madhu tight from one side while Maji held Madhu on the other side in her yet bliss fully trembling hands. Rajeshwar watched the sight to which Namrata billions were not worth nothing.

Maji rang up Jumbo uncle that very night; gave the good news of Madhu saying yes to Rajeshwar. At his end of the phone Jumbo uncle jumped high phone in hand shouting at the top of his voice "YES IS BEST, this yes is the best yes I have heard in my life, Jeena, Niku, where are you all."

In the middle of the night every one came running to Jumbo uncle's bedroom; his two sons, their wives, their young and very young children and of course Jeena. As Jumbo uncle got busy telling everyone about the 'yes' his wife got busy getting tea prepared for the family; the late night turned young and alive. Maji phone on the other end was continuously busy, some one or the other from the family calling to congratulate her.

Full three car loads full Jumbo uncle and family and maids and servants reached Rajeshwar bungalow early morning. Jeena jumped out dancing from Jumbo uncle's car, Maji was up standing with the support of her walking stick, Jeena froze at the sight; stepping out of the car one by one, Niku, Jumbo uncle and wife, all were pleasantly surprised to see Maji out of wheel chair standing. Jumbo uncle exclaimed "Maji what is this, a miracle?"

"Yes this is a miracle and the one who has made this miracle happen is my daughter in law Madhu." Maji declared to one and all.

Jeena started dancing again, Pinky joined her and then Niku and the rest of them all including Jumbo uncle danced merrily.

Using his authority of CEO Wild Life Kingdom Park; Jumbo uncle sanctioned special three days leave to Rajeshwar. Pinky cried and forced her school off.

New paint for Rajeshwar official bungalow, new furniture, and new draperies all was ordered officially by Jumbo uncle. Jeena kept hugging and kissing Madhu on slightest excuse till Madhu got fed up; Niku had to shout at her to stop it; absolute jubilation the day began with. Maji felt that the weight lingering at her heart was no more there.

As the news of the waiting in the wings marriage spread, there was a general talk; Maji clutched wheel chair at Namrata leaving and is back at her feet at Madhu coming.

Yes when her daughter in law left. Annulment papers came, divorce happened. All this must have tormented her mind when she had the fall at the staircase.

Doctors' diagnosed shock was more severe than the wound. It was the shock which had crippled her. How right doctors were. Madhu came; shock retired and Maji walked.

Namrata was back again, she was very much there in the vicinity of Wild Life Kingdom Park.

It was afternoon. Amar was driving her Mercedes. Namrata was sitting beside him. Passing through the jungle road the car was speeding towards the forest resort. Namrata looked around, the area looked familiar to her she popped the question "Does this road lead to Forest Resort?"

Agreeing Amar replied "Yes Madam we will be staying there."

Namrata frowned making her disapproval very obvious "Why there?"

Very simply Amar explained "Rajeshwar sahib's house is close by. It will be convenient for us."

In a sharp voice Namrata cut in "I am not going to put up in that third class Resort; you turn the car towards hotel Marriott."

Without changing direction Amar requested "Madam if you are going to stay at the Marriott how will we meet Mr. Rajeshwar?"

With total indifference Namrata said "That is your problem."

Amar very politely admitted "I am very much there at your service Madam. But Madam right now need is ours."

Namrata hit back "Need is not ours, need is yours, you want to get back your girl Madhu. As for my daughter, I will get her anyhow legally; I have full right on her. Turn the car towards the hotel. If you want you can stay there at that Resort."

Helpless Amar turned the car towards the hotel. Once again he realized that Namrata was a hard nut to crack but then the hard nut was his only hope. Only Namrata could turn the tables right for him. There were two very big plus points; Namrata was Rajeshwar's First Love; Namrata was Pinky's Mother.

Rajeshwar got up from his bed and walked to the terrace hoping to find Madhu there. But she was not there. It was a long day, all the marriage details were worked out, Jumbo uncle and Niku taking charge telling Maji not to worry about anything and just relax and Maji was relaxed, more than anything for one thing; her would be daughter in law.

Jumbo uncle and family had gone back with the promise of keep visiting frequently.

Taking a stroll at the terrace Rajeshwar was thinking about his first meeting with Madhu.

He had slipped and fallen Madhu helped him and he rebuked her. How rude and crude he was with her, thinking so he looked up. Madhu was standing right in front of him. He never knew when she came.

This is exactly what happens in our lives. When somebody good steps in into our existence we never understand. And when we our self invite somebody wrong that too we do not know. And we think ourselves to be the ace of spades.

Once again Rajeshwar and Madhu found themselves at the same spot from where they had moved past long time back. Rajeshwar along with Namrata and Madhu with Amar but then, as they had promised to be faithful with each other, they were just white plain blank paper, Rajeshwar to Namrata, Madhu to Amar had sworn to be with each other in good or bad, however as of that day so much of print had come on that plain sheet of paper that the previous precious candid easy going attitude was missing.

When Rajeshwar took Madhu hand in his hand she merely asked "Promise me that you will slash and throw away my past memories from within my heart."

Reassuring her he said "What you have already accomplished that why can't I achieve?"

"You mean I have completely obliterated Namrata memories from within your heart?" Madhu in doubt inquired.

"The good ones yes but the bad ones will remain as they are."

"That means never ever you will have any fond memories of Namrata."

"What I really mean is we should not waste the precious moments of our dear left over life thinking and talking about those past nasty entities which cracked a good part of us."

"But what if you ever happen to meet Namrata?"

"Same as what happened to you meeting that Mr. Amar, stranger, total stranger."

Rajeshwar laughed; Madhu joined him laughing, and then said "Ability to laugh is such a blessing."

"Laugh and the world laughs with you cry and you cry alone."

Madhu with down cast eyes uttered "Thanks to you I am not alone anymore."

Winning Madhu into his arms Rajeshwar whispered in her ear "Maji had called our panditji (priest) to finalize our marriage date; I want it to be the earliest you are so close yet so far."

Madhu smelled whisky, very much remaining in the warmth of his arms she casually said "Your compulsive drinking can I talk about it?"

"You have to talk about it, if you don't I will be hurt." He said drawing her more close to him in the tight grip of his arms.

She giggled "I have treated alcoholics at hospitals."

"I know I am in safe hands."

Rajeshwar lips closed in for the bliss of a kiss. Madhu shied away. He insisted "Just one..."

Madhu whispered blushing "Better wait for punditji's date."

She tried to wriggle out of his tight grip, he held her "If I promise to be a good boy; promise to drink only occasionally that too with your permission then can I?"

"No."

"Why?"

"Pundit ji date."

"I hate myself for uttering Pundit ji."

"And I love you for that."

"Then let us consummate our love by at least a touch of your delicate lips."

"Go ahead." Madhu whispered permitting.

His lips touched her lips gently. Then he let go her very slow from the firm hold of his arms. She eased out her eyes looking straight into his eyes; both pair of eyes exchanged a message of faith, love and sincerity.

Rajeshwar smiled watching Madhu rush to her room somewhat shy but very happy. He looked up at the sky and said "Thank you God."

At hotel Marriott, Namrata booked the princess suite for herself. Once again she asked Amar if he wanted a room there. Amar declined saying he was already booked at the Resort by his channel. Namrata once again turned rancorous. She was not use to hearing no anyway. She admonished "Look I am not going to be here for long. You will have to forget your channel work and talk to Rajeshwar first and then have him talk to me. Whatever the decision I want it fast. In this wilderness I am not going to get bored, sitting alone here in this room."

Amar made an attempt to make her understand "Madam Channel job is totally in my hand; I am the director; I am the camera man; I am the anchorman. It is a total one man show. I will do it as and when I want but yes this particular work for which you have taken the trouble to come here I don't have any control on it."

Namrata got all the more annoyed, belligerently she got up from the couch she had positioned herself and stood dominating Amar "If you don't have any hold on it then why did you persuade me to come here?"

Amar had had enough. He smiled and said "Just for a try Madam and I am sure if you cooperate then we will definitely succeed in this try."

Namrata sensed the defiance in Amar; she deemed it not right to be taut any more. She realized that things should not sour further between her and Amar both required each other. She wanted to settle the matter grace fully, wanted it to end well. She wanted to win back Rajeshwar at all costs. She as per her attitude and nature dismissed Amar "I am extremely tired, will take some rest, you meet Rajeshwar and initiate the talks. Tell him that I am here then we will see what is to be done."

Amar bowed his head in a mock respect and harmony as if agreeing with Namrata advice then turned and walked out of there.

Jumbo uncle had send Niku to Rajeshwar house with a load of sweets. He had instructed Niku to go with Maji and distribute sweets to one and all their acquaintances.

Reaching Rajeshwar house she got the sweet boxes stocked in the hall and told the servants Ramzan and the maid "You people eat as much as you want and distribute to who so ever you wish as much as you want. Your sahib is getting married."

Seeing Maji coming with a walking stick she happily said "Oh Maji how good to see you out of that wheel chair walking again."

Maji was happy, very happy; her face which had in the recent past forgotten the pleasure of smiling was radiant with smiles at the smallest pretext. And she looked forward to the slightest opportunity to mention Madhu name and refer to her as 'my daughter in law'.

"This is my daughter-in-law's phenomenon, my Bahu-Rani's wonder miracle. It is her good coming."

Niku very much agreed "Such a good coming that she had put life in your legs, where is your Bahu-Rani I want to stuff her mouth with sweets."

Laughing Maji said "She has gone to drop Pinky School."

Niku got worried thinking of the man eater still at large.

"Had any armed guard gone with them?"

Maji reassured her "Yes, yes, every day an armed guard goes with them."

"Jeena has also gone to school under heavy escort. This Madhu's Sher uncle has become a big bother. Maji Baba has ordered me to go with you and distribute these sweets to all our friends and foes; I have security with me you please get ready."

"But beta the cards have not come, the marriage date is not yet fixed."

"With the cards we will go the second time right now we just have to announce the marriage."

That was the extent of jubilation at Rajeshwar camp; no one knew about the awaiting predicament.

Namrata was restless in her bed; the thought was again and again coming to her 'Pinky must have come to her school.'

Pinky was a student of St. Joseph convent this Amar had told Namrata. She was contemplating that whether she should go to the school and meet her daughter. Anxious she rang up hotel reception and inquired "Where is St. Joseph convent?"

She was told that the school was very close to the hotel. Namrata failed to hold the mother in her back any more; quickly she got ready.

Driving her car straight she reached the school. School she did reach but standing there she was thinking 'How to meet Pinky, if suddenly I tell her that I am her Mother God knows how the child may react. Who knows how much Rajeshwar had told Pinky about me and what he had told? It is quite possible Pinky may hate me or she may be totally ignorant of me?'

Just then the interval bell rang, children rush out of their classes into the open ground in front of the main school building where Namrata very much stood. Very young to young girls shouting, screaming ran playing in to the compound of the school.

Mothers and maids had brought food for their wards were in a huge hall where dining tables were lined up for the purpose. Some children came rushing there directly to eat food, some thought better to play for a while..

Namrata eager eyes were searching for Pinky. At a place at some distance she saw her daughter playing with her age group girls. Namrata heart beats increased, tears sprang up in her eyes. Without giving any more thought she moved towards her daughter.

Her eyes fixed on running and playing Pinky. Namrata was approaching her daughter, reaching Pinky she was about to hold her and pull her in her arms and embrace her and kiss her when Madhu all of a sudden appeared taking Pinky arm. Madhu took her away from right in front of Namrata eyes. As if Namrata was no one to Pinky. As if she was no relation to Pinky, was a total stranger to Pinky.

A statue like stunned Namrata was standing there watching Madhu lovingly feed Pinky. Pinky was laughing and talking to Madhu and at some exchange of pleasant and loving words Pinky lovingly put her arms around Madhu and kissed her tight. This Namrata failed to accept. Her own daughter, her own flesh and blood kissing and exhibiting such love for her stepmother; would be second wife of her husband. It was too disturbing a sight for Namrata. She had understood that it was Madhu, who had come into Rajeshwar life.

Namrata's pride again took hold of her. Angry she turned, started her car and left without meeting her daughter.

Amar was fast asleep in his Forest Resort cottage he was exhausted. Mentally Namrata had drained him out and physically he had driven her car at a stretch for four hundred miles. And in that duration he had either endeavored to endure her silence or sharp exchanges.

He was in deep slumber when constant ringing of door bell woke him up. He sat up in his bed; to ease fatigue stretched himself and yawned. Bell rang again.

He got out of his bed, went and opened the entrance door to his cottage. Maji along with Niku was standing in front of him, he smiled wide delighted.

Since the time he had reached Forest Resort he had been thinking that it was Maji only who can understand him well and straight in pulling down the wall between Rajeshwar and Namrata; putting together mother and daughter torn apart; getting back her lost daughter in law. Maji must be yearning for all that. Maji could help him best, so he had thought.

He was absolutely sure that Maji was going to help him. And see what a good omen. Maji was standing right in front of him. It just slipped out "What a good luck Maji, you have yourself come to my place."

Then as if observing something, looked at Maji head to toe and said "Oh! Maji you have come literally here walking? How come this miracle?"

Maji entered his cottage along with Niku carrying a sweet box Niku said "First you taste these sweets then we tell you."

"Yes beta, God has finally heard me, come first you eat this sweet."

Maji took the sweet packing from Niku, began to open it. Not knowing why Amar heart skipped a beat. Nervously he inquired "Maji sweets what for?"

"Maji is getting a daughter in law." Niku furnished the information which was specific enough for Amar.

Color drained down his face. Niku was observing him. She had been noticing him since the time he was covering the marriage at her place. He was always around where ever Madhu was; his movements were not clean; in fact he in totality seemed quizzical and weird to Niku. But she had no inkling as to why, and he was a no body so she had dismissed her premonition, but there he was, color draining out, Niku instigated "My Rajeshwar Bhaiya is getting married; all our wishes are coming true."

Offering him the sweets Maji insisted "Come take… first you eat sweets."

She pushed a piece in Amar's mouth. Trying to swallow the sweet Amar asked, since voice was not coming out so he gesticulates asking

'Sweets are for what?'

A happy Maji announced "Niku told you Rajeshwar marriage had been fixed."

Amar's breathing stopped for a moment. Scared to death he gesticulated once more asking

'With whom?'

A very happy Maji informed as alert Niku watched a desperate Amar trying to swallow the sweet "Of course with my Madhu."

The shock made sweet enter Amar's windpipe. He started coughing violently. Face turned red, eyes bulged out Maji was patting him hard but Niku was standing still, very much her doubt clearing; sure of herself. Maji poured a glass of water and helped Amar drink it.

"What happened Beta?"

Niku knew what had happened, however she was confused as to what the past could be; was it a one sided affair or both were in love. If both were in love so many questions at a time were plunging in Niku mind. Maji was hitting Amar hard on his back and saying "Someone must be thinking of you, remembering you real much."

Amar uttered trying to regain his breath and posture "No one...no one Maji...I told you I have no one, so be it."

"A young man like you must never think and talk like this, at least be happy for us." Maji observed.

"I am very happy Maji for you, will be there to cover the marriage of your dear son." Amar blabbered.

Niku was observing all through, she wanted to get out of there and think peacefully. She reminded Maji "Maji we have to go to so many other places."

Amar heart was screaming 'Whatever had happen should never have happen'

"Beta, remember you have to cover my Rajeshwar and Madhu wedding with your camera, I like your work, you have done a splendid job. Now you take rest I think you were sleeping I woke you up."

Amar suffered a passing thought 'It was better to sleep forever than to wake up like this'

Niku helped Maji out. Amar sat there brooding holding his head in both his hands.

Whole day distributing sweets with Maji Niku thought and thought and came to one conclusion;

'Madhu was too good to be so gravely wrong that in the presence of a lover and having an affair with him, would go ahead and say yes to marry someone else, however there was definitely something fishy, with time she promised herself she will find out; remove the fishy part and cast the smelly fish away.' The more bothering concern was, Rajeshwar was family and should she take him in confidence or not.

It was early morning when Maji had fed Amar sweets. As of then it was past noon. Amar had not eaten anything nor had a cup of tea. Forearm on his forehead he was

flat on his bed. Mercedes stopped In front of his cottage. An angry Namrata got out and banged the door shut.

Cottage door was wide open as Amar had not bothered to close it after Maji and Niku departure. Taking quick steps Namrata entered. Amar was lying prostrate on his bed she remarked "Whose death are you mourning?"

Serenely Amar replied "My death."

Annoyed Namrata rebuked "What is all this shit? Why didn't you come to the hotel? Why didn't you call me? And why is your mobile switched off?"

Amar continued in a mournful tone "My life switch had been switched off Madam so it doesn't matter at all to me if the mobile is on or off."

Namrata was all the more annoyed "Stop acting quizzical with me. Tell me straight. What is it?"

Amar picked up the sweet box kept near him and offered it to Namrata saying "Have some sweets."

Alarmed she questioned "Sweets? What for?"

Amar simply said "Rajeshwar sahib's wedding is fixed and final with Madhu."

Namrata turned pink. With an angry swift movement of her hand she hit the sweet box. Sweets spilled on the ground. She burst out "Let him get married. I am going to call my lawyer for my child's custody. I will straight away file a petition in high court and you will see I will get Pinky custody like this, like this."

Saying so she snapped her fingers and continued "My particular lawyer had not lost a child custody case till date, before coming here I had a detail sitting with him."

Amar now sat up in his bed and once more requested "Madam just please allow me fifteen days time. After that you may do whatever you feel like."

"Why, in fifteen days do you have a magic wand which will set things right. I know Rajeshwar well he will never understand."

"I know Madhu well she will certainly understand. Madam Madhu is an angle; she is too good a person. She will not come in between a mother and her daughter."

"She had already come in between me and my Pinky."

"Exactly, this is what I am going to make her realize. More over I am her first love. No one forgets first love. Have you forgotten your Mr. Rajeshwar?"

"Nevertheless he has forgotten me."

"How can you be so sure? He knows not you are here. Allow some time. Let things come in proper prospective. Please permit me to go my way; with your help I guarantee all to be well. In these fifteen days if I fail to convince Mr. Rajeshwar I promise Madhu will certainly understand."

With a lot of effort Amar convinced Namrata for those fifteen days as well as made her agree for her complete cooperation. To save her daughter Pinky from the tortures of appearing in court Namrata acquiesced.

The Man eater lion had not killed again nor had been spotted even after intense search. Finally every one began to believe Jumbo uncle's theory that the Man eater is no more. But he was very much there with his brother, taking rest, waiting for his wound to heal completely. Brother hunted and he filled his belly. But he did miss that particular human taste. People were once again moving freely in the jungle doing their daily chores.

CHAPTER EIGHT

Amar had to meet Madhu somewhere alone. He found out that daily Madhu took Pinky's lunch to school and after feeding her stayed back till the school got over.

That was the only possible time when Madhu could be approached alone, and a chance for Amar to attempt his exercise.

The school compound was a long drawn garden. Under huge shady trees there were some benches where the guardians of children sat and passed time waiting for their wards.

Madhu had made some lady friends. She was talking to them. As she saw Amar coming towards her she got nervous. Noticing this one friend inquired "What is it.?"

Glancing at Amar Madhu said "He, who is coming, I don't want to talk to him.

"No problem. We will just call the security, he will be thrown out."

During that time Amar had come somewhat near. Not knowing why Madhu stopped her friend from calling security "No let it be, it is no big deal. Let me see what he has to say."

Madhu got up and walked to an empty bench; sat at one corner. Amar followed her and sat at the other corner of the bench.

Somewhat understanding friends were laughing and commenting 'It seems; sweet love gone sour.'

Madhu in a have had enough tone inquired "What is it now?"

"Congratulations; your marriage with Rajeshwar is all set."

"Yes."

Amar came to the point directly "Madhu do you know other than me there is one more life which is being devastated by this marriage of yours."

"I don't know and I don't care." Madhu bluntly replied.

"Do you care about Pinky?"

"What do you mean; of course I do care about Pinky?"

"Then you have to also care about her mother Namrata, she is here."

Madhu was taken aback, even though she had a premonition but still in the wildest of her dreams she had never thought of Namrata coming back. Madhu questioned "How do you know her?"

"Same, as by chance you came to know Rajeshwar sahib. This life itself is a matter of chance."

"What does she want?" Cutting the matter short Madhu questioned; her heart pounding.

"Namrata is repentant, very regretful."

"All of a sudden and why are you advocating for her?"

"For the obvious reason Madhu, both our lives will be wreaked by you marrying Rajeshwar sahib and Madhu Namrata is also a mother."

"A good for nothing mother, she had left her two years daughter behind."

"Madhu, parting ways with Rajeshwar sahib has made Namrata realize her mistake that is why she never got married again and she is terribly guilty of leaving her daughter behind."

It was a very different ground for Madhu, she had never thought of it, mentally she was not at all prepared for an argument where the defendant was the mother of a child and a repentant ex wife. Madhu blabbered "It is too late now; she just can't step in at will?"

"Madhu she is not stepping in at will. She has come here because you are getting married to Rajeshwar sahib, she does not want a stepmother on her daughter."

A jolt Madhu received. Stepmother the term, she had never ever imagined herself in the roll of a stepmother. Pinky was like her own child but of course she would be her stepmother in terms of designation, in terms of relation label of stepmother was to be there for her. Madhu was dizzy with such reflections. Amar knew Madhu well, he knew that she was too good a person, capable of thinking from others point of view so he went on to touch her right nerves "You know on the basis of Rajeshwar sahib's second marriage with you she was bent upon filling a child custody case for Pinky, I stopped her."

Madhu was prepared to have it out with Amar she cut in sharply "Now I understand it is all your doing. The fact is, the reality is, you are the reason for Namrata being here. She is here because of you. You want to poison our life."

A confident Amar came forward in his defense and explained "No Madhu in fact I have convinced her not to go to the court and file a child custody case for Pinky. I made her understand that court proceedings will have a very terrible effect on Pinky."

"Oh! Come on! Why will a woman like Namrata listen to you?"

"Madhu Namrata is a mother she will not want tears in bargain for her daughter."

Madhu was helplessly confused she failed to give any reply. Amar noticed her restiveness. He embarked on the other line of action to convince Madhu "Madhu Namrata loved Rajeshwar once and Rajeshwar loved her, they were both very much in love as we were. Then Namrata committed the same mistake as I did, I agree that our fault is very grave. Nevertheless is there no pardon for such a mistake?"

"Tell me, had Reena married you; had you achieved your ambition; would you be sitting here right now?"

"Sooner or later yes, Reena was a blunder of my life. Sooner or later I was to realize it. Possibly it would have been too late by then."

"It is too late even now, listen Amar, I and Rajeshwar love each other. We are going to get married." Madhu said so more out of desperation then out of conviction.

Amar retorted charged with emotion "Yes indeed marriage is on the cards. You both are about to get married. However this is a lie that you both love each other. Madhu you have loved me so much that you cannot ever love anyone else. Of course you can get married, Madhu remember one thing, Rajeshwar will also just marry you because love today also, he loves, Namrata only. Madhu true love only happens once in life and that had already happened to Rajeshwar for Namrata and for you to me."

Madhu was totally confused, she hated confusion, she hated double mind but the circumstances, the situation, was too intricate, there was only one way out, she had to be ruthless emotionally, which she could never be. She did not know what to say, Amar beseeched "Madhu please let this estranged family be united again please do not come in between them."

Madhu was suddenly conscious that Namrata was the one who had given birth to Pinky, she had a definite right on her and today if Namrata had realized her mistake wants her daughter back; wants her husband back then was Madhu doing the right thing? This question shattered Madhu.

A ray of hope rekindled in Amar. He noticed a nervous Madhu, as habitual, biting her nail.

Just then the school bell rang, children rushed out of their classes. Amar got up from the bench. While leaving said earnestly, with all the sincerity in him "Madhu, there are always two sides of a picture, you having seen the bad side of my picture, I promise, there is a good side to it also, Just give me one chance."

Amar went away leaving Madhu in a state of confusion and uncertainty.

As Rajeshwar got free from his work he drove straight to Jumbo uncle's place. Niku had called him up and asked him to see her as soon as possible.

Niku and her husband Daniel, Jumbo uncle's eldest son, were waiting for him in the privacy of their bedroom. Tea was kept ready at the centre table of their room. They had decided to let him relax and then tell him.

Rajeshwar came along with Jeena in their room "See big brother what a surprise." said Jeena.

Daniel cuts in "No surprise we have called him, we have something important to talk you please go."

"Why?" came the instant query.

"We have to talk business, you better go." Elder brother ordered.

"Ok...Niku come along let the men talk business." said shrewd Jeena.

"Niku is not going anywhere; you listen to me and go."

Jeena saw the warning and left stamping her feet in protest. Daniel closed the room door shut. Niku had prepared a cup of tea for Rajeshwar by then. Rajeshwar was silent all through the odd scene, sensing something took the cup and said "Ok now shoot."

Niku began "This Amar..."

Rajeshwar was about to take a sip of tea but stopped, kept the tea cup back at the table and asked "What about that Bastard?"

Daniel and Niku had never heard a bad word coming from Rajeshwar, but they did not react surprised. Daniel said "Bastard he is, Namrata is here, Niku saw her at his cottage."

It was news for Rajeshwar but then he was prepared to expect the worst from Amar and probably the rendezvous of the two was it. Their intent was also very much obvious. Niku was saying "His character always seemed dubious to me, is he an agent of Namrata?"

"He is Madhu's lover, a faithless lover who has betrayed her, now wants her back, it is all his game." Rajeshwar summed up the riddle for the benefit of Daniel and Niku.

Both good meaning husband and wife were silent, contemplating. Rajeshwar put forward a suggestion "I would request you both to come over and live with us for some time. Madhu must not be left alone."

Along with Pinky Madhu came back from school with a heavy heart depressed and upset, at home Daniel and Niku were there with their bag and baggage. Pinky was happily surprised, she ran into Niku open arms. Niku announced "We are here to help out the wedding fast."

Pinky shouted "Hurray!!"

Maji was standing without her walking stick she said "Yes, yes as soon as pundit ji comes back from India I will get the marriage date fixed."

Daniel cuts in "Oh Maji, forget your pundit from India, tomorrow itself I will arrange for a very good pundit here."

"Beta my pundit ji is from here only. He has gone to India on a visit, within two days he is coming back."

Niku saw Madhu quietly going up; Daniel looked at Niku who whispered "Rajeshwar Bhaiya is there; let him talk to her first."

Madhu was in Pinky's room, taking out her change of dress from the cupboard, Rajeshwar had seen her come from down the hall. He was anxious to talk to her, forewarn her. So as soon as she entered Pinky's room alone, he came after her. Hearing him come in Madhu turned.

A confused and flustered Madhu was proof enough for Rajeshwar that Amar has beaten him in the game, he had met her first or may be both he and Namrata have met her, to make sure Rajeshwar asked the straight question "Both met you together or one of them met? I am referring to Amar and Namrata."

Surprised Madhu asked "How do you know? Did someone meet you also?"

Taking a deep sigh Rajeshwar said "They do not have the courage to face me so soon; yes meeting you they will definitely explain their point of view."

Madhu started crying. Tears rolling down her eyes she told Rajeshwar "Namrata ji is against you marrying again and opposed to a step mother for Pinky, she will file a court case, if you marry me,to get Pinky's custody."

Rajeshwar retorted angrily "Let her go to the court, I will fight it out, for last five years she never thought of Pinky now suddenly her mother hood has come alive."

Crying Madhu went on "Because of me if things go to the court and innocent Pinky is dragged to the court what will befell her. God knows what sort of and how many questions may be put to the little child; and may be compelled to answer."

This even Rajeshwar had not anticipated. For a moment he too was lost. Madhu continued "The court on the basis of you getting married again, for taking a [points towards self] step mother for Pinky; on these grounds if the court grants custody of Pinky to Namrata ji then how will you and Maji suffer the loss of Pinky and how will Pinky, I mean, how she can live away from you and Maji."

Rajeshwar putting up a brave front said "No such thing can ever happen."

Tearful Madhu said "God forbid if it happens I will never forgive myself."

Daniel and Niku entered the room, Madhu dabbed her tears with her sari border attempting not to show her grief to them, and Rajeshwar simply said "They know about your tears, no need hiding them."

Madhu did not know how to react; she had always taken it to be a well kept secret between her and Rajeshwar. Niku came forward with the explanation "Madhu we are family now. Amar and Namrata together here is very much our concern also. We never knew

Amar but we know him now; all by his ambiguous doings."

Niku closed in and held Madhu with a comforting arm around her. Daniel said "Sister in law you are no more alone, no more an easy target, together we will make them our target."

Madhu tried to smile but failed and said "But they are threatening."

"We know, we have heard, very much like Namrata, to use her own daughter." said Niku.

Rajeshwar puts in "There are only two options; one like the past let Namrata have her way when she had gone ruining our happiness, leaving us at will. The second alternative is not to allow Namrata and that Amar have their way, oppose them, and give both of them befitting counter."

Fight back was the consensus. Madhu still shaky but acquiescing. Rajeshwar very well sensed the turmoil in Madhu.

Upset Madhu, in the middle of the night was once more at the terrace. All that was coming to her mind repeatedly was 'What if Namrata files child custody case and succeeds in getting Pinky's custody?

Rajeshwar was at his bar, Daniel giving him company. They were agitated and concerned not only on account of Pinky's custody, they were very much reading into the whole charade.

They knew Pinky was being just used as a contrivance, as a means to accomplish personal win of lost relationships.

Rajeshwar always had worst expectations from Amar and now that he had met his kind in Namrata together they could be lethal.

Daniel said "To me our first concern should be Madhu; she must not collapse under their pressure."

Rajeshwar agreed "Very right you are, I very well read into Amar; the term Stepmother, Madhu could never have uttered it unless well underlined to her by one and only, that Amar."

Daniel said very well meaning it "Just give a hint, that Amar will not see tomorrow sun rise."

"That will be no way out of this mess, the best way out of this difficulty is through the difficulty, and things should be settled once for all."

"Ok, tomorrow morning we should begin making our own camp strong. Madhu must be convinced that she is not at the wrong at all. She will not be a stepmother but a mother to a motherless child."

"That's it, let me try right now."

"She must be asleep in her bedroom." Daniel guessed.

"No she will not be in her bedroom." Rajeshwar said confidently.

Rajeshwar left his drink half finished at the bar. Daniel watched him go then took his own drink to his bedroom.

Rajeshwar came to the terrace with full anticipation of finding Madhu there and Madhu was there sitting petite in a corner, bothering and torturing herself over welfare of little Pinky.

Rajeshwar came and sat besides Madhu, looked at her and smiled. Madhu in reply reciprocated a weak smile. Rajeshwar asked "Do you know what good I see in what had transpired because of Amar- Namrata duo?"

Surprised Madhu shook her head in a no.

"They have given us an opportunity to understand each other better."

Once more bowled over Madhu asked "How do you mean?"

"Adversity is the biggest teacher; since the time we have met this is the first adversity to come our way and it is their gift; so as we learn we certainly will in the process enhance our understanding. All thanks to them."

Madhu smile was a little expansive as she said "This is height of positive thinking."

"Yes, with you once again my positive thinking is back; so much for your influence on me. Now may I ask about mine influence on you?"

A thought struck Madhu; with downcast eyes she said "It makes me shudder to think how lonely and isolated my life would have been had I not come to South Africa and met You, Maji and Pinky. You all have given me so much in such a short time that I am scared."

Madhu failed to hold her tears; they trickled down on her face. Rajeshwar with his bare hands wiped her face clear of the flowing tears. Held her delicate hand into his strong hand and said "You will be the only mother to my motherless child. Keep this in mind and please don't scare yourself of worthless good for nothing people."

"All I am bothered about is Pinky."

"Madhu we have only one choice left open for us. We will have to fight our way out to our happiness. Pinky nobody can take away from us. With this firm belief we have to face them come what may."

"Maji is of age because of me she also gets burdened with problems."

"Problems Maji faced when you were not here. For her the biggest problem was me, my life, you cleared it so well that Maji is fit enough to give a befitting reply to one and all, agreed?"

Madhu feeling inhibited replied "I don't know."

"I know and I know it very well, but the problem for me is that one by one someone or the other is trying to scare you away. First Sher Uncle, then Mr. Amar, and now Madam Namrata, all are bad villains."

Madhu laughed forgetting all else. Rajeshwar who was still holding her hand kissed it. Madhu stopped laughing. Rajeshwar stated "Madhu if you stand by me then you will see that this battle which they have begun we will take it to its end, our way."

Her smile was confident. Rajeshwar had given her back the confidence which Amar had shaken. She uttered "Thanks."

"Thanks for what?"

"For making me feel light. The burden of confusion is gone."

"Do I deserve a reward?"

Madhu sensing some sensuality conveyed a silent reply as if permitting without uttering 'You merit whatever is there to me.'

Rajeshwar gently gathered Madhu in his arms. Madhu softened in his loving hold. As his lips approach her lips her eyes were almost closed as if she wanted to live that moment to its full.

In Rajeshwar room, behind closed door they sat in a meeting Rajeshwar, Madhu, Niku and Daniel. Madhu was the first to express her opinion "I think Maji should be told about Amar, she must know my background."

Rajeshwar cut in "What background? Amar is not your background; your background is that of a nurse, who treated and helped the sick and weak and that Maji knows."

Niku agreeing with Rajeshwar said "If at all time comes Amar background should be told to Maji; that of a cheat and a bastard."

"Matter ends there." Daniel summed up.

"What about Namrata and the child custody threat?" Rajeshwar braced the subject.

"Maji should not be kept into dark, sooner or later she will know that Namrata is here." Daniel suggested.

Rajeshwar agreed "Yes to fight this out she must be made to understand."

Madhu said almost with a resolve "I want to do it my way, this I take as my personal responsibility." Rajeshwar once again felt proud of Madhu.

Madhu sat massaging Maji's legs which were stretched relaxed on a divan. Niku was all eyes trying to study the skill with which Madhu was doing her job.

"Beti, I am ok now, I can very well walk so why this massage every day?" Maji queried.

"Maji how strong you are?" Madhu asked lightly.

"I will certainly dance at your wedding." Thinking ahead Maji said.

Niku was about to say something to add to the pleasure of Maji but a look at Madhu face stopped her. Madhu had stopped massaging Maji legs, she said serious in tone "That is great. But tell me are you strong enough to take a stand?"

"Stand, what stand?"

"If suppose I tell you; ex daughter in law is very much here and is at creating problems will you take a stand for me?"

Maji was lying down she got up and sat alert and angry "What problem she can create? She has no right?"

"She has a right over Pinky, she is her biological mother."

"She had given over that right five years back."

"Maji if she wants to reclaim that right, on the basis of your son getting married again are you strong enough to fight back?" Madhu asserted her question again.

Maji was old and experienced, she confirmed "If she is at it again then this time she will get it right back."

"That's it Maji. I wanted to hear this from you." Madhu exclaimed and Niku saw how efficiently Madhu generated the fighting spirit in Maji.

When Rajeshwar reached his office he found a Fax from Forest Ministry waiting for him. It read that the poaching incident which Amar had recorded, on the basis of that, all the poachers were under arrest. The Ministry was going to bestow a bravery award to Amar. Rajeshwar was instructed to give this good news to Amar himself and to help Amar further in his full capacity.

Rajeshwar reached Forest Resort to give the good news to Amar as well as admonish him. Amar was not there. He had left early morning driving the channel's Jeep.

Rajeshwar wondered where that devil of a person Amar could have gone; deep in to Forest to make documentary or somewhere else.

Amar knew of only one place where he could find Madhu alone, Pinky's school. His last meeting with Madhu was positive. Knowing Madhu he was in no doubt that at the most he required one or two meetings more. As a writer he knew that children do play a big role in keeping parents together. Had there been no Pinky it would have been very difficult for him to convince Madhu. There was no other ground; he himself was groundless.

At school, when he reached, his eyes met with a very big setback. Niku was sitting besides Madhu. And he also saw Madhu laugh at something she said meaning Madhu had relaxed, an unexpected counter. When he tried to enter through the gate of the school he was rudely stopped by the security "No outsiders allowed."

"Well I was allowed the other day."

"That day was that day this day is not that day." had come the curt reply.

Jumbo uncle was a trustee of the school; Daniel's instructions carried weight. Nothing of that sort Amar knew.

Next day was Pinky's holiday. Monu had come and triumphed and she was up early morning.

In the extensive compound of her bungalow was a huge mango tree. Monu was leisurely picking and eating its leaves and fruits. Bholu was eating the fallen ripe mangoes. Suspended from a heavy branch of the tree was a swing. Swinging at it safely in the company of her two trustworthy, dependable and physically powerful friends was Pinky. The two hands propelling the swing early in the morning were those of Amar. Doing the job Amar was trying to enlighten Pinky "Pinky beta you must know that very soon your Madhu aunty is going to be your Mother?"

Innocently Pinky replied "She is already my mummy, I call her mummy."

Amar questioned again "But do you know who your real mother is? The one who had given you birth is someone else."

Pinky simply said "Yes, The mother who had given me birth is Namrata ji Ok, and she is here with you to take me away."

Amar was totally taken aback; Pinky was saying "I know everything. I have heard Niku aunty talk. Daddy talks to Daniel uncle but I am not going to go with her."

Amar realized that after all she was Namrata's daughter, it won't be easy to deal with her also, giving a nice push to her swing to cover up he said "My dear she is not here to take you back. She had just come to meet you. She is after all your mother. She is longing to see you. She loves you the most."

Pinky questioned bluntly "Then why did she leave me and go?"

Amar was perplexed, what to reply? But after a thought he said "See, you see, it is like this, your Mummy and Daddy were angry with each other, it is not that earlier she never wished to see you, in this world no mother can live happy away from one's child."

Pinky shot back "Then why didn't she come earlier?"

This time Amar was prepared for her question he quickly and confidently replied "She was scared that if she ever came here your Daddy may not allow her to meet you. I convinced her that it is not so, Rajeshwar sahib is a very fine person, he will definitely let her meet you. So she has come now."

Pinky suddenly stopped the swing with her feet, got off it. Stood defiantly in front of Amar, her little hands on her waist and pronounced "You are a liar, you are lying and you are a bad uncle."

Then she turned and ran away. Monu and Bholu simply followed her. Stunned Amar was watching this. The look on his face seemed to be of losing hope. As he turned Rajeshwar was standing confronting him.

He had seen everything, heard everything. He admonishes Amar "Mr. Amar I am an upright person, don't take my decency as my weakness. I have tolerated you enough but now you are going overboard. Please go away from here otherwise you came here on your two feet but will go back on four shoulders."

A well shaken Amar replied "Mr. Rajeshwar what are you getting so angry at? What have I said so wrong to your daughter? It is a fact that Namrata loves her daughter very much."

Rajeshwar questioned "Why are you so much bothered about Namrata, Pinky and me?" Then starring hard at Amar he continued "You are a very wrong type of a person Mr. Amar."

A very repentant smile and feel came over Amar face as he said "Mr. Rajeshwar is there any one person in this entire world who is totally right and had not wronged ever. I agree my mistake is very grave but I am been penalized evenly, gravely."

Rajeshwar sneered at his rival "You call it severe punishment; just a few days of severance and the realization of your mistake?"

With a deep sigh Amar said "Not few days, a mere moment is enough to die on the realization of one's mistake Mr. Rajeshwar go and asks those who suffer this nightmare."

Rajeshwar looked at Amar from head to toe trying to understand him once more. Hefty burly Daniel had come there by then he was standing, his threatening totality, not far away. Rajeshwar finally said "You are a man of words that is why a girl like Madhu became your victim, I am not going to fall a prey to your web of words, it is my first and the last warning to you."

Then he took out the fax which had come from Forest Ministry, out of his jacket pocket, gave it to Amar "This is the approval of your bravery from the Forest Ministry, congratulations. In your work whatever help you require from me will be made available. But remember not to forget my warning. I am on my way to Forest Resort for my official work, do you need a lift?"

"Thank you Mr. Rajeshwar, my channel's jeep is parked outside your compound."

Amar walked away with the fax in hand.

Namrata had had lunch at the hotel, sitting idle she was getting bored, All at once something came to her mind, and furrows appeared on her tense burrow. Sharp expression came to her eyes. Blood gushes up her face, giving pinkish look, she picked up her car keys. Briskly walked to her car; sat in and drove off.

She was going to meet her daughter Pinky. Pinky was her own flesh and blood, she had given her birth, and she had every right to meet her, then what for the dithering. Why the tension. She will straight away go and tell Pinky who she is to her. Hold her in her arms and kiss her to her heart content 'I will see who dares to stop me.'

Driving her car this she uttered all by herself, speeding car's speed increased.

That valley of flowers with butterflies; that day also Pinky was playing there. Madhu was standing at a side of the bushes and watching a smile on her face. On the other side of the shrubs was the road from where Namrata car happened to pass. The sight of the valley of flowers and the butterflies hovering all over, the pink, yellow, white and red flowers ornamental the dense green bushes was so beautiful and eye catching that Namrata had to slow down.

Then she spotted her Pinky. It looked as if a little angel had descended on that beautiful piece of earth and was playing among the flowers and butterflies; a perfect paradise model on earth.

Namrata stopped her car and stepping out of it; appreciated her little angel a smile on her lips; her agitation gone, pleasure on her face.

It was so arranged by the Almighty that on one side of that flower valley was Madhu and on the other side was Namrata. Both however unaware of each other were engrossed in innocent Pinky.

On Madhu face was a wide open happiness; a spread out full smile. Namrata was also happy on seeing Pinky. But people like her of high society, at high places, expressed their happiness with restrain with control and not expansively, so that commoners do not take advantage. Such elevated people rationed their smiles and laughter. Namrata was doing the same.

Namrata was deeply involved and related to the high society. For this particular society only she had left her husband her child. Of course she was happy to see her daughter but she would not express her happiness like illiterate dark aged people. In her delight there was also a definite sense of pride like 'See she is my daughter so beautiful so charming.' With a raised head she was watching her daughter proudly.

Suddenly Pinky tripped. There was a ravine, screaming she fell into it and went slipping down vanishing from the sight of both Madhu and Namrata. From their respective positions both Madhu and Namrata noticed Pinky falling and disappearing? Shaken both rushed to see what has happened.

Madhu was running frantically without any care. She even tripped and fell but got up and ran again. There were thorny growths which cut her pricked her as she rushed through them, at times even slipping through them. In her rush and anxiety to find little Pinky she cared not for anything; was thoughtless to any impediments.

Namrata was also running but cautiously taking care of uneven slippery ground, fearing thorny bushes, going round them to avoid any thorny prickly scratching, catching hold of shrubs to take support while at a decent. Daunt self-care and caution defined her rescue effort.

When she reached where Pinky had landed she was outraged. Pinky was in Madhu arms. A very worried

Madhu was looking all over Pinky to see where she was hurt. Pinky had stopped crying she was saying "Mummy, I am ok, fine, not hurt mummy."

She was calling Madhu mummy. Hearing this something exploded with in Namrata. Angry tears appeared in her eyes. Madhu happened to see her. She had never seen or met Namrata. Nor there was any photograph of Namrata at Rajeshwar house. But then too she immediately recognized Namrata because of Pinky. Pinky was the child hood of Namrata. Her looks were of her mother with the character of her father.

As Pinky saw Namrata she clung to Madhu tight hiding her face in Madhu warmth. Madhu whispered to her "Pinky see your mother."

But Pinky never moved her face away from her lap to turn and look at Namrata. She began to cry. All this was out of bounds and far too much for Namrata.

Once again she came to meet her daughter; once again she went back without meeting her.

Reaching her hotel Namrata rang up Amar and summoned him immediately.

When Amar reached there, Namrata was pacing up and down her hotel suite. Her eyes were angry red and puffed up crying hard. Never anybody ever had made her cry as that day her own daughter did. She was definitely disgruntled with her but in this chagrin of her was hidden the love for her daughter Pinky. This she was realizing slow and steady, little by little.

When Amar came she poured her heart out to him though in anger "You know I was missing Pinky too much, how restless and eager I was to meet her. I drove all the way, I just wanted to embrace her, kiss her, and hug her. But when she slipped and fell in that flower valley and I ran like mad to help her, you know, you know she was already in that Madhu arms. She my Pinky; never bothered to look at me also."

Thus narrating Namrata complained "I am her mother. Her real mother, I gave her birth, keeping her nine months in my womb. But seeing me she clung to that Madhu as if I am going to eat her up; she hates me."

Amar liked the bubbling mother hood in Namrata. Taking opportunity he once again came forward to explain to her "Madam this is why I don't want you to file a court case. If in court the child behaves like the way as she does, the jury may draw wrong conclusions."

Namrata rebuffed him contempt in her tone "You don't worry about the legalities. If things reach court I have hired the best lawyer. He says I have a very strong case. Who will want a child to grow up in jungles and who will allow a step mother on her child and once Pinky comes to me I will win over her love."

To pacify her Amar said "But Madam things will never go so wrong if..."

Namrata cut him short "You do worry just for one thing. I have given you fifteen days. Today is the tenth day; five days remain with you to get your lovely Madhu back."

Feeling very odd about Namrata, Amar asked "Namrata Ji if I lose Madhu you will also lose Rajeshwar sahib. Please tell me honestly; keeping aside your anger and self esteem, losing Rajeshwar sahib for ever will you be able to live happily with your daughter?"

A very defiant Namrata retorted "If Rajeshwar with Madhu can live happily without his daughter then I can also live happily with my daughter without Rajeshwar."

Hearing Namrata Amar instantaneously clapped saying "You talk great, full of ego, full of pride talk. I am beginning to understand; my life had reached this stage because of my needs, greed, and my ambition. But you have reached this junction in your life because of your ego; because of your arrogance and vanity. The difference is I have realized my mistake but you are still not conscious of the wrong you have done because you still have with you your status and money power the might of which is not letting you sight the truth, the reality."

Somewhat perplexed Namrata retorted "What is all this trash?"

Amar explained further "This is no trash madam. It is a fact. Poor and needy realize their mistakes quite early but the rich and affluent realize it very late. Sometimes they never realize it at all. O.K. madam I did whatever I could to make you understand, if you do not appreciate then you are your own master."

Amar bowed and wished Namrata a final good bye and walked out on her.

Amar left leaving Namrata in complex. First time in her life she was entertaining doubts 'Is she herself wrong. All along she had been dead sure that Rajeshwar was wrong and this Amar what rubbish he had talked?'

'I have realized my mistake but you are still not conscious of the wrong you have done because you still have with you your status and money power the might of which is not letting you sight the truth, the reality.'

However in his rubbish Namrata did see some truth. She would have to seriously rethink about it 'If she is wrong that means Rajeshwar is right. How can this be possible? Rajeshwar never realized her worth, her value, left her for this jungle, for this two bit job of his, but why today that remembrance is coming back to her again and again when Rajeshwar had very specifically put across to her 'The rest of your life you will have to live with me in these green jungles among the wild animals.'

This particular confabulation had completely escaped her mind. Then why today it had come back to her? Amar had said that she had not realized her mistake; was this that realization which was coming so late to her which she had so conveniently forgotten?

On the other hand Amar's fortitude had given way. He decided that now he would just finish his documentary job and leave.

He never would be able to forget Madhu, would always miss her but then it serves him right. The total blunder was his. He will have to endure the penitence.

Next day, early morning he was lost in these thoughts. Namrata car came and stopped in front of his cottage. Through his window Amar could see her coming out of the car and looking at his cottage. He was sure that she had come to inform him that she was going to town to file her child custody case. Namrata rang the bell. Amar opened the door she said "Good morning Amar Ji."

Why today Amar ji, she was standing right in front of him in a very simple dress. No trace of any hard look on her face. On her lips was a soft smile. Amar was watching her. She inquired "Can I come in?"

Stepping out of her way Amar welcomed her "Yes, yes please Namrata ji, Come in."

Entering Namrata looked around the interior of the cottage. Cottage was quite neat and clean. All the necessities were there. To sit there was a cane sofa set; on it were placed comfortable cushions. The center table was quite beautiful, there was also a dining table and four chairs, the flower vase adorned fresh flowers. Namrata made a comment "Cottage is not bad I feel like shifting here in this Forest Resort, can I get a cottage like this?"

Amar was skeptical if he was really seeing whatever was happening or was he dreaming but he said "Yes why not I will just book a cottage for you. Forest Ministry is very happy with my work. The entire staff had been instructed to take good care of me including your Mr. Rajeshwar."

Surprised Namrata looked at Amar with questioning eyes. Amar opened a show case drawer and took out the fax of the Forest Ministry and handed it to Namrata with a sense of pride "Here take a look."

Namrata carefully read the fax "This is something great Rajeshwar sahib must be very happy with you."

Amar sarcastically smiled as Rajeshwar admonishing him flashed through his mind, he replied "Yes he is very happy with my work, but not with me, he has given a strict warning, I must cut off my other activities."

Namrata questioned feigning innocence "What other activities?"

Amar replied "Creating hurdles in his and Madhu marriage."

Namrata questioned again innocently "Have you done any such thing?"

Amar replied smiling at her cute little game "Getting you here, is it not enough?"

In agreement with Amar Namrata said "So it is so. Why didn't you tell me earlier?"

Amar clarified "Had I told you earlier things would have gone from bad to worse."

"And now why are you telling me?"

Meaningfully Amar replied "I see some great change now."

Namrata came clean and straight telling Amar "Yes Amar, last entire night I kept thinking that this ego and arrogance they don't allow a person to think right and straight. They suffocate and limit human intelligence and reasoning power."

Taking a satisfied deep sigh Amar said "How nice it is to hear all this from you."

Namrata laughed and then told Amar "I am going to help you your way. Tell me what is to be done?"

Happily Amar said "First of all shift here, at this Forest Resort and just please remember one thing the tongue that talks love is much more effective then the gun which shoots bullets."

Amar and Namrata both knew that Pinky was the key to their happiness. Amar as an aspirant writer director very well understood human behavior, their needs, and their feelings, the ways they function and live their lives. Amar explained to Namrata "The linkage of off springs is very strong especially if the kids are young. Parents may differ and separate but the kids have the power to bring them back together. They feel the need of both the parents."

"Agreed, but will it not be using an innocent child for ones selfish needs?" Namrata asked.

Amar looked at her amazed "Great now you are talking like a mother, this is what was required, the feel of a mother to touch the hearts. I mean that of Madhu and Rajeshwar and Pinky."

Tears surfaced Namrata eyes as she said "Mother I am to Pinky. Leaving her and going away was the biggest blunder I committed. I fought my parents for making me leave my daughter behind. When I saw Pinky's photographs, you send through my P.A. I just can't explain what I went through."

"This is what I told Miss Chatterji that blood linage is God made not man made so we just can't cut it off. I am very sure Pinky must be also missing you at times; in school watching other mothers feed their kids or when talking about their mothers kids may be questioning her about you."

Amar goes on further giving lift to her motherhood, justifying their need to rekindle Pinky's emotions and love for Namrata "It is not only our need to win over Pinky but also very much the demand of a mother's mother hood; reaching out to your daughter's heartfelt desire you will be full filling your forsaken duty."

Namrata agreed nodding a yes. Her heart ached for her daughter, tears rolling down her eyes she uttered "But all this is possible only if I get to meet Pinky. She hates me and I am nowhere near to win her love."

Amar was very happy with the motherly tears of Namrata. He was sure that these tears will go the long way to Madhu heart and may be if these tears succeed in rebounding even a couple of tears from little Pinky eyes then Rajeshwar will also have to think twice. Amar said "Yes you need time with your daughter; you need to have her company."

"It is not possible without Rajeshwar permission and consent." Namrata summed up.

As Namrata shifted at the Forest Resort, Amar thought and thought, there had to be a way to bridge the gap between her and Rajeshwar. Some contact, some meeting ground was required. Rajeshwar house was not far from the Resort yet the distance between the hearts was wide and deep. He had to fill in that gorge; find a way out, what could be it? He thought.

Suddenly like an electric current it came and gave light to his thinking 'Goodness' was the name of the game.

Good people understand the language of goodness much better and the plus point was Namrata will not have to act well; she was a bad actor he had made out on the very first meet, so she would have to play as she felt, that is motherly. He immediately went to Namrata cottage to brief her.

"Namrata ji you must go and meet Rajeshwar sahib very honestly with an open heart."

Confused Namrata asked "What do you mean?"

"I mean tell him that the mistake you committed leaving him you cannot undo now, can't put right, because he belongs to someone else now."

Namrata looked at Amar as if he had lost it but Amar continued "Then you must also tell him that yes one thing you definitely want and that is to stop your daughter Pinky hating you. And this can be only done by you taking care of your child, giving her the love of which she was deprived of. Request him that you want to put right this blunder of your life and to do so you need his help."

"And why will he help?" Namrata asked more sad than sarcastic.

"Rajeshwar sahib is a very nice decent person he will never say no I am sure. He will certainly permit a daughter to meet her mother, and that mother is no one else but his first love; the one with who he was very happily married once. Believe me it would be a very good beginning for us."

Chapter Nine

Namrata was getting ready to go to Rajeshwar house, her one time home, where after marriage she had thought of living the rest of her life. The lipstick in her hand shook. As she looked at herself in the mirror of the small dressing table at the Resort cottage she discovered her lips trembling. Inadvertently her hand reached her heart. She could hear it pounding, nervous she got up, walked up and down the cottage. She was thinking; had she become so feeble.

Yes this is what happens in love. Love has so much power that human body trembles in front of it. The heart throbs hard to rush blood into the veins to reach human brain so that the love stricken victim not loses sense. This is why true love is not the cup of tea for one and all. It is not the possibility for every one; it is meant for only those who are strong, very strong only they can appear authenticated at its testing grounds.

Today it was her test, very soon she would find out whether her trembling lips, tear full eyes and pounding heart convey her massage of love to Rajeshwar or not. That love which he had once showered on her its defunct spark rekindles again or not.

Not knowing why, Namrata set on foot for Rajeshwar place leaving her Mercedes parked. On the way was the same valley of flowers full of butterflies. Today Pinky was not there, though the valley was looking beautiful as ever but Pinky's absence was conspicuous by her absence. Namrata stopped there for a moment and smiled then proceeded towards Rajeshwar dwelling.

The huge gate of the bungalow was shut. After years together Namrata was standing there and watching it. It was the same house where she had happily come after marriage. This was her house. Very many priceless lovely moments flashed through her mind.

She had missed her periods; Rajeshwar had taken her to the hospital for pregnancy test. She tested positive. Rajeshwar's happiness knew no bounds. All the way back from hospital to their home Rajeshwar sang his favorite song 'phoolon ki bagya mehke gi..' (Flowers in the garden will bloom) The song was still ringing in Namrata ears. More than the song Rajeshwar's sweet melodious voice was haunting her.

When they had reached the house it was late night. Rajeshwar carried her in his arms to their bed room; laid her down gently on their bed; then kissed her passionately.

It was Pinky's first birth day. Her parents had arrived unannounced. She had refused to see them. Rajeshwar in trying to convince her to see them told her that it was he who invited them. Namrata blew her lid off on Rajeshwar; told him "You have no right to invite them. They are my parents. I know them much better than you do. You think they have realized their mistake; changed. No they will never ever change; they want me back with them; with you or without you."

How right she was; they took her back without him.

She was running high fever. Rajeshwar was up whole night, by her bed side. Entire night he took care of her; fed her medicines; applied cold iced water soaked napkins on her fore head; rubbed the sole of her feet with ice wrapped in towel. By morning her fever had subsided completely. She slept, when she woke up Rajeshwar was there at her bed side ready with her breakfast all caring and loving.

All through the way she had restrained herself but tears were running free on her face. The memories of her marital bliss were back in full strength.

She was standing right in front of the gate which was the doorway to the heaven of her life.

She wiped her face clean of all the grief; took a deep breath to compose herself. She never rang the bell to get the gate open. She pushed both folds of the gate forward and backwards, a gap was formed, putting her hand through it she opened the latch of the gate, exactly the same way as when returning from her routine morning walks she used to.

Sitting in the lawn of the bungalow were Rajeshwar, Madhu, Daniel, Niku, Maji and Pinky; comfortable and relaxed having their breakfast. Watching the gate open by it, Rajeshwar reacted concerned. Madhu was applying butter at a toast for Pinky she turned and looked the way Rajeshwar was looking. Maji was blowing at her hot tea she also looked towards the gate surprised. Daniel and Niku also were watching the gate tea cups in hand. Namrata entered.

All looked at each other totally taken a back, then slowly they got up from where they were sitting, at a distance Namrata was standing looking at them and they at Namrata. Rajeshwar instructed Pinky "Pinky you go in."

Obeying her father Pinky moved to go in but Madhu held her hand restricting her. Rajeshwar noticed this and kept quite may be thinking what Madhu had done was right; whatever was to be exchanged should be right in front of the child. Gathering her courage Namrata walked to them. All of them were just thinking one thing 'For sure Namrata was there to talk about Pinky's custody. May be she had come with the court notice.'

The manner in which Namrata came to them belied that. The way she smiled looking at them and said 'hello' was all confusing. She was not the same Namrata who they knew. This was a broken abated Namrata. Every bit of her seemed to be submerged in her repentance.

Rajeshwar had decided that he will talk to her just standing but now he moved a chair towards Namrata asking "Please sit Namrata."

Joining her hands in a Namaste to Maji Namrata sat. Madhu asked "Tea ...?"

Namrata pointed towards a glass of water kept there.

"First, please a glass of water."

Madhu offered her the glass. All of a sudden Namrata realized that her hand was not steady. Nervously she took a deep sigh to take control of herself. Proffered glass of water was still in Madhu's hand waiting for Namrata. The situation was turning very embarrassing.

There was no other way out so finally somewhat flustered Namrata extender her hand and took the glass from Madhu. To hide the trembling of her hand she took support of her other hand as well, and sipped water from the glass.

Excepting Pinky, nobody was obviously watching Namrata because everyone was conscious of her nervous condition. Pinky was enjoying looking at her Mother. As she kept back the glass at the table the tremble was very evident and obvious. Pinky laughed out and laughing ran away from there, tears sprang up in Namrata eyes but smiling she said "I have come here to congratulate you all for the coming marriage and I also have a request to make."

Rajeshwar was now watching Namrata very intently as if trying to figure out what she was up to; whatever he saw he did not believe. When Rajeshwar did not speak up Madhu said "Yes please go ahead tell us."

Namrata said "The mistake which I committed leaving Pinky, I want to set right."

Hearing this, menace of court case became very obvious on the faces of Madhu, Rajeshwar and Maji. Namrata as if read this and hurried to clarify "The court case problem, I mean you people might have heard about, is not there at all now. I will not bargain tears for my child. As it is I have given her enough to grieve so no more problems. Yes I have thought so once but not now, coming here, seeing Pinky had changed everything. My happiness lies in Pinky's happiness, all I want is that she stops hating me and in this I need your help."

All this Namrata said her eyes and head cast down. As she raised her head and looked at them with requesting eyes she noticed tears in Madhu eyes, in Niku and Maji eyes, while Daniel was confused. Rajeshwar was sitting stunned looking at Namrata. He said "Namrata Pinky cannot hate you she is a child and children are not capable of hate, at the most they can be resentful or angry. Given love they concede and forget and above all you are Pinky's Mother."

Now Rajeshwar came on the main point, he questioned "But you stay away in town and Pinky lives here you see all this will need some time how will you both be together? Are you thinking of taking her with you?"

Namrata hurriedly replied "No, no, not at all, she is studying here; her school is here more over if I take her away from you people she is going to hate me more. I have booked the cottage at the Forest Resort, I will stay there I, I, just need your permission to meet Pinky as and when possible and some help."

Before Rajeshwar can say anything Madhu who was very much touched by this approach of Namrata, spoke up "Namrata ji we are there with you in every way and why will you stay at the Forest Resort, this is such a big house please you are most welcome. Come stay with us."

Now Namrata was looking at Madhu with tears in her eyes. Madhu continued "Adjacent to Pinky's room is my room I will vacate it for you."

Trying to control her emotions Namrata said "Whatever I heard about you I find you even better than that. To meet Pinky I will come here or if you are free you can come with her to the Resort."

Saying so she got up to go away, Rajeshwar also got up asking "How did you come? Where is your car?"

"At the Resort, I came walking."

As if remembering something Rajeshwar said "Morning walks?"

Namrata nodded a yes Madhu said "Come, we will drop you."

Smiling Namrata replied "Thank you very much, I will go walking, walking is my hobby."

Before leaving Namrata touched Maji feet and then walked away. Maji and Madhu were very emotional but Rajeshwar was still looking at going Namrata bewilderment in his mind.

Namrata reached the open gate. Monu and Bholu had come from somewhere, they were entering the gate. Namrata was taken aback. Monu stopped for a moment raising his trunk he smelled her then not caring moved in, she took a sigh of relief as even Bholu followed Monu. She walked out of the gate.

Pinky was hiding somewhere. As Namrata went out of the gate Pinky ran straight to Madhu and put a question bluntly "Why did she come here?"

Madhu trying to make Pinky understand said "Pinky she is your mother, talk about her with respect."

Pinky shot back "What mother, I hate her."

Rajeshwar and Maji, Daniel and Niku looked at each other blankly but Madhu questioned "Why?"

Angry Pinky replied "She left me and went away ok? "

Madhu tried to explain "It was a mistake and she is very much sorry about it now, did you not see what state she was in. She loves you very much."

Pinky retorted "I don't care."

Saying so she dashed away to play with Monu and Bholu. Rajeshwar told Madhu "Don't believe so much on what your eyes have seen, this change in Namrata I see a significant hand of that Amar."

Maji was surprised to hear this she asked "Amar, what had that Amar to do with it?"

Maji was totally ignorant of Amar and Madhu past. Rajeshwar and Madhu had told her nothing. Simply for the reason; just not to disturb her. But today Rajeshwar warned her saying "Maji this Amar is not good person. It is he who had brought Namrata here. You please just keep this in mind."

Seeing her son's demeanor Maji choose to keep quiet for the moment. But she had also seen the world. She made out that there was for sure something to it.

Namrata was shocking. All of them didn't move an inch, kept sitting where they were sitting, when Namrata went. As soon as Pinky's episode got over every one huddled together expressing shock.

Maji was the first one to speak "What a relief, Namrata is not going to file child custody case."

Madhu opined "To me she looked genuine, I am sure she meant every word she said."

Niku put forward her point of view "This much I can also vouch for Namrata, as far as I knew her she was always straight, at times too straight." She laughed.

Daniel gave a straight explanation "I think the mother in her has come alive."

Relieved all kept discussing Namrata, Rajeshwar merely smiled occasionally; he was thinking or may be worrying.

Daniel and Niku went back home. Dangerous Amar was considered tooth less. The change in Namrata was a knockout blow for him. This was what they thought. Sadly mistaken they were.

After dinner that night when Pinky as usual came to Maji for her bed time story session, Maji asked her "That Amar uncle of yours, that one with the camera, how is he? Good or bad?"

Spontaneously Pinky replied "Very bad."

Maji sat up in the bed alert her mind saying yes to her doubts "Why?"

"Dadi he is the one who had brought that one here."

Maji very well understood that Pinky was referring to her biological mother. Nevertheless Maji choose not to reprimand her right then and disturb the flow of information coming her way, Maji carried on "How do you know?"

He only told me this. He was saying that till now your mummy never came because daddy will not let me meet her, he convinced her to come here."

"But my dear that Amar why the hell is he taking all this trouble, what is his game?"

Innocently Pinky replied "I don't know."

"We will have to find out, there is certainly something fishy."

Interested Pinky put in "I will find out and tell you. He is all the time trying to talk to me, I think Dadi he is a 'chammach' I mean yes-man of that Namrata."

Then Maji immediately reprimanded Pinky "My dear you should not take your Mother name like this, very bad. However you definitely try and find out what his game is. If possible tell that Amar that I want to meet him."

Happily Pinky said "Ok."

"But remember it is a secret between us."

Pinky shook hands with her Dadi saying "Ok promise."

Dadi hugged her Pinky.

Next morning Madhu and Pinky mounted on Monu were out on their ride. Bholu was also coming along. Madhu told Pinky "Pinky shall we go to the Forest Resort."

Pinky reacted happily saying "Yes, yes, sure, Amar uncle will be there I have to meet him."

Surprised Madhu asked "Why?"

Pinky reacted holding her tongue in between her teeth, then blabbered "Oh! Just like that." saying so she patted left side of Monu jaw "Monu, right, Monu right."

Obediently Monu took a right turn. Madhu was suspicious; she inquired "Why do you want to meet Amar uncle?"

Excusing herself Pinky said "Oh, Baba, it just slipped of my tongue; after all I am a kid. I like him, what's the problem? If there is a problem please tell?"

Now Madhu was nervous she said "No, no problem. There is no problem."

They reached Forest Resort. As usual tourists rushed out of their cottages appreciating the sight of Monu and Bholu with Pinky, feeding them with biscuits, fruits and cakes while photographing the unique union of human and animal co- existence.

Madhu was looking around for Namrata so that she can make mother and daughter meet but instead she saw Amar coming. Pinky was all excited seeing Amar. Waving exuberantly to him she called out

"Amar uncle!!!"

Amar also waved back to her though he was a little surprised at her over friendly behavior. Pinky signaled Monu to sit, the elephant obeyed. Madhu and Pinky alighted, Pinky ran to Amar saying "Come Amar uncle make friends with my Monu and Bholu."

Amar looked at Bholu saying "Well Mr. Bholu, I have already met."

The chimpanzee right away put his hand in Amar coat pocket, when he pulled his hand out it was empty. Angry Bholu growled at Amar showing pointed teeth, Amar laughed and said "Mr. Bholu your requirement is not in this pocket it is in the other one."

Amar took out a hand full of dry fruits and spread them at a clean place. Bholu got busy picking and eating the dry fruits. Madhu eyes were still searching for Namrata. Finally she spotted Namrata coming out of her cottage with a huge basket full of fruits. She dragged the basket to Monu. Other tourists were also around. Monu and Bholu were being continuously fed, photographs taken, Video recordings done. Madhu said "Namrata ji we have come to your Resort, will we get some tea."

"Yes, Yes, why not."

Namrata cottage was just right in front of them. Holding Pinky's hand Madhu lead to take her along, Pinky struggled to free her hand saying "I don't want her tea, I want to go back home."

Namrata had moved a little ahead but her total attention was at Pinky. Madhu was telling Pinky

"Pinky please, she is your mother and you must not behave like this."

Pinky retorted "She is not my mother. You are my mother."

Pinky was so loud that every one heard and reacted; Namrata as if froze in her steps. She felt a piercing ache in her heart which made her dizzy but she took control of herself, taking swift steps rushed in to her cottage.

All eyes were at Madhu and Pinky. There prevailed an eerie silence. Madhu not caring at all sat right in front of Pinky. Looked into her eyes, taking her small hands in to her hands she began in an explicit tone "If I am your mother and you are my good daughter then listen to me, now right now you will have to say sorry to Namrata ji. She is the one who has given you birth, she is your biological mother, this in itself is such a big deal that the rest, your father me or the rest of the world all are secondary. This you have to understand well and if you will not understand then I will understand that I failed to educate you well l and if I can't educate you well then I have no right to be called your mother and live here."

During this discourse tears sprang up in Madhu eyes and when she talked of not giving right education and leaving tears trickled. Little Pinky wiped them with her hands.

Pinky had started loving Madhu so much that her feel, this emotion was enough to dislodge innocent Pinky. She may not have understood Madhu completely but the truth in Madhu utterance had definitely reached her. She had understood this very well that Madhu was very good that was why she was making her understand something very well and that was that a mother can never be bad.

Namrata was packing her things, she was not distraught with Pinky nor was she angry. She understood that she was to harvest what she had sown, she left a two year child, that child was eight years as of then, with the growing years of the child how could Namrata expect anything other than hatred to grow; hate was bound to be there. Husband and wife do fall out and part ways. A woman leaves husband not children but she left her two year old daughter just for the reason that her parents preached to do so. Later on she often fought with them on this issue but of what use it was. Whatever had to happen had happened, she would have to go away from there. Just then Pinky's sweet voice rang in her ears "Please don't go mummy."

Namrata without looking up kept packing, thinking that her ears were ringing, it was her wishful thought, again that rhythmic voice came to her "Please mummy, please do not go stay here."

Now Namrata looked up. Pinky was there along with Madhu. Namrata was not crying till then but at the sight of her daughter tears rained out of her eyes. Madhu, with a slight movement of her hand suggested that Pinky go to Namrata, Pinky moved towards Namrata. Namrata sat on her knees and opened her arms towards coming Pinky. Pinky moved into Namrata welcoming bosom. Vehemently Namrata embraced her. Madhu appreciated that priceless moment with tears trickling down her eyes. A click was heard she turned. Amar was there with the camera to his eye capturing that touching and beautiful scene.

Chapter Ten

Namrata's parents, Manohar Shivdasani ji and his wife came back from London. Miss. Chatterji, Namrata's P.A. informed them that Namrata had gone along with one Mr. Amar to meet and contend with Rajeshwar.

Mr. Shivdasani was a sixty years old absolutely fit aristocrat, though he was only 5 fit 6 inch in height even then he had not allowed any fat to load on him. He ate well measured, no oil, no spice food. Precise exercise as advised by his personal trainer, and was very fastidious about his designer's clothes, everything was very accurate, limited, to the point, in his life. But to earn money there were no limits for him, there was no point of measure, no bound, discipline and principal. Money was God, money was relation and money was the purpose of life to him.

That was why when Namrata had married a man of bits, Rajeshwar, he was extremely disappointed. His dream son in-law was king of trade Vivek Shiv Dasani. Now that dream had once again become a possibility. Vivek had divorced his wife.

Vivek was nuts for Namrata since child hood but when Namrata married Rajeshwar Vivek also got married. Now he had divorced his wife. The view in general was that Namrata was the reason of his divorce. But how come this had happened again, once again Namrata had gone to that jungle to meet that Rajeshwar and her daughter.

Manohar Shivdasani ji and his wife were on fire, they ordered their driver to ready their Hummer. Both husband and wife picked up some necessary things and departed to get Namrata back from that jungle.

Man eater had recovered from his leg wound completely, of course he limped a little but the strength and vigor was back. With his brother he was on the rounds of his jungle.

Both the brothers were hungry. They were on the rounds in search of some prey. They found some spotted deer grazing. Taking caution brother started closing in, after a few moves he turned to glance at his Man eater brother just to know his line of action but he felt very strange. His brother had not moved at all. It seemed he was not interested in the hunt. Confused but with a never mind attitude the brother alone pounced on the prey.

The deer ran for their lives. The lion targeted one but after an exhaustive chase through the meadows finally failed in its attempt. The deer escaped. Exhausted and panting the lion turned its lordly full of majestic main neck towards his lame brother and looked. That fellow had not moved an inch. With a limp but gracefully he moved towards a direction, silently the other brother followed him.

Deep into the dense woods on a giant tree was a massive honey bee hive. A stout well built black villager on spotting that hive was very happy. A happy smile spreads on his thick lips. Quickly he collected some dry wood. Piled it under the hive and put on fire the wood. As the wood caught fire he hurriedly gathered some leaves and covered the burning wood with it, dense smoke build up. As the smoke reached the beehive the bees were disturbed. They began to fly away. The villager covered himself top to bottom with a thick blanket. He was waiting for the bees to abandon the hive but he knew not that this wait was not of bees to go but of death to come.

Man eater smelled human scent. He raised his magnificent head and took a deep sniff then moved following the human scent. His brother whose stomach was flat with hunger followed him.

The villager was sitting totally covered with the blanket. He heard rumbling of the leaves and dry wood being shattered under heavy paws also with a gush of breeze came such a stench which through his nostrils gushed in and crash into with his brain set in the safe hollow of his skull. Shocked and scared he threw the blanket away. He beheld his death right in front of him.

Sharp smack with the open paw of the Man eater lion smashed his brain from his safe skull and it flew on to the green leaves of the tree and shattered all the strings of his existence.. The remaining brief moan suffocated in the tight grip of the strong jaw of the lame Man Eater Lion.

That night the villager's mother, wife and kids kept waiting for him, thinking he must have found some big beehive; must be busy extracting it. Then he would sell it to some tourist at the Forest Resort, the money he will get with it he will buy some ration for his family. But they did not know that instead of providing for them he had provided and satiated the hunger of the lame lion and his brother. Yes for the first time the lame lion's brother tasted human blood and liked it.

Namrata had asked Madhu if she can do some shopping for Pinky in a shopping mall at some distance. She wanted to take Pinky there and buy her some toys and clothes; she had requested Madhu to get Rajeshwar's permission "I want to see Pinky wear my choice of clothes, will you do this for me, I mean ask Rajeshwar permission." Namrata had requested very humbly.

Madhu loved to oblige, she was very much conscious of the fact that Pinky was Namrata's daughter; she had full right. Once they were apprehensive about Namrata taking them to court and legally try to take away Pinky from them. But Namrata had really changed. She was a good mother, so when Madhu put forward Namrata request to Rajeshwar there was no question of a no. He asked Madhu "When she wants to take Pinky?"

"Today only, it is Pinky's holiday."

"Ok, but you also go along do some shopping for you also."

Saying so he took out some cash from his jacket pocket gave it to Madhu saying "This is some cash, pundit ji [The priest] will be here today evening, I am sure Maji will persuade him for an early date of marriage."

Hesitating to take money Madhu said "It is alright, if I have to do shopping I have some money."

Pressing the money in her hand Rajeshwar said "Whatever you have is yours and whatever I have that too is yours"

Taking her in his arms he said "Madhu why didn't you come earlier in my life. The character you have demonstrated, I mean to bring together Pinky and Namrata really portrays the golden heart you have and the open mind you posses. Really Mr. Amar lost a lot in losing you but then some body's loss is some body's gain."

Saying so he laughed holding Madhu, just then Pinky came in running. They stepped apart from each other as she entered "Daddy, Daddy Jumbo uncle is here."

Fondling Pinky hair Rajeshwar said "Ok, I will be down."

Pinky ran away. While going Rajeshwar told Madhu "Madhu if possible put some sense into that Namrata also, please make her understand that this change in her is absolutely apt for her to settle down again, certainly there is no dearth of good homes for her, her parents must be having many in mind she must not procrastinate anymore."

Madhu in agreement shook her head in a yes. Rajeshwar walked out of the room to meet Jumbo uncle.

Jumbo uncle was there to inform Rajeshwar that one of his villagers had not come back home last night. He had gone to jungle in search of honey but had not returned.

Namrata parents were on their way to the Forest Resort when Vivek's phone call came. He had come to know about Namarta leaving to meet Rajeshwar. He was in America with regards the settlement of his divorce. Getting rid of his wife he was happy to be free to propose to Namarta and marry her with all the pomp and show.

His company and Manohar Shivdasani ji's company were to merge. Total diamond trade was to be dominated by Vivek. Manohar Shivdasani ji had now come of age and Namarta was his only daughter. After marrying her Vivek would be the natural beneficiary. All this Manohar Shivdasani ji had himself given him to understand. That was one reason Vivek had divorced his obese wife of American origin, paid heavily for the divorce. He threatened Manohar Shivdasani ji "You will be liable to settle all my account if there is to transpire some chicanery." This he had conveyed to Manohar Shivdasani ji on the phone.

As soon as Vivek had switched off his phone a nervous Manohar Shivdasani ji had called Namrata. He had not gone into any details just told her that he and his wife were reaching there. She must wait and not go anywhere.

Madhu was to come to Forest Resort with Pinky to Namrata cottage and then together they were to proceed on the shopping spree.

When Madhu with Pinky reached there the huge Hummer was parked right in front of the cottage. Amar was sitting in the veranda his hand on his forehead. From inside the cottage some loud voices emerged.

The altercation taking place inside was being pronounced in three different languages. The most used dialect was Sindhi; the other one was English and the third one was Hindi. Amar gestured a confused Madhu and Pinky to take seats. Perplexed they sat on the cane sofa kept in the veranda. Inside Namarta father was shouting in Sindhi, what Madhu could make out was this that some Vivek will ruin him. Namrata shouted back at her father in English "Before making such a promise to Vivek you should have asked me."

Namrata mother shouted back at Namrata in Sindhi and kept on shouting. May be she was putting forward that Namarta was their daughter and they have full right on her.

Namarta hit back once again in English "If parents have authority, they do have some obligation also."

Father shouted back in Hindi "What have we not given you."

Namarta retaliated once again in English "You have given me a ruined life, torn me apart from my family, my child."

Namarta was heard crying. Pinky was all ears, on hearing her mother refer to her as 'My Child' and cry, Innocent Pinky's heart for the first time sensed a strange vibration which at her young age she failed to understand. Madhu hearing Namrata fight her parents and cry over Pinky was very much touched. Amar noticed this and in his heart thanked God for His sent opportunity. Mother was shouting at the top of her voice this time in English.

"Why blame us you have yourself left your husband, your daughter."

Namarta shot back "And you people rejoiced at my devastation because you people wanted to use me as the queen of your business."

Father shouted back in Sindhi somewhat meaning whatever he did was for the benefit of Namarta so that she could live like a sovereign. Namarta retorted "I don't want to eat your diamonds and rubies. The happiness the pleasure I felt embracing my daughter, it is, it is not in the concept of you people."

Pinky was confused as to why she was feeling what right then she felt; somewhat sad and sympathetic towards Namrata. Madhu was extremely moved, Amar took a deep sigh. Namrata voice was heard "That's all I don't want to talk any more, I have made my decision, please leave me alone and go now my life belongs to my daughter Pinky."

All of a sudden little Pinky was scared; her young mind thought; what Namrata means by 'my life belongs to my daughter Pinky? Does she mean that I belong to her?' Pinky wanted to leave.

Madhu also decided not to stay there any longer. Holding Pinky's hand she got up to go home.

"Pinky, your shopping we will do some other day. Let us go home now."

Pinky happily agreed "That's ok mummy." Amar also stood up to join them "I will walk you both home; I don't see an early end to the drama here."

But Madhu said "It's ok, we will go. "

All of a sudden Pinky spoke up "Oh, Amar uncle I forgot, Dadi wanted to meet you."

Madhu was nonplussed. Amar walked along with them.

Back in the cottage the drama continued. Namarta mother was a very shrewd woman; she took an about turn all of a sudden. She all of a sudden realized that Namarta's mother hood can be dealt only with motherhood and love. Demonstrating tears in her eyes she told Namarta in the language Namarta was most comfortable with that was English "You talk about daughter's happiness to us, you are our only daughter and Pinky is our only grandchild. Interest is dearer then the principal."

Manohar Shivdasani ji very well understood the change in this wife and added in Hindi "One promise I make to you right now, I will manage Vivek understand that Pinky is your daughter, If he wants to marry you Pinky he will have to agree to."

Cutting in Namrata said "There is no need to make Vivek understand anything. I never liked that person and now I am repulsive to him."

Namrata's mother cooled down further. Her husband following suit "Nobody is forcing any one on you. It is your life you have to take final decision."

"Yes as parent we were just trying to help." Mother brought the matter to an end for the day.

The altercation at the cottage Pinky could comprehend little though her heart was touched at times but she felt more scared of the emotion than emotive, walking towards home with Amar and Madhu she inquired "Who were they? Fighting Namrata ji?"

Madhu reprimanded "Again Namrata ji?"

Realizing her mistake Pinky innocently caught her tongue in between her teeth for a moment then said "I mean my other mother."

Madhu exhaled a sigh, and then went on to tell Pinky "Your grandparents."

Trying to put two and two together, Pinky asked "You mean my other mummy's mummy and daddy?"

Her tone was strange, it was not sarcastic nor had a pinch of impishness in it; it had a feel of something lost or missing. Madhu gave a look but said nothing, just nodded a yes. Amar intervened saying "Pinky you must have heard, how much your mummy Namrata ji loves you?"

Pinky lost somewhere said "Yes."

"When Namrata ji goes away will you ever think of your other mummy?"

Pinky very innocently replied somewhat lost again "I don't know uncle."

Saying so as if scared with the ongoing confusion in her mind she held Madhu hand, Amar took it in the other sense and remarked "Yes this is it, you have one more mummy but she has no other daughter."

"Will you stop it Amar?" Madhu warned.

Amar took no offence and ignored her warning walking along casually said "Madhu you know, Namrata ji was saying she will never forget the affection, love and understanding you have displayed towards her, well I know this all to be very much you, and I thank God that you have not changed. But you know Madhu, Namrata ji will change so much this I had never dreamt in my wildest dreams. I bow my head to Motherly love." He glanced at Pinky may be to read her reaction.

Little Pinky was again very much lost in her innocent thoughts. Madhu also noticed the change in the child. Amar continued "Namrata ji is very happy Rajeshwar sahib is getting a worthy life partner like you."

Madhu inquired of Amar rather sarcastically "Amar you tell me about you? Are you happy or not?"

Amar smiled sadly and said "I am happy just for one thing; you got saved from a bad man like me by a very thin margin."

Pinky was walking at some distance from them but she heard what Amar said however she failed to comprehend the complete significance of it, but it certainly took her mind away from the confusion of her other mother. She decided to ask her Dadi. Madhu also felt that Amar is going too far; he should not have talked so in front of the child, she once again admonished Amar glancing towards Pinky. Amar smiled a very cool smile and said "Why the hell are you getting angry? You are the one instrumental to bring together mother and daughter. See we have reached your home."

Madhu turned and looked at the house. Suddenly the thought occurred to her 'Yes this house which belongs to me now, once belonged to Namrata ji. Am I depriving her of it?'

Madhu froze in her steps. Amar was unaware of the effect his pinch had had on Madhu, holding Pinky hand he entered the gate to meet Dadi ma.

Lost in thoughts Madhu was still standing there. Monu and Bholu approached from behind. Madhu reacted on the heavy steps of Monu turned and looked. Monu was shaking his head as if telling Madhu to go in and not mull over.

In the living room Pinky entered with Amar and sat down on a sofa thinking something. All along their way from Resort to the Bungalow Amar had been watching Pinky's behavior. The writer director in him was telling him that he had scored a major point. The God send opportunity had not only influenced Madhu but also the little child 'God is with me' Amar thought and said reminding lost Pinky "Pinky beta go call Dadi, you said she wanted to see me?" Pinky as if wanting to get rid of the confusion in her mind jumped up from the sofa.

Leaving Amar in the hall Pinky ran up straight to Maji and asked the other question which was bothering her adolescent mind "Dadi, Dadi tell me one thing what does this mean 'I am happy that you got saved from a bad man like me' what does this mean?"

"But who got saved from whom?"

"Amar uncle said this to Mummy."

"You mean to Madhu?"

Shaking her head rapidly in a yes Pinky insisted "Dadi please tell?"

As if coming to understand something Dadi said "This means my dear that my doubts are not baseless. Madhu and Amar very well know each other."

"Amar uncle is down, I got him here."

Maji immediately got up exclaiming "Ok!"

Down, sitting in the hall Amar was thinking as to why Maji wanted to meet him 'May be she wants to offer me the job of covering Rajeshwar and Madhu marriage, great, the one I was to marry today the time has come to cover her marriage.'

He laughed at himself. Maji was coming with Pinky, he got up as Maji approached he touched her feet. Maji blessed him "God bestow all happiness on you, may you succeed well in life, make a big name for yourself."

Amar smiled broadly saying "Maji now I understand why till date all my jobs got jeopardized? Why success eluded me, just because your blessings were not with me."

Smiling Maji sat down. Amar also settled himself. Pinky sat clinging to Maji just then Madhu entered and directly went to the kitchen. Maji remarked "What is wrong with Madhu? Why is she off mood? Yes Pinky you and Madhu were to go shopping with Namrata?"

Cheeky Pinky said "Yes Dadi, but my grandparents came."

All the more surprised Dadi asked "Grand parents? You mean Manohar Shivdasani ji and his wife are here?"

Naughty and laughing Pinky said "Yes and there at Forest Resort some fighting is on."

Shocked Maji looked at Amar and questioned "Fighting on, but why?"

Amar replied in a very straight forward manner "Maji Namrata had realized her mistake fully; she was giving her parents back, left and right."

Maji as if reminiscences "Yes she is too good at giving back."

Amar immediately realized that he had touched wrong cord. Changing topic he said "Maji pundit ji had come or not? When is Madhu marriage date going to be fixed?"

Maji kept looking at Amar silently. Amar once again realized that he had again committed mistake; he was talking to Rajeshwar's Mother about marriage of her son and instead of mentioning Rajeshwar, had asked about Madhu marriage. A solemn Maji replied "Pundit ji had gone to his native town in India, by tomorrow he will be here. Tell me one thing my son. In India you come from where?"

"Mumbai Maji."

"Very strange, you are from Mumbai; Madhu is also from Mumbai did you both ever meet there?"

Amar was in a confused state of mind, whether to tell the truth or not? Madhu entered with the tea tray saying "We did meet Maji. In fact we know each other very well. Please forgive me; I never told you so earlier, Rajeshwar sahib had prohibited me to do so"

Madhu prepared a cup of tea, all was silent, she gave the cup of tea to Amar and said "Here Mr. Amar, have some tea."

Then she told Pinky "Come Pinky you have to do your lesson if you study now you will have time to play with Monu and Bholu in the evening."

Taking Pinky by hand she went away from there. Silently Amar was sipping tea. All of a sudden Maji facial expression was totally indifferent to Amar. She got up to go, but before leaving told Amar "In this house, after many- many days happiness has come, if you want blessings of a mother please don't disturb it."

Maji departed. The tea which was in Amar's mouth, with great difficulty it went down his throat.

Now one thing was very clear to Amar, getting Namrata there had not helped him at all. Madhu was all the more angry with him now. But the other side of the picture seemed bright; one new eventuality had cropped up; it could be of benefit to Amar. Namrata had changed, was a better person and a much better mother. That good occurrence was of Amar's benefit.

The good change of character in Namrata was bound to affect a fine girl like Madhu. Her compassionate heart will certainly hold her to be responsible for coming in between a mother and daughter. A repentant Namrata will weigh more and more on Madhu heart and this weight might rock the boat of Madhu and Rajeshwar.

Also according to Amar's concept first love was all power full and Madhu's first love was he himself. Rajeshwar and Madhu were in a sort of an arranged relationship. Circumstances had brought them together. If those very circumstances changed then the marriage can alter. This could be the win for Amar.

He was sure with time Madhu would forgive him. As for Maji blessings, Amar was certain to avail them. Maji wanted the happiness of her house, she would get that, only instead of Madhu Namrata would be there; her first daughter in-law; the real mother of her granddaughter; Rajeshwar's first wife, his first love. Amar felt complacent, good and encouraged.

Chapter Eleven

Namrata was not in the know that Madhu had heard her argument with her parents. She felt that Rajeshwar must not have permitted that was why Madhu and Pinky never came. She was in a double mind whether she should go and talk to Rajeshwar about Pinky or not.

Rajeshwar's jeep came and stopped in front of her cottage. Alighting he said "I was passing this way so I thought I better check if you ladies were back from your shopping?"

Once more Namrata realized that how wrong she had been about Rajeshwar. Rajeshwar had permitted them, then why didn't they come. All of a sudden she got the entire picture; her encounter with her parents in the cottage while Madhu and Pinky may have waited outside. She was engrossed in her thoughts. Rajeshwar inquired "Namrata where are you lost Madhu and Pinky, did they come here or not?"

Somewhat still lost in her thought she said "They did come but went away."

Confused Rajeshwar questioned "Why?"

She very simply replied "Well my mummy daddy had also come. A heated altercation happened between us. I think during that time only they came and went."

Dwelling into their past Rajeshwar said "I thought after I shift out of your life it must have put an end to all the differences between you and your parents."

A sad smile spread on Namrata face she said "Bad people disparities never come to an end. The disputes of good people resolve. See you have someone much better than me in Madhu while I have no one."

Rajeshwar had once loved Namrata very much. As of that day seeing tears of regret in her eyes he was touched. He asked "Won't you offer me a cup of tea? Patrolling around the jungle I am exhausted."

Controlling her tears and pointing towards the sofa Namrata said "First sit, you are standing as if you are in a hurry to leave?"

Rajeshwar sat. She switched on an electric kettle kept in the veranda. She was trying her level best to subdue her emotions but the tears were not listening. She turned away from him. They had lived together for so many years, loved each other so much, Rajeshwar very well understood her feel and plight. Trying to help her out he said "Namrata this change in you is really great; I mean it is best for you to settle down again."..

Eyes brimming with tears she turned and looked at him; plight of her heart reached her lips "Then give me a chance to settle down again."

The call of her heart did reach Rajeshwar. But in the past also this had happened. Namrata had made many promises but failed to comply. She had sworn to live life Rajeshwar's way but failed.

In a way if you see Namrata was not in the wrong. The environment, the milieu in which a person is born and brought up leaves a very profound stamp on the course of a person's life; this is where arranged marriages score over blind love marriages. Blind meaning; love confused with infatuation. In arranged marriages; the culture, the upbringing, the back ground all is given a very serious consideration. This is why, in bygone days, while arranging marriages, people were very particular about blood line also. so that the environment remains one, up brining same, culture same then naturally thinking was bound to be somewhat similar and sailing after marriage smooth, however in this modern world of today all is mixed up; love with infatuation; boys with guys; girls with ladies. Pair of loving eyes meets, love evolves, marriage takes place, then eyes open, love evaporates and divorce happens.

This is the reason curse like divorce is so rampant all around us because true love that can overcome all hurdles is in short supply, so scarce.

Namrata got married to Rajeshwar when she was 26 years of age and those twenty-six years she had lived full fledge in the cream of the society; in the beautiful cask of that stinking rich society. Just for some time Rajashwar's love had put a blind on that glitter and glamour. Nevertheless with in only three years, when her daughter Pinky was just two years the veil of infatuation slipped down her eyes and she failed Rajeshwar.

That day also may be the memories and love of Rajeshwar was over whelming her. Rajeshwar was rather sure of that. So he tried to explain "Namrata please don't misunderstand me and feel bad, the fact is the mistake which we committed earlier we must not repeat. My life and my work are in this wilderness. Here you can come for a visit or a holiday but cannot live life."

Tears rolling down her eyes Namrata beseeched "Once more, just once more try me."

But Rajeshwar was firm. Looking away from her he said "Namrata we have past the age of being blind in love, life is just not beautiful flowers It is also a path full of thorns at times, and when two different people with two deferent point of views together are forced to walk on that thorny path it happens so that they often hurt each other more than those pricking thorns, constrained they do live through it together for as long as they can but that is a life full of sorrows, full of differences, full of retributions."

An indignant Namrata wiped her tears. Took control of herself and questioned "And you are sure that this Madhu will live ever happily with you? There will never be a discrepancy, no diversity; no bloody thorn will ever prick you both at all?"

Rajeshwar smiled, at once again angry Namrata and concluded "Yes thorns can always be there to hurt but we will put up with them together or if possible remove and throw them away."

By this time Rajeshwar had finished his tea, he got up to go "I will send Pinky along with Madhu."

Namrata by now was sitting her head down she raised her head, looked at him and said very coolly "Thanks."

Rajeshwar drove away in his jeep. Namrata was sitting quiet. Suddenly she struck hard. The kettle and the crockery flew and crashed.

Madhu found Pinky crying. After coming back from school Pinky sat at her desk in her room doing her home work. She was crying while doing her home work. Madhu thought in her school something might have happened but the happening was at her heart. This Madhu came to know when she inquired "Pinky what's wrong? Why are you crying?"

"Mummy can I call my other mummy Mama?"

"Yes certainly you can, but why are you crying?"

"I want to meet her, I miss her."

She kept crying, Madhu was happy the blood ties were calling. The relation had become alive. The inevitable has happened. Madhu was happy for mother and daughter at the same time a premonition was knocking its presence, the double mind, the state of confusion, the weakness of mind, Madhu hated the most was again establishing itself. Madhu cursed it out of her mind.

Pinky asked "Mummy can we go and meet Mama?"

"Sure my love, we will go today itself."

Madhu rang up Namrata and told her the good news "Namrata ji your daughter is missing you, she wants to meet you."

Namrata never believed her ears when she heard it on her mobile "My daughter is missing me or you are being good once again?"

"Well if you don't believe me talk to her yourself."

Madhu gave her cell to Pinky who crying said "Hello Mama."

The mobile slipped from the trembling hand of Namrata she picked it up with trembling hands, trying to hold it right to her ear and mouth, Namrata blabbered "H…H…hello…hello my sweetheart so good, so lovely to hear your sweet voice." Namrata was crying as she had never cried before "Mama don't cry, I am also crying for you." said Pinky.

Namrata cried all the more saying "I am coming to meet you beta right now, right this moment."

Madhu very well witnessed the emotional patch up between mother and daughter; all that was happening to mother and daughter she was delighted to see and was happy at her for being instrumental.

Rajeshwar had just come in. Madhu had dressed Pinky in one of her prettiest dresses. He inquired "You both are going somewhere?"

"Yes we ladies are." came the vague reply from Madhu.

Namrata Mercedes entered the compound and came to a halt with a jerk. Rajeshwar reacted surprised; he had just come back meeting her. Namrata alighted. Pinky ran from near Madhu to Namrata. Namrata also ran for her daughter. Rajeshwar saw mother and daughter meet and go into each other's tight embrace. Rajeshwar turned and looked at Madhu; she was standing all smiles. He also smiled; he had made a very good choice in Madhu but at that point of time he never knew that excess of everything was bad including goodness.

Center Point Shopping Mall was an extensive cooperative; from pin to elephant all was available. The needs of Pinky were no problem but the choice of little Pinky was a big problem. She wanted sport shoes to play with Monu and Bholu; Reebok and Nike were her favorite brands; to get them in the shade she desired proved impossible; red was offensive, Bholu didn't like red, white would get dirty very fast, black she hated. At her age Pinky was the most difficult customer to please. Namrata was ecstatic, enjoying every moment of her daughter's coming together. She whispered into Madhu ear "I can't believe it, I shopping with my daughter all thanks to you Madhu."

"Namrata ji, hundreds and thousands of thanks to you for being so understanding."

Namrata laughed as she said "You know Amar says we should open a mutual admiration club as we keep appreciating each other to him."

"I hardly talk to him," Madhu said dryly.

Pinky was busy trying two pair of shoes which she has finally short listed, two sales men were at her service trying their level best to help her make up her mind. Namrata asked Madhu "Will you never forgive Amar?"

"Forgiven are those who you wish maintaining some relation with. To me he does not exist."

"Madhu you are too good at heart, be a little generous to him as well; just being friends will not hurt you but certainly will ease out some guilt in him."

"Guilt what guilt had he succeeded in his designs he would have made a story out of that guilt and made a film." Describing so, her first love, Madhu laughed.

"You mean he has not changed?" asked Namrata seriously.

"He is not capable of change." replied Madhu confidently.

"Will you forgive him if you feel that he has changed?"

"Machines do not change they break down and slump to be dumped in junk yard."

Talking they have moved a little away from Pinky. She called out to them showing her selection of the two pair of shoes "Which of these two should I go for?"

"Take the one you like." Namrata suggested.

"I like both of them."

"Then take both." replied Namrata.

Excited Pinky called out "You mean you will buy me both pairs?"

"Your Mama can buy you the entire Mall she is a very rich woman." said Madhu genuinely in good humor.

Pinky lovingly clung to Namrata asking "Is it true Mama?"

Namrata took Pinky in her tight embrace, her voice chocking with the upsurge of emotions, she said "Yes my angel it is true; I am a very rich woman but a very poor mother." she said looking at Madhu who really was feeling sorry for her.

Innocent Pinky failed to understand the real sense of 'poor mother' objected "I wanted one pair of shoes you bought me two, you are not a poor mother you are good Mama."

Namrata just couldn't hold her tears they trickled out of her eyes. The sales men who were attending on them, sensing some sensitivity, thought it wise to move away from there.

Pinky gently brushed her Mama's tears with her cute little hands "Mama everyone is looking, why are you crying?"

Taking control of her Namrata said "Sorry my love, I am really sorry.

Shop they did till Pinky was sated and exhausted. Shoes, outfits, electronic items, games, and gadgets, all sorts of variety of choice a child could wish for and even new furnishings for Pinky room; they had to hire a carrier. Namrata Mercedes dickey could not contain her daughter's first shopping extravaganza with her.

After sunset they reached home. Mercedes plus two other vehicles; one carrier that carried Pinky shopping's the other one transported show room workers who had come to assemble some of items. Rajeshwar was back from work, Maji was wide awake waiting for both, her very dear granddaughter and her most precious to be daughter in law Madhu but along with them came Namrata her ex daughter in law.

Namrata on her part was apprehensive coming to her ex home so late at night. Madhu the good soul had insisted that Namrata should come and set up Pinky's room with her new things,

Workers immediately got busy offloading little Pinky's consignment. Rajeshwar and Maji stood in the hall as things were transported up to Pinky's room. They certainly did not appreciate what they saw. Such a shopping extravaganza; what was Namrata trying to prove? Was she trying to win over Pinky by her wealth? Or was she making an attempt, once more, to show off her riches? However they also saw Pinky and Madhu very happy so they kept quiet for the moment. Namrata who knew them well sensed their disapproval, she came to them "Please forgive me; I just couldn't hold myself shopping first time for Pinky. I am really sorry it will not happen again."

There was so much of motherly truth in Namrata utterance that both Rajeshwar and Maji were perplexed as to how to react. They just couldn't get themselves to raise any objection. On the contrary Maji found herself saying "Namrata Beti, Pinky is your daughter you have full right on her."

Tears filtered in Namrata eyes, emotions charged her face, the realization that she had abandoned such wonderful people hit her hard; not able to restrain herself from breaking down she rushed up to Pinky's room leaving Rajeshwar and Maji at a loss once more.

In Pinky's room Namrata entered trying hard to conceal her teary eyes. Pinky had been unpacking her toys one by one and playing with them all around the room. Right then she was playing with a remote operated helicopter, it went flying out of the room, and with it went Pinky not noticing distraught Namrata. Madhu did detect some upsetting change in Namrata body language "What is it?" she asked.

"Nothing." replied Namrata but her eyes said otherwise.

"Down there did Maji or Rajeshwar object to the little shopping you have done for your daughter?" asked Madhu with the hint of her good humor.

Namrata cried, tears rolling down her cheeks she said "They are too good to object and I am too late to know it."

'She is too late because of me' the pinch in Madhu heart said. However to Namrata she said "You must not hurt yourself like this Pinky is your daughter and you are very much in time for her."

Namrata smiled, wiped her tears and shook her head in a 'yes'.

Namrata was setting up Pinky's room; Madhu was helping her in whatever she desired in the room set up. The oriental bed was moved out by the workers, a new fancy child double bed was assembled by expert hands within minutes and put in place; new mattress was laid on it. A packing was cut open; it contained a dozen bed sheets, bed covers with pillow covers, new pillows which sprung to their full size as soon as binding straps were cut open. Namrata picked up a pink bed sheet, looked at Madhu as if asking approval, Madhu nodded a go ahead and helped Namrata stretch the bed sheet over the bed. Out of the bedcovers Namrata asked "Which one?"

"Your choice?" Madhu said.

Happily Namrata selected a bed cover with gigantic paintings of Mickey Mouse and with Madhu help furnished it on top the bed.

Madhu approved "This looks youngish, perfect for Pinky,"

Pleased Namrata hugged Madhu.

New wide screen TV, with games gadgets in place, was set on a new show case brought and assembled by the workers. Namrata objected "The TV should not be right in front of the bed. Pinky must not go on watching TV till late night."

Madhu agreed "Right, where you want the TV set to be?"

"Beside the bed, so that she has to come out of her bed and then watch TV sitting on this sofa," Namrata pointed to the sofa.

"Perfect." Madhu said agreeing.

Madhu on her part simply assisted Namrata; letting her set the room of her daughter as per her discretion, Madhu reveled on the sight of happy Namrata.

This was Madhu not only a nurse by profession but also a human who loved to nurse the hurt feelings of fellow humans; who felt happy on making others happy and she knew how to make others happy.

Rajeshwar and Maji were there in the room watching all this with silent apprehension. To them compromise with Namrata should be in limit; however Madhu was going all out 'Was she being naïve?' That was what Maji thought but all that what Rajeshwar thought was; 'I am very lucky. Madhu is the best thing that has ever happened to me, she is too good a person. I must never lose her.'

Workers finished their job at Pinky's room, fast and efficient and were gone. Namrata thanked Madhu, Rajeshwar and Maji "I must say the feel I experienced today I was never aware of, and I must thank you all for it. It is quite late, I shall leave now."

"Not without having dinner," Madhu said with finality.

At the dinner table Namrata sat after years together but not at the head of the table where she used to sit; Madhu sat there ordering the maid to serve soup to Maji and Pinky first. Rajeshwar came carrying his whisky glass. This unexpected development surprised Namrata; Madhu noticed the shocker in Namrata look.

"He will quit compulsive drinking so he has promised." Madhu said.

"When you can make Maji walk then this is no problem," Namrata said smiling.

"Madhu has to tell me once and I will give up forever." Rajeshwar said in a rather challenging tone.

Maji spoke up "Madhu Beta, please tell him to give up the nasty habit,"

"OK Maji, Rajeshwar sahib, please give up this nasty drinking habit,"

Rajeshwar called out "Johnny where are you?"

From nowhere Johnny appeared and came rushing "Yes sir;"

Handing his whisky glass over to him Rajeshwar said "Johnny this peg is all yours and go to my room right away there is a full case of whisky kept there that is all yours as well."

Johnny stood flabbergasted, Rajeshwar smiled at him and repeated himself "Johnny please do as you are told,"

Johnny immediately finished the peg of whisky in one gulp and then rushed up to Rajeshwar room.

Every one sat still astounded. Pinky not believing asked "Daddy will you never ever drink again?"

"Never ever; solemn promise." Rajeshwar said extending his hand to her, Pinky jumped from her chair and came rushing to him and flung her into his embrace.

Maji was so happy that she joined her hands in prayers to the Almighty, Madhu knew not how to react; had Rajeshwar done this on purpose? Just to make Namrata realize something? Namrata sat quiet fighting the jealousy which was creeping into her against Madhu. Coming back to her chair Pinky said "I am so happy today; my Mama is here and my Daddy will not drink."

The relation between the two and little Pinky was very much obvious in her innocent deliverance. Each one felt it and most of all Madhu.

After late night dinner finally it was time for Namrata to leave. Pinky insisted "Mama why don't you stay the night with us? We will together sleep in the bed you have bought me."

They were there in the hall, standing, Namrata about to leave; the thought of sleeping in one bed with her daughter send exciting shivers through her body, for a second she felt her legs giving way, Madhu was beside her, she kept her hand on Madhu shoulder to regain her balance. Madhu sensed the tense application of her hand and looked into her eyes, Namrata eyes; the eyes of a mother said it all.

"Yes Namrata ji, it is very late now, Sher uncle must be on his prowl. Please stay the night with us." Madhu seconded Pinky's request.

Namrata stayed back in the house, where once upon a time every night was her right.

Sleep evaded the three of them. Pinky was fast asleep with wide awake Namrata next to her. Her room was situated in between the rooms of Rajeshwar and Madhu. Beyond these set of rooms was the staircase leading to the terrace. Namrata, lying on the bed with her dear daughter saw Madhu silently cross over towards the stairs to the terrace. She wondered if Rajeshwar was there at the terrace waiting for Madhu.

Rajeshwar had called Madhu on her mobile. When rest of the world slept the terrace became their favorite romantic rendezvous. It was Rajeshwar who always called her there. Madhu also enjoyed the private moments there with him. However that night she was not in a romantic mood, she wanted some human answers to her questions from her would be husband.

As she entered the terrace Rajeshwar appeared from behind her and held her in his arms. She remained in his arms but questioned "What did you want to prove, I mean to Namrata ji?"

"Come on Madhu, let's not talk about her and upset the beautiful full moon watching us." he said tightening his grip on her.

She turned in his firm arms to face him "You purposely said that you will give up drinks if I asked you?"

"And I purposely want to kiss you." he said attempting to kiss her.

She moved her face away "Let us not rub salt into some body's wounds."

Rajeshwar sat on the floor of the terrace forcing Madhu to sit along; on his lap "Stop bothering about others as it is we have wasted half our lives."

Madhu said shifting from the warmth of his lap on to the cold floor of the terrace "we must not forget that she is Pinky's biological mother."

"Sure, that is why she can meet Pinky as and when she wants."

"A mother might want more than that."

"Well, during Pinky school vacations she can take her along to live with her."

"Can she come and stay with us?"

Rajeshwar pulled her close to him "Madhu you know, this good part in you scares me and I love it too."

"Nothing can scare you this much I know about you by now, and if you love my human part then please be good to Namrata ji." Madhu said solemnly.

Rajeshwar laughed and said "Oh my God, you think I am not being good to that lady, I tell you why you feel so because you are extra good to her."

Suddenly he became serious "I have a gut feeling; the lady and that friend of yours Amar are exploiting you emotionally."

"Now you are being extra what should I say, skeptical." Madhu said annoyed.

"No my love on the second thought, I am sure, the two are using you, that Amar knows you well so he in connivance with Namrata is trying and creating situations where in you feel as if you are coming in between mother and daughter."

Exasperated Madhu, jerking herself free of his embrace got up "I can't believe, you thinking in these terms?"

Rajeshwar also got up "Why, do you think your Amar is good enough for such an exploit?"

"Amar is a good for nothing man but Namrata ji is a mother, she can't be so mean so as to use her own daughter, exploit her for her own benefit."

Namrata was there standing in a dark corner of the terrace listening to the exchange. On hearing Madhu defend her she felt guilty. Though she had not planned any move to use her daughter however still she felt culpable. She just turned and left as quietly as she had come.

Rajeshwar gently kept both his hands on Madhu shoulders, looked into her eyes and in a very sincere tone said "Madhu, why are we fighting for those who have betrayed us?"

"I said Amar is a good for nothing man."

"That you said because you are very angry with him and you are very angry with him because you loved him very much."

"What do you mean?"

"I mean we should stop fighting for either of them,"

He again took her in his arms but she jerked herself free "I want to know what you mean by; I am very angry with him because I loved him very much?"

"I mean exactly what I said," Rajeshwar replied rather off mood.

"I do not think so." Madhu said tears in her eyes and walked away to the confines of her room.

Rajeshwar stood there thinking 'I must take care, not let them succeed in their nasty designs.'

Chapter Twelve

Rajeshwar was driving when his mobile rang. Switching it on he said 'Hello' He shivered on hearing from the other end, color drained out of his face, beads of perspiration appeared on his forehead taking a sharp turn he accelerated his jeep towards the village of Jumbo uncle.

Jumbo uncle's village was a scene of catastrophe. People were screaming, wailing, shouting for help. Bloody and gravely hurt human bodies were lying here and there all around. Some were dead. Some were unconscious. Some were writhing in agony. Rajeshwar jeep screeched to a halt. Villagers rushed to his jeep surrounding him.

He was told that it was not one but two lions that did the carnage. They invaded the village attacking and killing people. To save them some ran into their homes but the lions chased, caught, and killed them there. Jumbo uncle rushed out with his rifle, was about to shoot one lion when the other one attacked him from behind. He suffered severe injuries.

Jumbo uncle's mansion was close by. Rajeshwar ran to it. Out at the gate Jumbo uncle was prostrate on a bed his back severely cut. Women of the house were wailing. Jeena rushed to him "Bhaiya Baba is very hurt."

Rajeshwar had informed the city hospital on his way there. But for the help to arrive, for the ambulances, the doctors, the nurses to come it would take some precious time.

"Help is on its way, I have informed the city hospital."

Rajeshwar was checking on Jumbo uncle, he opened his eyes and said "I am ok, help others, Daniel, how is Daniel?"

"Where is Daniel?" inquired Rajeshwar.

"There in the field." Jeena pointed out towards an open field where at a spot some people could be seen crowding "The lion dragged him out there; he tried fighting the lion to save Baba." Jeena wailed and cried.

Rajeshwar ran to the field, tearing people apart he forced himself upon the scene. It was too bad a sight; Daniel was severely mauled; worst than Jumbo uncle; his face, chest, abdomen, thighs were clawed and bitten by the beast, at places chunks of flesh was missing. Niku sat beside him stunned and shivering. There was an immediate need of first aid. How Rajeshwar wished Madhu to be there.

Namrata Mercedes came and stopped right in the middle of the village. From the driver side Namrata appeared and from the other side Madhu rushed out. On receiving the news Namrata had brought Madhu along.

The gory blood bath all around shattered Namrata, dazed she was about to fall. Madhu quickly helped her. Namrata tried to take control of her but threw up. Rajeshwar had seen them reach he called out to Madhu "Madhu come here fast."

Composing herself Namrata beckoned Madhu to go. Madhu ran towards the field, with the help of other villagers Rajeshwar had picked up critically wounded Daniel and was carrying him; reaching them she was taken aback for a moment. As they reached mansion exterior Madhu composed herself. The women were still wailing doing nothing to help. Madhu shouted at Jeena and other women telling them to stop crying and get some hot water and some clean cloth. The African women failed to understand her. Niku and Rajeshwar explained in their dialect. They rushed to their respective houses. Then Rajeshwar said to Madhu "Madhu all the injured, I will get them here. Till hospital help arrives we have to take charge,"

Rajeshwar ran to his jeep, on the loud speaker attached to it he instructed the villagers to carry all the injured men at Jumbo uncle's mansion.

At the mansion Madhu with professional expertise was tearing off the tattered clothes from over the injured body of Jumbo uncle and Daniel, Niku took heed from her and helped her. Rajeshwar was guiding and helping villagers fetch injured men. Namrata was still sitting dazed.

Some hot water containers were brought to the exterior of the mansion. Whatever anti-septic available

Madhu poured into the containers and then exhibited the empty bottles to villagers asking them to get as many as they find. Rajeshwar noticed how efficiently Madhu has taken charge. Then he glanced at Namrata, she was sitting all exhausted after bouts of nausea. The compatibility of Madhu and the vulnerability of Namrata were there; very evident.

A Forest guard's jeep reached there. Whatever medicines available at Rajeshwar small hospital they have brought along. Rajeshwar and Madhu got busy cleaning the wounds of the wounded. Namrata took courage to stand and help but her legs gave way. They trembled so bad that she sat back where she was sitting. Caught in the scene of annihilation were two women, one Madhu the other Namrata and both were so poles apart, they were almost each other's antithesis.

Amar was busy shooting for his documentary in the jungle. Forest guards met and warned him to leave immediately. They informed him about the carnage at Jumbo uncle village. The first thought which struck Amar mind was that 'I must shoot this carnage before any other channel team reaches there.'

Amar sped his jeep towards the village thinking his career was sure to be made there if not anywhere.

When Amar reached the village it was a little late. The help and media had arrived. Helicopters, police jeeps, doctors, news men and channel teams were busy. Injured were being loaded in to helicopters and flown, losing no more time Amar also got busy covering it.

Amar discovered that special orders had come to hunt down the Man eaters. Some professional hunters would soon be arriving. Police personal were already deputed there. Lions have to be killed immediately. Amar vowed to catch this hunt in his camera better than any other channel team.

Right then Amar was very effectively covering the devastation at Jumbo uncle's village. While at the horrific job a thought was persistently crossing his mind 'unto the time the two dangerous lions are eliminated Rajeshwar will be kept busy day and night. His marriage with Madhu will have to be postponed and I will gain some more time to make Madhu understand.'

Rajeshwar had finished transporting Daniel to a helicopter, right then he was running with a severely wounded child in his arms. Amar was running along capturing this shot in his camera. Reaching Madhu Rajeshwar laid the child on the bare ground. Madhu shivered at the sight of the mutilated child, after examining the young one, Madhu declared the little soul no more. Amar covered this through his camera. A switch clicked on in his mind illuminating one more helping deliberation 'Here, Madhu is just witnessing what life with Rajeshwar is going to be, the trailer is right in front of her eyes. I am sure she must be already re- considering her decision and choice.'

However what Amar never knew was that this happening had not scared Madhu at all. She was a nurse by profession. She very well knew and had seen worse mishaps happen. Man kills man. One bomb explodes and thousands perish. Bullets are fired butchering and slitting people. At hospital she had seen hundreds and thousands of dead body's come in. Lay on the hospital floor. Hundreds of people writhing in pain, crying for help, sometimes during some riots, sometimes after some bomb blast.

In this speechless and brainless jungle world only two lions have gone berserk, they have killed seventeen people and injured twenty six. After years together such a mishap had happened, brainy, intelligent, wise and resourceful human beings kill every other day, sometimes in the name of religion or sometimes to defend or extend their territory, border lines down on this earth. And also sometimes just for trade; to sell heavy fire arms, bombs and ammunition.

Those two lions, who have transformed into Man eating lions that too because of human mistake, would very soon be killed. Madhu knew that as crestfallen Rajeshwar was about the villagers similarly desolated he would be on killing those lions.

That was why; on the contrary to Amar wishful thinking she was appreciating and all the more feeling for Rajeshwar. But people like Amar would say that it was sympathy not love. Nevertheless, to whom so ever it may concern, sympathetic is one who shares pain and without love how can one share pain therefore in a way sympathy and love are very much interrelated. In some picky cases two faces of the same coin.

When Namrata reached her Resort cottage she was very badly ...shaken. Her parents were waiting for her. They had seen the news of Jumbo uncle's village devastation on their hotel TV.

Watching their pale and very distraught daughter they choose just to keep tight-lipped. To them it was very well obvious that witnessing the carnage had left her traumatized. Once again she must have realized that this jungle she could not belong to. They wanted to hear exactly that from Namrata. They wanted Namrata to speak up first.

But Namrata was their daughter only. She remained silent, did not utter a single word. Finally Shivdasani ji broke the ice, initiated the talk "The place had become even more dangerous. We must not leave Pinky here."

Mrs. Shivdasani seconded her husband "Yes my love, we have had talks with our lawyer, you also have consulted him. He is sure of getting Pinky custody. Rajeshwar second marriage is a very solid ground for us."

Manohar Shivdasani ji added "We will admit Pinky to some good boarding school; her upbringing will be in right hands, in right environment."

Mrs. Shivdasani put in "Yes, this way Vivek will have no objection, we have already talked to him."

Now Namrata replied back "You people may have had so many other talks also with Vivek. Please I am very tired I do not want any arguments, sorry mom sorry dad."

She went into the bed room of her cottage and closed the door behind her. Disappointed parents kept looking at each other.

Jumbo uncle had simply refused to stay put in the hospital. He got his wounds dressed by the doctors and came back to village; had drank two full bowls of native herb preparations. Holding a rifle in his hand and a belt of bullets all around his waist was ready to go for the lion hunt. Madhu came to him with an injection and said "Have you heard the good news Daniel is out of danger, I just had a talk with Niku."

"Yes I have been to the hospital myself, seen with my own eyes he is doing fine, after all he is my son." said Jumbo uncle.

Madhu smiled appreciating and said "Jumbo uncle if you have to go for the hunt then go. But this injection is also a must. Doctors have prescribed one for you every eight hours."

Jumbo uncle bared his arm saying "Oh! Give the injection, I am not scared of injections, whatever, I am not going to leave those lions they have killed so many of my people."

There were angry tears in Jumbo uncle big red eyes. Madhu administered the injection "Jumbo uncle just remember, hunt or no hunt, every eight hours you have to be here for this."

Amar was there with his camera recording this. It was a very good matter for his documentary. A man who had been wounded by those lions was going to hunt them in his wounded condition. He told Jumbo uncle "Jumbo uncle in this hunt you are my hero, I and my camera will be there with you all the time. I am sure you will hunt down at least one lion."

Jumbo uncle disputed "Why one? I will shoot the two of them. But you better listen to me, if you want to be on the hunt, carry a rifle not this camera, with this thing you are inviting your own hunt."

Amar said meaning fully may be for the benefit of Madhu "Jumbo uncle death is for one and all. Nevertheless the death of a person like me would make no difference to anyone. It is so that there is no tear to my account."

Madhu ignored him. Jumbo uncle a little confused walked away in search of Rajeshwar. Madhu also turned to go Amar intervened "Namrata is running very high fever. I have just been to her cottage. There is no doctor here to attend to her."

"Yes, all doctors are busy. She may be having some fever, too much tension."

"Not some, she is running very high fever. If you can visit her and give her some medicine it will be very nice of you."

Thinking for a moment Madhu nodded a yes.

When Namrata had shut her door on her parents they had waited for some time then finally had gone to their Hotel. Witnessing the blood bath at the village the fever had nabbed her, when Amar came it was as high as may be hundred and one degrees.

At that moment it was not less than hundred and three or four. She was shivering and was hallucinating about Rajeshwar and Pinky.

Pinky is standing in the valley of flowers. Namrata is running fast to reach her but the distance between her and Pinky keeps on increasing.

Namrata is standing at a barren desert like place. All of a sudden Rajeshwar appears with a bouquet of flowers in his hands. Looking hard into Namrata eyes he hands over the bouquet to her. As she takes the bouquet a thorn pricks her hand. Drop of blood oozes out on her finger.

Fidgety Namrata turned in her bed. Her heart and total self ached.

Madhu knocked at her cottage door slightly then entered without waiting for a reply, some medicine in her hand. She was a very experienced nurse. She was at this job since the age of sixteen. One look and she understood Namrata condition. Namrata eyes were closed she was somewhat in a restive sleep. Madhu kept the medicine at the side table opened the fridge took out some ice cubes, kept them in a bowl, walked to Namrata cupboard, removed some napkins, soaked them in the cold ice cubes. Sitting beside Namrata touched her forehead, realized the fever was really high. Folding the icy napkin she placed it at Namrata forehead. Madhu continued with this routine, gradually fever began to recede. Namrata opened her eyes to find Madhu next to her. Madhu offered her the medicine saying "There are no doctors here but I have brought this medicine for you, three times a day; your fever will go down."

Namrata tried a smile and said "Thanks how Pinky is? No more shopping?"

"You get well first and let things get better then we will go shopping with your dear Pinky."

Namrata smiled ruefully saying "Now she is your Pinky, I am her mother just for name sake."

"Why for name sake? Rajeshwar sahib has said this time in Pinky's holidays he will send her to live with you."

"What when her holidays end?"

Very open hearted Madhu said "Then you too come back with her and not here at this Resort, you will live with us at our home as Pinky's mother. That house if it belongs to Pinky it belongs to you as well."

A surprised Namrata watched Madhu with open mouth. She was thinking that in this world were good and open hearted people like Madhu also? Noticing Namrata starring at her like that Madhu inquired "What are you looking at like this?"

Namrata very honestly replied "I am not looking; I am thinking that this world is safe to live because of good people like you otherwise people like us, who have just learnt to take and only take, we would have just plundered this world and put an end to it."

Taking Namrata both hands in her hands Madhu said "Namrata ji don't take yourself to be so wrong, you just had some weaknesses and they are no more with you now. God has bestowed so much to you; see if I can get Rajeshwar sahib you can also get somebody else equally good."

Namrata once again came out clean and straight "Madhu there is no equation of you and me, I have lost a very good man of this world because of my mistake where as you have lost an average man because of his mistake. This is why what you have lost can be replaced but in my life Rajeshwar sahib's absence can never be filled again."

Amar entered saying

"Just the same way in my life your absence can never be replaced."

Amar came and sat on the floor where Madhu was sitting. Beseeching kept his hand on Madhu knees. Suddenly Madhu discovered that her both hands were in Namrata hands and Amar was holding her knees with his hands, she could not even brush them aside. Both were looking at Madhu with entreating eyes. Amar pleaded "Madhu please just give us one chance to expiate our sin, please for God sake test your first love once more."

Saying so he placed his forehead along with his hands in Madhu lap, Madhu was sitting statue like. She was a very emotional girl and her emotions were stirred up by her first love and Namrata's helpless repentance who was begging now "Madhu I know what I am asking you is very much and I also know I don't have any right to asks for it. But what to do this heart within me is compelling me that I should at least beg of you once may be you may have pity on me. I may get my daughter and my Rajeshwar back and your Amar may get back you, please Madhu have pity on us. Save our lives from being wrecked and ruined."

A very fidgety Madhu getting up and said "But all this is not only in my hand, Rajeshwar sahib should also agree."

Amar put in "Rajeshwar sahib knows that Namrata ji has changed; only there is need of some time to revive his lost first love."

Though in fever Namrata got down her bed and stood folding her hands begging forgiveness "Please Madhu, please you are the only one we can plead to; you are a woman with a large heart please have pity on us and forgive us. Think of Pinky; give her a chance to live with her parents together, she is very young right now but as she grows up like any other child she would like to see her parents united. Please for my sins don't let my daughter suffer; the Pinky you love so much suffers; I beg of you to please have mercy on us."

Saying so she cried bitterly, Madhu was very tense and distressed; she knew not what to say and what not to say. On one side her humility was shattering her and on the other side was her past which had broken her, given her so much pain. She said "I, I, need some time to think."

Amar could see the crack in Madhu, he sensed the dilemma in her tilting to one side, his side and he was right. Her double mind was almost reduced to thinking one way, that of Namrata and Amar way. He invigorated

"Madhu you have been thinking all along and you have the reasons to think as we have the reasons to suffer; to suffer for the wrong we had done for the blunder we committed. If you think that it is not enough then I am ready to be penalized to any extent for the rest of my life but Madhu please, I beg of you, do consider Pinky, don't penalize the next generation, don't let the suffering be carried on to the next generation, now is the time for decision at least for Pinky."

Madhu was very much considering not only Pinky but also forgiving and forgetting. Brand new questions were also coming to her mind; will it be sweet revenge if she married Rajeshwar? Has she said yes to Rajeshwar in rebound? Madhu got up and left abruptly, without giving any inclination. Namrata was confused but Amar was confident. A smile came to his face.

Hunting tribe Africans had assembled in front of Rajeshwar house. They were professional hunters. These tribe's men had migrated deep into the far interiors jungles since the time restriction were imposed on wild life hunting. The authorities knew that the profession of these people from generations together was only hunting so they were to some extent considerate with them. Tribe's men were also conscious of this lenient attitude of authorities like Rajeshwar. They hunted with caution. Some had even taken up agriculture as means of lively hood.

However that day an opportunity had come their way, the authorities have had themselves invited them for the hunt. In fact Rajeshwar was waiting for them to begin the pursuit.

Some expert hunters had also arrived. In the entire Forest Resort there was not a single cottage available at that point of time. The poachers who used to steal hunt they too had come today openly.

Michkle was also there. He was the same Michkle who had killed Monu's father and mother, who Rajeshwar had had an encounter with but then Michkle had managed to escape. Because he had escaped so there was no proof against him. So he had come openly to hunt the Man eaters with his some new and some old colleagues. He knew that Rajeshwar can do him no harm but what he did not know was that Monu had grown up. Monu was an elephant and the phrase 'elephant memory' very much applied to Monu. He had not forgotten the killer of his mother and father.

A lost Madhu reached home. She was not conscious how and when she covered the distance between Forest Resort and would be husband Rajeshwar house. She passed through the tribal people and the villagers heedless of their din and clamor. She straight away went to her room.

Rajeshwar was looking for her. Before departing for hunt he wanted to inform Madhu that pundit ji had arrived. The wedding date was fixed. Next week Monday on the first of the month was their wedding.

He saw Madhu entering her room. He came after her. Madhu was standing at the open window staring blankly in to the sky. Entering the room Rajeshwar said "Where were you? I looked for you all over. Pundit ji had finalized our wedding date, next week on the first of the month."

Coming close to Madhu he lovingly kept his hand on her shoulder and as if trying to explain said "Because of this mishap there is not much to celebrate. We will get married in a simple way but when things get right we will paint the town red. What say you?"

He gently turned Madhu towards himself. One look at her face he immediately understood where she had been, keeping his anger in control he questioned "How is Namrata? I heard she has high fever."

Walking a little away from him Madhu said "I have given her some medicines. She will be ok."

"She will be ok but you are looking sick?"

Madhu looked up at Rajeshwar. Though there were no tears in her eyes but tension and despair was written large all over her face, she asked "I ask a matter of heart. Please don't reply using mind. Namrata is your first love or not?"

Rajeshwar replied in a matter of fact tone "Yes."

Looking into his eyes Madhu questioned "Then how can you forget her?"

He gave a blunt reply "I will never forget her; the poison of her memory will always remain in my heart."

Madhu tried to reason "But Namrata has changed now."

Rajeshwar came face to face with Madhu, kept his index finger under her chin, gently lifting her face in level with him said "Namrata has changed or not, I have got nothing to do with it. You tell me have you changed?"

A nervous Madhu uttered "Why should I change?"

Now Rajeshwar walked a little away from her saying "This lamenting about first love; Amar is also your first love. Are you failing to discard his memories even after dismissing him from your life?"

Now Madhu moved to face Rajeshwar there were tears in her eyes as she said "I am talking about Namrata ji, who you had married. Who was your wife. And by her you have a daughter Pinky. The stature she had in your life had never been that of Amar in mine."

Rajeshwar confronted Madhu saying "You want me to accept her because of that past marital title so that Amar's rank in your life may increase?"

"I have told you Amar is like a stranger to me, he means nothing to me now. Namrata is above all Pinky's mother and Pinky loves her now; has already started missing her."

"Madhu tell me straight, do you want me to call off our marriage?" Rajeshwar put forward the question he hated the most even to think of.

The question had lingered somewhere back in Madhu mind. It hit her hard, the impact made her legs tremble. She sat on the bed in her room, her face went pale as she went on to say "What I meant to say was that Namrata has really changed, realized her mistake and is very much repentant. It will be nice to give Pinky her mother back."

"No one is forcing mother and daughter away; they are free to meet each other whenever they please. However merely for your information, if for you your first love that Amar is a stranger, then for me my first love that Namrata is dead and is set on fire on a funeral pyre; the ashes have also blown over this jungle. Now you tell me (Rajeshwar cut in very sarcastically) if in case I do oblige you how long you think she, that Namrata, will tolerate this jungle because of Pinky. She will leave and go again and this time will also take away my Pinky. You want me to go through a worst hell time again." Madhu was all puzzled and confused; she had no answer to Rajeshwar.

Suddenly Monu's very loud triumphing reverberation up surged from down below. Along with it a very great clamor and pandemonium bounded up as if people were running helter-skelter. Rajeshwar and Madhu both rushed to the window.

Down below was stampede and hysteria. Monu was infuriated, triumphing he was running after a man. That man was Michkle.

Michkle ran into his jeep. With the might of his tusks and trunk Monu over turned the jeep. Monu missed Michkle just by inches; he crawled out of his jeep and ran for his life.

Michkle was running desperately to save himself. Monu was after him and after Monu was Pinky, shouting "Stop! Monu! Stop...!"

Calling, she was running after Monu towards the jungle and after them running was the mass gathering assembled there.

Rajeshwar and Madhu came rushing down. By that time Jumbo uncle had reached Pinky and caught hold of her. Pinky was struggling in Jumbo uncles strong arms and crying "Leave me Jumbo uncle! Leave me, what had gone wrong with my Monu? Why is he running after that man?"

Rajeshwar had recognized Michkle. He knew why Monu was after Michkle. Suddenly some voices arose in African dialect "The elephant is gone mad! Shoot him Kill him!!!"

Pinky wriggled in Jumbo uncles arms "No! ... No... My Monu is not mad!!!"

Rajeshwar had reached them. Pinky shouted to him "Daddy! Daddy! My Monu is not mad! My Monu is not mad...!"

Rajeshwar emphatically nodded a yes. Then in a thundering voice announced in African dialect "This elephant is not mad, I have raised him since it was a baby. My little daughter rides him daily."

A man, who may be was Michkle colleague questioned "Then why is he running after Michkle? Why he is after the life of Michkle?"

Staring back at that man Rajeshwar yelled back "You go and ask Michkle this. Why leaving the rest of the people the elephant is just after him? Why didn't he crush anyone else under his feet? Why he over turned Michkle jeep only? Why he did not touch any other vehicle? You go and ask Michkle? It is because Michkle has killed Monu's father and mother for their ivory in front of Monu eyes when he was a baby. "

Michkle's friend replied "It is all bullshit... before this elephant kills Michkle we must shoot the elephant."

Rajeshwar thundered "If any one shoots at this elephant then with the authority of a Forest Conservator I will shoot him. All the hunts men present here are permitted to hunt and kill those two Man eater lions only. If anyone even injures some other wild life then that particular person will be arrested under Forest preservation act. All the hunts men please note this well. And the ones who do not agree to this, they can return back to where they came from. I and my guards along with the tribe men are force enough to deal with those two Man eaters."

Forest guards, the tribe's men and villagers shouted in unison supporting Rajeshwar. In their language they yelled loudly 'Yes! Yes!'

They admonished the hunts men come from elsewhere raising their spears, rifles, their bows and arrows. Michkle's friend disappeared in the crowd. Madhu also reached there. Rajeshwar took crying Pinky from Jumbo uncle and passed her to Madhu pacifying her "Pinky my love, you don't worry nothing is going to happen to your Monu."

CHAPTER THIRTEEN

Michkle was running like mad deep into the woods. Monu was after him like death. Michkle was exhausted and breathless. He knew that running he won't last any more. As he approached a huge tree he jumped and climbed it. Monu was just behind; he flung his trunk to grab Michkle but merely missed him by a fraction.

Michkle, getting lucky, escaped climbing the higher branches. His trunk raised Monu was in infuriated agony. He pushed the tree with his head, endeavoring to uproot it. The tree was too big and strong. In his attempts Monu injured his head. Not caring with all strength and fury Monu was trying to uproot the massive tree.

Hearing his fury Rajeshwar, Jumbo uncle, Amar and others reached there. They found an exhausted Monu sitting under the tree watching Michkle's every move up the tree. Michkle was just trembling.

Rajeshwar stopped his jeep near Monu. He fetched a long rope from his jeep. Without any fear, without any doubt tied it around Monu's neck, Monu also exhibited no resistance, was sitting quiet only occasionally glanced with his small eyes at Michkle still perched up the tree and shuddering. Rajeshwar tried to pull Monu by the rope saying "Come Monu, come, come with me."

But Monu refused to move a bit. Amar was busy with his camera. Jumbo uncle asked Rajeshwar "What will you do now? He is not in a mood to move from here."

Rajeshwar tried once more but Monu was stiff and still. Thinking something Rajeshwar untied the rope. Collected it put it back in the jeep. Everyone was waiting and watching in suspense as to what Rajeshwar was up to.

Rajeshwar opened a medical kit kept in his jeep. Took out a syringe, arranged an injection then came to Monu. Lovingly patting Monu on his jaws said "Sorry Monu. There is no other way; this injection will put you to sleep for a while. And when you wake up this Michkle will be behind bars."

Rajeshwar administered the injection under Monu's ear. Within moments sleep over came Monu. He slept lying stretched on the ground. Amar had shot the whole incident. Now he recorded Michkle getting down the tree.

Some of Michkle's men have also reached there. As Michkle landed down the tree, once again Rajeshwar and Michkle stood confronting each other "Michkle you are under arrest. "

"What is my crime?"

"Seven years back you have shot and killed Monu's mother and father, he is the same little Monu who was crying and wailing when you were cutting the tusks of his dead parents, cutting their ivory to sell."

"What is the proof of what you say?"

Amar intervened "In this camera is the film that shows Monu recognizing you in hundreds of people and then without harming any one, chasing just you. The truth of this film and the witness of an esteemed officer like Mr. Rajeshwar plus your old record I think is enough for any court and jury to form a definite bad opinion about you."

Michkle knew that all the villagers will willingly testify against him. Most villagers' lively hood depended on tourists. Tourists came to see wild life. Poachers massacred animals. Reason enough for villagers to hate poachers. Also at that time there was no question or chance of running away from there. Michkle was engrossed in these thoughts when he was handcuffed.

The hunt began in all earnestness. All the huntsmen have been told that the two Man-eater lions are in the prime of their age. One of them was lame and both were always together. It was decided that pursuit would begin from east to west. Hunters would stalk on the west side while the tribe's men and villagers will enter from east; beating drums and making loud sounds, harrying the two lions. All knew that it was a tuff job to find the Man-Eater lions in the vast spread out jungle.

Medicine given by Madhu had helped Namrata. The fever subsided. She came to meet Pinky and Madhu. Amar had advised her to keep in touch with

Madhu. He was confident that they have touched the right cord; the vibrations should be kept alive. He knew that Namrata silence would also speak to Madhu the language of her heart, to which Madhu has become very much alive.

But the ways of God are strange; the emotional outburst of Pinky for her elephant of a friend Monu; that anecdote had made Madhu forget all for time being. She was totally engrossed in Pinky crying bitterly for Monu when Namrata arrived. Namrata took it for granted that Pinky was crying for her; she came rushing to her daughter "Pinky my darling don't cry see Mama has come."

"My Monu has not come yet."

Pinky cried in Madhu's lap, Namrata was taken aback, her ego hurt, she had changed but the streaks in her character would take time and die hard. Her point of view in life had been very much centered on her; she would have to learn to look at life from the prospective of her child at times such as of then. Madhu told her about Monu and the killer of its parents Michkle.

The flash back flashed to Namrata when Rajeshwar had brought one month old baby elephant and she had protested defying Rajeshwar. That Monu was so dear to her daughter now that she grieves bitterly for it.

Settling down on Maji bed along with Maji and Madhu she took Pinky in her lap. Pinky weeping said "They say my Monu has gone mad?"

Pacifying Namrata said "How can your Monu be mad, he is so sensible, you know when he first saw me at the gate he sniffed at me I am sure he recognized me."

"And he recognized that Michkle also who killed his parents, and that is why he ran after him." Said Pinky tears rolling down her cheeks then all of a sudden she asked Namrata "Mama, do you hate Monu?"

"No my love I love everything you love." Replied an understanding Namrata.

"Will you touch him and ride him with me?"

With all her faults Namrata had one outstanding quality; she never lied. She laughed and told her daughter "I can't promise you that but if you insist I might try."

"Nothing will happen, even Mummy was scared the first time but now you see how she enjoys ridding him."

"Your Mummy is great; I am not as good as she is." Namrata said smiling at Madhu. Pinky had stopped crying catching hold of Namrata hand she simply insisted "You are also good, when Monu comes I will bring him to the forest resort, and you will have to ride him with me ok."

"Ok baby but now you go to sleep you seem so pale and drained."

Namrata said fondling her to help her go to sleep. Tired and exhausted Pinky went to sleep in her mother's lap within seconds. Madhu watched the eternal picture of a mother and her daughter.

As exhausted Pinky slept Madhu Maji and Namrata came down to have a cup of tea.

The back of the hall had an opening towards the animal hospital. The iron cages were quite clearly visible, in one such cage Michkle was locked in. The three Maji, Madhu and Namrata were stunned to witness a human locked in an animal cage. They came to know that Johnny and a Forest guard have locked Michkle in there. The cook Ramzan gave them this information.

The three discussed that it was all most past noon. Michkle should be very hungry, should they serve him meal or not, of course Michkle was thirsty and hungry.

Gaining consciousness Monu was neither hungry nor thirsty. Raising his trunk he was trying to smell Michkle restlessly running here and there.

When Michkle had climbed the tree Monu trunk had almost reached and caught him but Michkle was lucky to get away. Now Michkle smell was well set in Monu trunk.

At the bungalow the three women decided that some food and water must be given to Michkle. It will be inhuman to keep him starved.

Carrying some food and water they came near Michkle's enclosure. It was the same cage where the wolf pups were kept. They had been since long sent to a zoo. The cage was made out of strong iron bars. Thick and impenetrable wire net was spread around the bars to keep poisonous reptiles and insects away. To pass food inside the enclosure door had to be opened which was locked. It was a number lock; Madhu very well remembered all the numbers of all the enclosure locks.

Fixing the numbers together she opened the lock. Pulled the door a little open and signaled Namrata to put the food and water inside.

Michkle mind was working fast. If he could succeed in his escape from there he could be free as ever. Namrata kept the food inside. Michkle kicked the door hard. The door flew open so violently that Namrata and Madhu were both thrown back, Maji who was standing at some distance shrieked.

Other than them the old cook Ramzan was in the house. He was standing at a distance and watching the show of humanity. He came running to apprehend Michkle. Michkle hit him hard on the jaw. The old fellow collapsed then and there. Michkle ran towards the open gate. But he froze.

Monu was once again standing confronting him. Trunk pulled up belligerently and ears drawn in fury.

First Michkle was running to escape out of the bungalow now he ran in the bungalow to save his life.

There were no two opinions about it, if Monu caught him he shall be torn and smashed into pieces. Michkle was looking for some place to hide while running for his life.

Petrified Namrata ran into the bungalow. Hearing the screams and wailing and her Monu thunder Pinky was up. Rushing she came out.

Michkle tried to get inside the bungalow but Monu was quick to block his way. Madhu and Maji were shouting and screaming at Monu trying to stop him in vain.

Finally When Michkle found no other place to save himself he re-entered that particular cage from where he had escaped, shut its door. Monu aggressively moved towards the cage, to tear that cage apart was no big deal for Monu. Madhu and Maji knew this but Michkle realized this too late. Monu was advancing towards him. There was no hope of Michkle survival.

Little Pinky came in between death and Michkle. Raising her small hands she ordered Monu to stop.

"I say Monu stop, Monu stop, stop, stop..."

Lifting his trunk Monu gave out a wild cry. But stop it did not. Little Pinky without any fear or inhibition ran to Monu; held its huge front leg with both her delicate tinny hands and pushing him back with all her petite strength kept saying

"Back Monu ... Back..."

Monu once again triumphed but stopped waving its trunk as if asking Pinky to let go. Not heeding Pinky kept up her monologue "Monu back...Monu back" slowly, slowly Pinky's Monu did heed, and it stepped backwards. Maji, Madhu and Namrata who had come down by then all were amazed at the spectacle of a wild elephant listening to eight year old tiny girl.

Dead scared crooked Michkle was also watching, eyes wide open, the huge monster of his death pushed back by a little angel of love.

Michkle felt that the little angel had restrained the animal. Opening the door he once again jumped and ran towards the open gate. Pinky screamed to stop him "Uncle! Don't run...Don't run...!"

Inadvertently Pinky moved away leaving Monu. Monu once again went out of control and ran after Michkle. Pinky ran after Monu once again shouting for him to stop.

Namrata ran after Pinky. Madhu was already ahead of Namrata calling for Pinky to stop. But Pinky was not listening and Monu was not listening to Pinky.

Running all proceeded towards the jungle, the habitat of two Man eater lions, Maji was watching helplessly.

Beating the drums, shouting, yelling and hounding the pursuit were on. The lions were in a thick spread out dense growth of trees. On one side were the armed hunters from the other side the hounding was being done; shouting, screaming, and beating drums natives were moving into the thicket.

The lame lion was extremely clever and shrewd. Though he did not know what a gun was but he knew well that the fire which came out of it made him a lame lion. The fear had settled in him. Annoyed, disturbed and nervous as well by the howling and the clamor he was about to exit the bushes when his sharp watchful eyes caught the sight of the two legged animals holding that same thing which bellowed and belched fire.

Exuding a loud roar the lame lion hid ducking in the safety of the bushes. His brother was running at a distance. Hearing lame lions roar he too stopped. Lame lion turned and looked. Two men sounding their drums were coming towards him. He once again looked towards the hunters. Some more hunt men with their guns had reached there by then. The roar had reached them also. They were aiming their rifles at the shrubs. The lame lion jumped back in to thicket. His brother followed him.

Suddenly the men in pursuit found themselves in confrontation with the lions. One sharp smack of the lame lion was enough for the two hounding men. Brain of one flew away from his skull the other's face that was, his cheeks, nose, lips all vanished.

As if the lame lion had shown his brother a way, physically stronger and aggravated brother attacked in a blitz. He felt a very different pleasure in hunting the two legged animals. They were damn weak and slow. They couldn't even run properly, did not have strong horns or hoofs to defend them. Just one slap was enough to show them the dust. Even that small spotted deer struggled better for his life. At least it threw some punches with its hooves in self defense. The two legged ones looked so tall and broad but there was no energy, zeal or fight back in them.

The hunter had become hunted. All were running helter-skelter in a bid to save their lives; mauled by the lions, stricken by terror.

The sixth sense in Rajeshwar signaled that something terrible had gone wrong. Jumping in to his jeep he dashed into the dense forest but soon the jeep got stuck in the thicket and in front of Rajeshwar eyes was the visual of another catastrophe.

The lions were nowhere in sight but yes human bodies were littered everywhere. Some were dead some were dying and some were writhing in pain. Rajeshwar had posted some gun armed guards also along with the hounding people. However in the face of the fury of the lions they turned nervous wrecks. Of course with shivering hands they have fired to save their own skin but wildly without being able to aim at their targets. One definite benefit of this random firing was Lame lion retreated and after him went his brother, further destruction got averted.

Four men were killed and nine injured severely, minor injuries were not accounted for right then. Packing off the dead and the severely wounded in jeeps Rajeshwar transported them to his make shift hospital.

Maji came rushing to him forgetting her walking stick not caring for her yet weak legs and begged him "Beta, go and save Pinky, Madhu and Namrata."

"Why what happened to them? Where are they?"

"They have gone after Monu, Michkle tried to escape, Monu ran after him, Pinky and they…"

It was another bolt for Rajeshwar; another blow for him. Madhu Pinky Namrata were in deep jungle where two Man eater lions thirsty for human blood were on the prowl.

Amar was very busy with his camera capturing and recording the images of the dead and the suffering of the wounded with professional expertise but this news shook him as well, for a change his concentration got confused between the scene in front of his camera and the predicament of the endangered three lives.

Chapter Fourteen

Michkle was hiding under the cover of some giant wild shrubs. Monu was searching for him pulling and uprooting the wild high rise bushes. Monu was coming the right way; Michkle scent was guiding him. Michkle sneaked and crawled into the adjoining lake and took a dip to save himself from Monu. Monu lost Michkle and his scent. Monu went on rampage; its elephant fury at its worst; stamping, crushing and pulling out the wild shrubs.

Pinky running after Monu was left way far behind; her friend has disappeared in the thick forest. Crying Pinky was calling for Monu and was searching him running around the jungle. Madhu and Namrata were together both shouting Pinky name at the top of their voices and desperately looking for her. They were very much deep into the jungle. Madhu and Namrata heard Pinky's distant cry, they ran towards it. They saw Pinky at a distance trying to climb a huge tree. Both ran towards her Madhu once more raced Namrata to Pinky, caught hold of her asking "Pinky what are you doing?"

"I want to climb the tree to find where my Monu is?"

"No, we must go back home immediately." said Namrata reaching panting and out of breath.

"No, no, I want to find my Monu." Pinky kept crying and insisting.

Suddenly Madhu realized they do not know which way their house is? They have come very deep into the woods. They have lost Monu as well their way home.

Where Monu was in the dense forest somewhere near the two lions were also there. Having lost Michkle Monu was furious. Both the lions were as it was in very bad rage, ready to kill.

All of a sudden the two adversaries Monu and the two lions bumped into each other. Challenging the two Man eaters Monu thundered in his elephant time fury. Both the lions circled him roared back defying him. This eco reached Madhu Pinky and Namrata searching their way out of the jungle. The three were petrified. They were under an enormous tree. Madhu suggested "We must climb this tree it is too dangerous to be down here."

Looking at the tree Namrata was diffident "But but how will we climb it?"

Madhu contended "We must try."

Back there at his hospital Rajeshwar was in a dilemma, on one side in his hospital were nine precariously injured men screaming in agony shouting for help. On the other side deep in the extreme danger zone of the jungle was his daughter Pinky, would be wife Madhu and first love and ex wife Namrata, facing grave danger.

Once again he had called the town hospital; had administered pain killer injections to all the wounded. Madhu need he was feeling very much.

Amar Jumbo uncle and Johnny had already left in search of Pinky Namrata and Madhu. Maji was crying but was not asking Rajeshwar to go and search for them. One man's stomach had been torn open he was bleeding profusely. Rajeshwar was trying his best to stop the bleeding by cotton wads and bandages. Help from town was yet to come. Rajeshwar knew not how to leave such critically wounded men struggling between life and death and go to save his own.................

Monu and both the lions were thundering, roaring challenging each other but were not actually attacking one and other. Somehow they knew well that attack meant a decisive battle unto death. Either both the lion get killed or Monu. An exhaustive session of threatening intimidations continued.

Madhu crouching down made Pinky stand on her shoulder and then taking support of the tall and enormous trunk of the tree slowly stood up giving instructions to Pinky "Pinky take support of the tree, use hands, hold tight."

Pinky with her hands propped up the tree to keep upright and in place said "Don't worry aunty I will not fall."

As Madhu stood up to her full posture Pinky took hold of a thick branch of the tree and pulled herself up to it.

"That's good Pinky, come on go up as far as you can go safely."

Namrata sat wide eyed watching, Pinky was in practice of climbing trees so it was not very much difficult for her to reach a top branch and sit safe.

Attention Namrata, Madhu said "Namrata ji your turn now come on I will give you a push."

"No I can't."

"You will have to; right now this tree is our only hope."

Namrata realized the fact, she got up from where she was sitting on the ground, came to the huge trunk of the tree, felt the tree bark with her hands, her hands bruised on the rough surface of the tree trunk. She looked at her hands in disgust; the tree had left its mark on her delicate manicured hands. Madhu patiently watched. Suddenly the roar of the lions was again herd. Namrata made hurried attempts to climb the tree. Madhu tried to help her climb the tree supporting her, pushing her with her hands and shoulder pads. Namrata was perspiring profusely. She was slipping again and again at the trunk of the tree. There were bruises all over her body. Madhu was encouraging her "Namrata ji, try, try again, yes you can do it, you can do it."

Namrata once more slipped and landed with a thud on the ground. She cried bitterly. Madhu tried to console her, encourage her "Namrata ji you can, try…"

Crying Namrata shook her head in a no, an idea struck Madhu. She suggested "Namrata ji you please hold on, now I will climb the tree and will pull you up."

Making a courageous effort Madhu climbed the tree then throwing her hand to Namrata strived to pull her up.

Too many people, too much of noise; Bholu had disappeared somewhere.

Michkle came out of the lake water. Monu was not there instead Bholu was present.

In the pandemonium at Rajeshwar house Bholu had perceived this much; Michkle was the person after whom his friend Monu ran. Bholu was Monu's friend so it was his duty to keep an eye on Michkle till as such Monu arrived. Bholu opened his mouth wide, growling showing deadly fangs to Michkle, Bholu rushed towards Michkle. Michkle once again jumped into the lake.

At the encounter sight between Monu and the two lions, the lions had finally backed off. Failing to deal with Monu had made the lions more pugnacious. They were in a very belligerent mood they challenged and intimidated each other. They roared at each other, threatened one another with menacing open claws and deadly fangs in their wide open jaws.

Namrata had not yet climbed the tree. The lions were anywhere near, as soon as their roar reached Namrata she hysterically tried to climb the tree, dreadfully nervous Madhu also pulled Namrata with all her might. One jerk, Namrata was up at the branched trunk. She looked at her hurting bruised elbow and knees Madhu said "Namrata ji this branch is quite low to climb further please take off your shoes, with bare feet it will be easier to climb."

Madhu and Pinky have dropped their shoes before making the attempt to climb the tree. Now Namrata was also compelled to do so.

From a close by bush both the lions appeared. They smelled human presence. They were not hungry but very angry with human beings. They felt pleasure in tearing them apart. They saw the humans on the top of the tree. They bellowed a belligerent roar. Petrified Pinky clung to a branch. Namrata lost balance, was about to fall, Madhu grabbed her tight.

"Take courage Namrata ji, come, and climb with me on this upper branch."

Shattered and shaken Namrata began the climb. The lions came rushing to the tree. Lame lion made no attempt to climb the tree but his brother with his sharp and strong claws helped himself up the trunk.

Madhu, Namrata and Pinky were not out of his reach. But at the same time being a lion he was not good at tree climbing; cautiously he indulged in the exercise. In a matter of moments he could get to them. From a top the tree Pinky shrieked "Monu!!!"

Monu was at quite a distance. But he heard and did catch sight of his dear Pinky. Pinky called him again and again "Monu Help! Monu Help!!!"

Monu raised his trunk, bellowed an outcry and charged running towards lame lion. Lame lion turned and defiantly faced charging Monu.

This time the look and body language of the lame lion was resolute, to take life or give life. His brother jumped down the tree forgetting the humans and joined him. Both plowed their front claws into the bare ground; raise their hind legs in readiness to charge.

Amar was with Jumbo uncle and Johnny. Johnny was wildly driving the jeep in search of the three ladies. Jumbo uncle was standing in the open jeep; rifle hung on his wounded shoulder and was looking out through his binoculars. Amar was sitting at the front seat, holding his camera tight. One of the jeep wheel bumped into a ditch camera in Amar's hand got just saved from being thrown away. Amar remarked "Johnny drive safe to find them we have to be alive."

Johnny never heard what Amar said, in his ears was ringing the roars of the lions and the thunder of Monu. He sharply steered his jeep towards the source of the wild confronting uproar.

The jeep, maneuvering the sharp turn was balanced on two wheels as of then; the other two wheels were raised up the ground. Jumbo uncle had tumbled down but was in the jeep. The camera was in Amar's one hand with the other hand he had caught hold of whatever he could. Johnny was trying hard to get the jeep racing on two wheels back on four wheels. Suddenly the jeep went over a huge rock concealed in tall grass. With a shattering jolt Jumbo uncle flew off and landed at a distance. Amar lost the grip on the jeep but not on the camera. He was flying in air with the camera still in one hand. The jeep was rolling away like a foot ball. Johnny may be was still somewhere in the jeep.

Landing, Amar had skid on the uneven and rough, thorny and rocky forest terrain but he had somehow managed to keep the camera raised in his hand. His back was badly bruised and feet injured but his camera safe and sound.

Then from somewhere near had come the thundering of Monu and the roar of the lions. Forgetting his injuries he rushed in that direction camera in hand. Had not even bothered to look back and see where Jumbo uncle was or what the fate of Johnny was? His total concern was the very big scene, the source of coming roaring thunders.

When Amar reached there of course the scene was very big. The battle which raged down and the three vulnerable lives perched at the tree; the relation between them Amar very well knew; making this linkage, the subject, he had begun to shoot the scene from behind nearby shrubbery.

Both the lions were encircling Monu from two opposite sides. When Monu turned towards one lion the other one attacked from behind. At times it clawed the hind side and sometimes brutally dug in fangs. But Monu's one jolt was enough to heave the lion away, though leaving back some deep gashes and wounds at the behind of Monu. Monu was not the least bothered about those injuries. Pinky was in danger and Monu had to save her. Michkle he was to kill, this he no longer remembered then.

This is the difference between a human being and an animal. Man lives thinking of yesterdays and the days to come mixing present with past and future there by not concentrating, exact, at the job at hand.

While Animals live just for the moment they are living, the present, their total rapt attention to what they are at. Monu was also at that moment totally focused at the two lions and live or die battle for the sake of his beloved Pinky; it was all that was right then to his existence.

Angelic Pinky was also living for that present moment. She wanted her Monu safe and sound. The battle which was raging down bellow she wanted her Monu to win. She was praying to the almighty with her heart and soul, folding her little hands together. Namrata was sitting clinging to a branch, it seemed that her hands and feet were frozen, mind had gone numb. She was unable to see anything hear anything. She was alive but there was no life left in her. Madhu had shifted near Pinky. She was consoling her "Your daddy will be here any moment; Monu will be alright, nothing will happen to your Monu."

Amar was there in the shrubs covering, capturing the entire scene in his camera to the best of his abilities; the battle of life and death between the three animals as well as the shattering reaction of the three humans for the benefit of whom the battle was being fought,

Both the lions were inflicting grave wounds on Monu. None of the lions was coming in Monu hold. If Monu could seize one of them in one strike he could put an end to it.

The lions were very swift and agile. Monu was much more powerful but his heavy self was not fast; very slow compared to the lions. Suddenly lame lion brother in one majestic leap was astride Monu enormous neck. With all his might plowed both his claws in. Locked his strong jaw on the base of Monu left ear Monu writhes in excruciating pain.

Pinky shrieked slipped and fell. Startled Madhu threw one hand towards Pinky. By luck she caught hold of Pinky's one hand. Pinky was dangling in Madhu hand. Amar did capture the dreadful moment however as Monu thundered his attention was drawn to the battle raging below that had taken a fierce turn and his camera panned to it.

Excruciating pain impelled Monu to summon all his strength and deliver a fierce jolt to his neck. Lame lion's brother lost balance, tripped, hung with one claw dug in Monu neck. Next moment Monu trunk took that lion in its tight grip and banged him on the ground. With a loud thud the lion landed on the ground at his back, his both claws and feet wide open. Monu bending his knee put his body weight on the lame lion's brother.

Countless bones of the lion smashed into splinters. Jaw opened, tongue jutted out. But at that particular moment lame lion clutched Monu wind pipe in his power full jaw, squeezing it near shut. Monu breathing stopped.

Pinky and Madhu both were shrieking. Pinky was still dangling from Madhu hand grip and Amar's camera was fixed to his eye in his hand grip. Namrata was statue like still. Monu eyes drooped; he was losing consciousness when two loud cracks off gun fire were heard.

Chapter Fifteen

Lame lion grip on Monu wind pipe gave way. Life trembled in the lame lion's body and began to jerk out of it.

Rajeshwar was holding the rifle still aimed at the lame lion. His finger pressed the trigger once more. One more shot echoed. This bullet put an end to the lame lion's existence; its grip lost its hold on Monu wind pipe. It collapses away, releasing Monu. Monu's breathing gradually resumed.

Rajeshwar rushed in quickly and expertly climbed the tree. His trembling hand reached his daughter dangling by Madhu hand. Tears were running down his eyes as he held his life's most precious thing, his world, his daughter Pinky in his arms. He embraced her tight.

Camera was attached to Amar's eye. Limping, his body bruised, shirt torn to shreds; he was taking different shots of Rajeshwar helping Pinky get down the tree. One more jeep of Forest guards had reached there, Amar paned his camera to shoot that.

Forest guards climbed up the tree and helped Madhu and Namrata come down. Monu though severely wounded but had stood up on his feet. Pinky came running to Monu, clung to one of his bleeding feet. Amar shot this touching moment.

Madhu and Rajeshwar also came rushing to Monu with tears running down their eyes. Pet him with great love and affection; then got busy checking his wounds.

Some Forest guards have helped Namrata to the jeep. She silently sat into it. Her body and mind were still without awareness.

Help from city hospital had had arrived. It was only then Rajeshwar had gone in search of his near and dear ones. Rajeshwar along with Amar Madhu Pinky and Namrata reached home.

In the jungle, Jumbo uncle was found unconscious. Villagers and Forest guards rushed him to the hospital. Johnny was very lucky, he was alive. One hand fractured and a mild head injury. Front two teeth were also missing.

Bholu had not permitted Michkle to step out of the lake. Michkle was still into waist deep water, he saw some Forest guards approaching in their jeep. He ducked back in to the water. Bholu failed to understand this funny behavior of Michkle. He got very annoyed and well tired of waiting upon Michkle Bholu plunged into the water. Michkle was dead scared and dead sure that now Bholu was not going to let go off him.

Another Forest guard jeep passed by. Michkle left with no other alternative was forced to call out for help. Michkle was arrested.

News of Man Eater Lions being eliminated was there everywhere. At Rajeshwar house Namrata parents had also arrived. They took a sigh of relief to find their precious daughter alive. Pinky was their granddaughter but they seemed not much concerned about her. They rushed to their daughter Namrata "It is enough Namrata. Let's go from here. If you have to come back we will come back again but right now we can't take it anymore." so entreated her father.

Namrata was still in her dazed state. Her mind was still not functioning. As if reasoning and thinking power had gone. Taking advantage of her shock her parents quietly lead her to their Hummer. Namrata in her stunned state simply boarded her parent's vehicle.

With great care Monu was being helped out of the forest department truck in which Monu had been transported. Pinky was already there calling to him "Monu come down, Please come down."

All this was happening right at the gate of Rajeshwar bungalow. The exit of the bungalow was crammed, crowded and blocked. Manohar Shivdasani ji's Hummer was stuck. He was in great hurry. He wanted Namrata to leave that damn place as soon as possible.

He and his wife were focused out, cursing the scene out there; to them it was a sense less drama. As silently as Namrata had sat in the Hummer the same way without a sound she got out of it. Suddenly Manohar Shivdasani ji and his wife reacted shocked to see Namrata passing outside through the crowd in front of their eyes. Manohar ji mouth was open it remained that way, shocked his wife jumped in her seat.

By that time Monu had been lead down the truck. Namrata straight away walked to Monu. For the first time in her life, without any fear without any diffidence she very lovingly held Monu trunk in both her hands. Raising her head Namrata looked in to the eyes of Monu and uttered

"Thank you Monu."

Amar was in his cottage. His camera was connected to the TV. With what expertise he had done the job then, he at that moment saw on the small screen of the T.V. Jubilant he made attempt to pat his back. A painful groan came out of his mouth.

Somebody clapped. Turning he saw Namrata at the open door clapping "Great, how well you have shot this entire mishap, this episode of our misadventure."

A happy Amar got up saying "Namrata ji all these shots are award winning shots. First time this world will see how an elephant saved three vulnerable human lives from two fierce Man eater Lions."

Namrata very sadly passed a comment "Yes an animal, an elephant saved three vulnerable human lives, where as a human merely endeavored to shoot this fight of life and death, just saw the lethal struggle through the eye of his camera."

Amar looked at Namrata his eyes questioning. But the next moment he understood the significance of what Namrata had said. Silently he flopped where he was standing. Namrata continued "Amar that was no filmy scene that you did capture in your camera and the three human lives face to face with death were no film characters. One of them is your love, your life, your Madhu. One a little child was dangling held by your Madhu. You totally forgot all this; no thought of saving any of us ever entered your mind?"

Amar, from where he was sitting very honestly nodded a no. He was realizing this fact completely, and absolutely, that when that camera was in his hand this world became a film set for him and the people living in it film characters that he had to mould shape and shoot that was all that mattered. More than that he saw nothing, heard nothing and thought nothing. His own life was worth nothing when his camera was on. He had experienced this couple of times.

Amar got up and slowly walked to his camera. Picked it up, looked at it with love twinkling in his eyes and said with utmost sincerity "What a fool I have been, I am already married. Married to this camera of mine then why all the while I am running after Madhu."

Namrata uttered "And I after Rajeshwar." Surprised Amar looked at Namrata who went on to say "Yes Amar. In last two days whatever happened, it gave me lot to understand. Madhu stood by Rajeshwar down right and absolute in thick and thin, firm. Whereas I just trembled, my love is no good for Rajeshwar. I was a mistake in his life where as Madhu is a blessing."

Going into the past Amar uttered as if to him "I very shrewdly brought in you, I mean his ex-wife, his first love into the scene, and then made Madhu feel that she was being a vamp; coming in between mother and daughter. I very well cashed on it; I really worked well my screenplay. However that Almighty sitting up there is the greatest screenplay writer, in one stroke of His pen He gave a true to life twist to my screenplay."

Namrata looked at Amar her eyes asking further explanation. Amar continued "Through the speechless wild animals He, the Almighty, taught me what no school or college could; Monu and those two Man Eater Lions while they were busy at their job I was busy at my job. For them their job was of prime importance for me my job was of leading importance. They saw no more and I saw nothing else. Almighty dawned on me my own meaning of life. He tutored me the most important lesson of life which is to know one own self, all very well knew me but I was so busy and occupied with my ambition; never had any time to discover myself. He held a mirror to me and I saw what I am."

Namrata smiled understanding and asked "What is to be done now?"

In Madhu marriage to Rajeshwar only two people participate from her side, one Amar as a good friend and the other Namrata as her elder sister. In their relationships such a twist would come this none had ever anticipated.

Namrata was to keep coming there to meet her daughter Pinky. Rajeshwar also promised to let Namrata take Pinky home during Pinky vacations.

Amar was to never come back. Along with Madhu memories he was taking with him a story; his story, Madhu's story, Rajeshwar's story, Namrata's story, innocent Pinky's story, elderly Maji's story, Monu and Bholu's story, story of two Man Eater Lions, the story of green and dense Forests. He was sure to get his directorial debut, curtsy this story. His relations with

Namrata have become exceedingly good. He was sure to convince her to finance this project of his.

Some people never change. Amar would also never ever change. What he was he always will be.

THE END

www.ingramcontent.com/pod-product-compliance
Lightning Source LLC
La Vergne TN
LVHW041014150826
845672LV00001B/87

* 9 7 9 8 8 8 8 1 5 3 2 2 2 *